LIES LOST AND FOUND

Also by Jacqueline Boulden

Family Ties Family Lies (A Lake Amelia Mystery Book One)

Her Past Can't Wait

Selected Praise for Jacqueline Boulden's novels

"Jacqueline Boulden's LIES LOST AND FOUND effectively straddles the space between charming, gripping, and impactful . . . It also has a strong thematic core: indignance at the plight of the immigrant labor force (both documented and undocumented), which supports the economy even in small, wealthy towns in upstate New York."
—INDIE READER PRO REVIEW

"The action begins in the first chapter, and the suspense never lets up . . . Those who appreciate cozy mysteries with some edge will eagerly race through Boulden's novel to see if the victims find justice."
—BLUEINK REVIEW

"Boulden's story (*Family Ties Family Lies*) presents small-scale but beguiling mysteries backgrounded by a vibrant portrait of a small town that's both warmly close-knit and slightly claustrophobic. It's also a meditation on family love, loss, and remembrance, conveyed in plangent prose grounded in rich, concrete detail . . ."
—KIRKUS REVIEWS (STARRED REVIEW) A TOP 100 INDIE BOOK OF 2024

"The people from this little town come alive, and the plot twists keep unraveling taking the reader spiraling to the riveting conclusion. I cared deeply for these characters, and Boulden has a great talent for writing good dialogue."
—JACK RIGHTMYER, ALBANY TIMES UNION

"A sweet slow burn—as past and present collide in this compelling tale of small-town drama, family ties, and life-changing surprises. When a determined journalist investigates the story of her own life—she unearths answers she never could have predicted."
—HANK PHILLIPPI RYAN, *USA TODAY* BESTSELLING AUTHOR

"You won't want to miss this heart-wrenching but uplifting story about the strength and flexibility of family. Complex, captivating and compelling. Fans of small-town dramas will love *Family Ties Family Lies*."
—TINA DEBELLEGARDE, AGATHA NOMINATED AUTHOR OF *WINTER WITNESS* AND *DEAD MAN'S LEAP*

"*Her Past Can't Wait* is a scathing commentary on how society treats women when they do something as simple as trying to set physical boundaries. Gut-wrenching, intriguing, and twisty, Boulden's thought-provoking story lays bare just how far we have to go as a society when it comes to believing and protecting women."
—LISA REGAN, *USA TODAY* & *WALL STREET JOURNAL* BESTSELLING AUTHOR

"In her fast-paced and absorbing novel, *Her Past Can't Wait*, Jacqueline Boulden illuminates the courageous and timely story of a woman facing her traumatic past and how EMDR eased her suffering. A must-read for all trying to live like the past is in the past, when it's actually still buried in their subconscious."
—DONNA KNUDSEN, PSY.D., EMDR INSTITUTE FACILITATOR & CERTIFIED CONSULTANT

"An engrossing tale about sexual assault that skillfully covers a tough and timely topic."
—KIRKUS REVIEWS

"An accomplished news journalist, author Jacqueline Boulden has applied her keen observation and reporting skills to telling a powerful story too many women know well, and one woman in particular must remember in order to live in peace."
—RENÉE BESS, GCLS GOLDIE AWARD & ALICE B READERS AWARD-WINNING AUTHOR

"The building of the suspense is excellent. The tension building steadily until it peaks at the culmination of the climax—that was brilliant. It was exciting and terrifying. A real page turner!"
—*Judge, 31st Annual Writer's Digest Self-Published Book Awards*

To Helen, always

To my readers: You are the wind beneath my wings.

To Vivian Lotz (1943-2025): thoughtful Beta reader, excellent dinner guest, and dear friend. You are in our hearts forever.

Lies Lost and Found

Library of Congress Control Number: 2025908216

Paperback ISBN: 979-8-9860384-5-2

eBook ISBN: 979-8-9860384-5-2

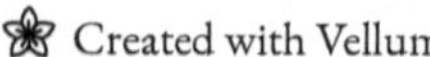 Created with Vellum

LIES LOST AND FOUND

A Lake Amelia Mystery Book Two

Jacqueline Boulden

Chapter One
Present Day

Rose Webster flicked her wrist and struck a match against the dark brown strip on the side of the box. The flame flared, dimmed, then began its journey down the wooden stick, heading closer to Rose's fingers. She held it against a small bundle of sage until it caught fire, smoldering and sending a small plume of smoke into the air. After giving it enough time to burn, she blew out the flame.

Then she walked around her father's den, waving the smoking sage in the air, clearing the room of negative energy, negative memories. No one had used the room much since he'd passed fifteen years ago, felled by a heart attack no one saw coming. His impressive oak desk dominated the room, with wall-to-wall bookshelves behind it and along the opposite wall. The bookshelves were empty now. The desk had been cleared out long ago, but painful memories remained. The most painful was discovering her father had another daughter. Rose had learned that shocking news recently. Some days, it felt like a lifetime ago. And sometimes it felt like yesterday.

Rose and her brother, Kirk, had inherited their childhood home in Lake Amelia after their mother had passed a few weeks ago. Kirk lived in Florida and didn't care whether Rose sold the house or lived in it. Rose wasn't ready to decide. Her home and career as a photojournalist were in Philadelphia, although she couldn't work right now because of injuries suffered during a recent assignment. If she stayed in Lake Amelia for much longer—maybe even picking up some freelance jobs when she could work again—she wanted to use more of the house, including the first-floor den.

First, she had to make it her own.

Sweeping the room with sage did more than clear any lingering negative energy. The earthy aroma invigorated Rose and sharpened her mind, helping her to focus on positive thoughts despite her fears that her injuries might not heal well enough to return to the demanding work of a news photographer. Once she'd covered every inch of the room with the healing fragrance, she left the sage bundle smoldering in the kitchen sink.

She opened the cupboard underneath the sink, grabbed a rag and the Murphy Oil Soap, and returned to the den where she wiped down the bookcases on the wall opposite the desk. She crossed the room and knelt carefully without putting much weight on her right arm. As she wiped a lower shelf, her hand hit a bump. Actually, it felt more like a round button, cool to her touch. Not wood. Maybe brass? She pressed it and pulled her arm back when a section of the wall popped open.

"What the heck?"

Rose reached into the compartment, ran her fingers around the inside, and pulled out an envelope. The flap gaped open, revealing a wad of money. She gasped and fell back as if shoved.

Rose stared at the cash, then pushed herself off the floor and dropped into the chair behind the desk. She turned the envelope over in her hands. It had no writing on the outside. When she flipped it upside down, hundred-dollar bills cascaded onto the desk, along with a folded piece of paper. Although eager to count the cash, Rose unfolded the note first. The person either had poor handwriting or had scribbled the message in a hurry.

My investigation must be making someone nervous. It's not just that someone ran my vehicle off the road the other day. Someone broke into my apartment. I'm pretty sure I'm onto something. They've tried to hurt me. I'm terrified. They know where I live and where I work. I need to disappear. I hope you'll use this to continue the investigation.

Rose's father, Randall Webster, had been a successful attorney, an advocate for working-class people and the growing immigrant population in upstate New York. He didn't take on domestic cases, divorces, family disputes, those sorts of things.

What was this about? What was the money for? And why had Dad stashed it at home instead of in the safe in his office near Saratoga Springs? If the money was for a case her father had been working on, was it even legal for him to keep the money at home?

What other secrets were you keeping, Dad?

Ben Franklin stared back at Rose. A lot of Ben Franklins. Rose had never seen so many hundred-dollar bills. To be honest, she'd never even held one.

She pushed the bills into a pile, then picked them up and counted as she laid each one back on the desk. When she reached five thousand dollars, she paused and took a deep breath. Was she halfway through the stack?

At eight thousand dollars, she took another deep breath and slowly counted out the remaining bills until she laid down the very last one.

"Holy crap, Dad, what were you doing with ten thousand dollars in cash?"

Chapter Two
July 2010

The late morning sun sparkled off the deep blue water of Lake George in the Adirondacks. Power boats towed skiers along the smooth surface until another boat roared by, creating sudden waves that challenged the skiers to remain upright. Jet skis raced one way, then circled around and flew off in another direction. Paddle wheel boats, filled with tourists leaning on the railings and soaking in the view, offered a calmer ride. And thousands of people on shore glanced at the activity on the lake while eating lunch or filling shopping bags with mementos.

Kelsey Jacobs and her friend, Millie Snyder, sat at a small table on the patio at the Western Inlet Inn on the lower west side of the lake, each drinking from a tall cool glass. Millie's contained lemonade and Kelsey's iced tea. Millie's boyfriend Josh liked fishing at Lake George, so they'd taken a few days off from work downstate. While Josh fished, Millie shopped and spent some time with Kelsey catching up on their lives.

A few drops of iced tea fell onto Kelsey's lap when she raised her glass to her lips, making her question her choice of white linen slacks. Kelsey dipped her napkin in her water glass and dabbed the spot on her right thigh.

"See that?" Kelsey laughed. "You can't take me anywhere." She focused on rubbing the iced tea stain, then looked up at Millie. "I didn't mean to interrupt. You were telling me about your work."

Millie waved her hand. "There's not much to tell. As an associate attorney with a few years of experience, I'm handed a wide variety of tasks, some interesting, some tedious—all of them have to be done immediately." She laughed. "They brought me into a fascinating case the other day involving an adoption agency and . . . Well, I shouldn't talk about it, but I'll fill you in once it's resolved. I work long hours, eat dinner at eight o'clock most days, then collapse on the couch."

"And you love it?"

Millie's smile lit up her face. "And I love it. How's your work?"

Kelsey opened her mouth to answer but stopped, distracted by a woman's voice coming in bursts of Spanish from behind the privacy hedge separating the patio from the nearby guest rooms.

Millie turned her head. "The woman sounds upset. Can you understand what she's saying?"

Kelsey nodded and put her finger to her lips. She leaned in and whispered, "The woman who's so upset is telling the other person a story. My Spanish is a little rusty, but I'm getting the gist of it." Kelsey gazed at the table as she repeated the conversation.

"The woman blames the owner for her husband's injury. He was climbing a stepladder while painting a two-story shed near the water when he fell. The man said the ladder was old and unstable. She said they couldn't go to the emergency room because they didn't have insurance. Her husband doesn't have documentation." Kelsey paused.

"She says the owner sent her and her husband to a friend of his, a doctor who could take care of his broken wrist and injured lower back. Despite their fears, they went to see the doctor because her husband was in a lot of pain. They told the doctor they didn't have much money. She says he told her, 'No hay problema.'

"Her husband didn't work for a week. When he visited the doctor a few days ago, the doctor said, "Perhaps you have a daughter who could clean my office to settle your bill." She didn't want her daughter to work for the doctor, but they had to pay him somehow." Kelsey paused again. "I can't hear every word, but she's saying something about what happened to another girl who lives in the same apartment complex." Another pause. Then she nodded. "When the woman's daughter came home late yesterday after cleaning the doctor's office, she went straight to her room."

Kelsey and Millie looked toward the hedges. The woman who'd been speaking was sobbing.

"She's afraid for her daughter," Kelsey said.

A man standing near the patio bar apparently heard the woman sobbing. He wore a polo shirt with the inn's name embroidered on it and had a walkie talkie clipped onto his belt. He glanced at Kelsey and Millie sipping their drinks as he rushed past them to the source of the voices.

"Vuelvan al trabajo," he commanded.

Kelsey whispered, "He told them to get back to work." The man walked and spoke with so much authority that Kelsey pegged him as a senior manager or member of the inn's security.

A woman hurried out from behind the hedge, wiped her eyes with a handkerchief, and scurried across the patio.

"Should we go after her? See if we can help?" Kelsey asked. Before Millie could answer, a server walked over with two large plates and set their salads on the table. They picked up their forks and began eating, glancing around the patio, distracted by the conversation they'd overheard.

"I'm not sure what we could do," Millie said. They ate quietly, then returned to their conversation about work, old friends, and life's daily challenges.

"Tell me more about what you're doing."

Kelsey nodded. "It's a small firm, so I get to do a lot more than a paralegal would at a larger firm. We address issues important to the community, like helping immigrants find jobs and decent, affordable places to live. It's one reason I'm so interested in the conversation we overheard. It sounds like some workers here are having a difficult time."

"It's challenging coming to this country to work, even if you do it legally." Millie sipped her drink. "What about Hal? Have you heard from him?"

"No, thank goodness. He got the message."

"Ending a relationship can be difficult. I'm glad you don't have to deal with him anymore."

"Yeah, me too."

The two women returned to their meals. When they finished eating, Kelsey asked the server where the restroom was. She looked across the table. "Do you need to go?"

Millie shook her head.

"I'll be right back."

The restroom was through a door off the patio and down a short hallway. When Kelsey walked into the ladies' room, the housekeeper was wiping the mirror with a blue spray and a cloth. The woman's eyes were red and swollen, the muscles around her jaw taut.

"¿Le puedo ayudar?" Kelsey asked. "Can I help you? I overheard you on the patio."

"No, no," the housekeeper said, her eyes as big as saucers. Her face turned bright red as she grabbed her throat and rubbed her chest. She dropped her cleaning supplies into the bucket and rushed out the door.

Kelsey started to follow the woman but stopped. She didn't want to push. When she returned to the table, she told Millie about her encounter.

"I didn't mean to scare her, but she couldn't get away from me fast enough."

"I don't think there's anything we can do," Millie said. "But I agree. Something's going on here with the owner and the doctor and the workers." Millie reached for her handbag and pushed back her chair. "I don't have kids yet, but I know all mothers worry about their children, wanting to do everything they can to protect them from falling into an unsafe situation. That woman can't help but worry something might happen to her daughter."

"Maybe something already has," Kelsey said.

Chapter Three
Present Day

"The money was in the envelope with this note?" Maxi stared at Rose across the small oak table in front of the sliding glass door in the kitchen. She'd barely crossed the threshold when Rose pulled her into the kitchen to show her what she'd found. Maxi held the wad of bills in one hand and the note in the other. "You said there's ten thousand dollars?"

Rose nodded at her sister. Well, half sister since they had different mothers, but Rose had thought of her as her sister the moment she found out about her. Rose had discovered books and a photo in the attic after returning to her childhood home to care for her ailing mother. She'd learned the girl in the photo with dark skin and a tidy afro was Maxi Stover, and the woman was Maxi's mom, a civil rights lawyer with the ACLU in Albany. The man in the photo was Maxi's father. And Rose's father. Rose and Maxi hadn't had a chance to explore what their new relationship meant. They were going to talk about it tonight, but the note and Ben Franklins pushed that aside.

"She's scared," Rose said, pointing to the note while

picking up the bottle of red wine off the kitchen counter. She walked over to the dining room table and set the wine down. This was Rose's favorite part of the house. Her parents had taken down the wall between the kitchen and dining room after Rose had left for college. They'd created an open space, with the kitchen at one end, a large comfortable couch in front of the fireplace at the other end, and the dining room table in the middle.

"What makes you think it's a woman?"

"Instinct." Rose shrugged. "She mentions someone ran her off the road and that her apartment was broken into. Plus, the tone and her handwriting."

"She—or he—said they *thought* someone tried to run them off the road," Maxi said. "It wouldn't be the first time someone claimed that happened. I've heard that story more than once after finding a car in the ditch."

As a deputy sheriff in Washington County, Maxi had plenty of stories to tell. If only she would. Rose sometimes tried to learn what cases Maxi was working on, but Maxi rarely shared any stories and never any that would interest a journalist.

"What should we do with the money?" Rose asked. "Should we look for the woman?"

"With what information?" Maxi asked.

Rose jerked her head back. Her eyes widened, then almost disappeared in her frown. "By searching for clues, the way most investigations start." Was she underestimating how difficult it could be to find the letter writer and why her father had stashed money in a hidden compartment at home?

"What's your goal? Do you want to return the money? Do you want to find out if something happened to the woman?"

Rose's mind raced. She could ask Brandt Statler, the lawyer her father had brought into the firm, intending to have Brandt buy out the practice when Randall retired. Except a heart attack stole those years from her father, and Brandt had assumed the practice sooner than intended. Brandt might remember something or recognize the woman's handwriting.

Rose couldn't just toss the letter and keep the money. That didn't feel right.

"For starters, you should tell Kirk." Maxi placed the note on the table and steepled her fingers under her chin. "Since the money was found in your parents' home—now yours and Kirk's home—you should let him know before you do anything else."

"That makes sense."

"Good. Can we eat now? I worked nine hours straight today with very little lunch and I'm starving."

Rose had made a simple dinner, perfect for the summer: a tossed salad with shredded carrots, roasted beets, shaved parmesan, walnuts, and chicken. Rose's Aunt Tess, owner of the Main Street Diner in Lake Amelia, had been giving Rose recipes, knowing she wasn't much of a cook and encouraging her with easy meals. Rose hoped the salad would be enough for Maxi. Her sister had a hearty appetite.

Rose pulled the salad out of the refrigerator and set it on the dining room table. She returned to the kitchen for a loaf of ciabatta and a bottle of extra virgin olive oil. Maxi walked over and sat at the table while Rose sliced the bread and poured some EVOO into small bowl.

"So, busy day?" Rose asked as she and Maxi filled their plates.

Maxi grunted. "Everybody on the road is in a hurry, as if Lake George will be gone if they don't get there faster than the family in the car in front of them." Maxi stabbed some lettuce and stuffed it into her mouth. "People think we pull drivers over for speeding so we can collect the fines and pump up the county's bank account," she said after a moment of chewing. "They don't realize how much we're trying to slow them down before they slam their vehicle into a fire hydrant, which a young man did today in Hudson Falls."

Maxi ate vigorously while Rose nibbled on salad and sipped her wine. Maxi wiped her mouth with her napkin. "This is delicious. Thanks for dinner, and for letting me whine. What else did you do today besides uncover more secrets?"

"I really could be done with secrets," Rose said, chewing a piece of grilled chicken she'd gotten at the grocery store. "I packed some of Mom's clothes into a couple of trash bags. I went through her things in the downstairs closet. There's so much stuff. I don't know whether to give it to the church or the Salvation Army."

"It's only been a few weeks. There's no hurry."

"I know, but I don't have much else to keep me busy. It's difficult to look at Mom's toiletries in the downstairs bathroom without crying, so I tossed them in the trash. And then I went across the hall and saw her stuff on the dresser in the bedroom. She had several old bottles of perfume even though she hadn't used perfume in years. She told me she couldn't bear to throw them out because of the memories they contained. Of Dad." Rose swallowed the lump in her throat. "Of Christmases. Mother's Days. Then I sat on the bed and sobbed." Tears filled Rose's eyes.

Rose couldn't ignore the pull to stay in the lakeside community where she'd grown up and had such wonderful memories, but her professional life and friends were back in Philadelphia. Exciting breaking-news assignments happened far less often in small-town Lake Amelia than in the fast-paced Philadelphia area. Of course, one of those exciting assignments was the reason her right arm was in a cast and the muscles in her right shoulder still ached if she raised it too far.

"Where'd you go?"

Rose looked up from her plate. "Sorry. Just thinking

about cleaning Dad's old office today and taking care of Mom's stuff. And wondering how long I'll be here."

"And?"

"I don't have a clue yet," Rose admitted. "I have some legal matters to wrap up and my surgeon hasn't cleared me for work, but I miss my home, my friends . . ."

"But?" Maxi pushed her plate toward the center of the table and picked up her wine.

"But life threw me a major curve when I discovered you're my sister. I want to get to know you. Find out if you want to stay in my life." Rose dropped her hands to her lap. This was a conversation she and Maxi needed to have, but now that they were, Rose was afraid Maxi wanted much more space than Rose did.

Maxi sipped her wine and cleared her throat. She set the glass on the table and leaned on her forearms. "Rose, I liked you as a friend. I'll like you as my sister. But we're different kinds of people—"

"Because I'm straight and you're gay," Rose blurted.

"No, because I'm in law enforcement and you're a nosy photojournalist."

Rose stared at her and pinched her lips together.

"Kidding, Rose. I'm kidding. See, you don't know me at all yet. I do like you, and it's a lot to take in that I have a sibling. Two, counting Kirk." Maxi's eyes softened as she glanced into the distance. "My life is complicated enough, trying to fit in where some people don't think I belong. You haven't spent a lot of time in Washington County lately, but it's one of the most conservative counties in the state. And I'm not. Far from it. I'm working hard to make friends at work and in the communities I cover. That takes time and energy. I want to get to know you better, for sure, but I need to go slower."

Rose smiled and nodded. "I know it seems like I'm on the

express train while you're on the local, but the most important thing is I want to have you in my life. I mean, we have the same father. We're both career women. We have a similar sense of right and wrong."

"Probably a little better than Mr. Randall had."

"Dad."

"Not Dad to me. You're all set to have me call him Dad. He's still Mr. Randall, no matter what the photos show. Or what my mother said. I still didn't have a father growing up. Never will. That was a great . . . sadness for me." There was a catch in Maxi's voice as she looked down at her hands, opened and closed them a few times. "Most girls my age had loving, attentive fathers who took them for ice cream or to the skating rink or to the matinee on the weekend. I wanted that. Until my mother begged me to stop asking because I would never know my father. She was right."

"But you can know him now. Through me. Through Kirk."

"When I'm ready, Rose. On *my* schedule, not yours."

Chapter Four
July 2010

Haunted by the fear in the housekeeper's voice, Kelsey drove to the Western Inlet Inn the next day. Millie and Josh had checked out that morning and were headed back home. Kelsey planned to find the house-keeper and offer to help her. She could wander the property and, if anyone asked, tell them she was checking out the space for an upcoming family gathering.

The lake was visible between the two and three-story buildings with dark brown siding that sat on a sloping hill. White pines provided a canopy of shade for some. People more interested in creating tan lines could stretch out on the chaise lounges scattered at the edge of the beach where they could enjoy the expansive view of New York State's fourth largest—and cleanest—lake. The beach at the Western Inlet Inn was just wide enough for two people to walk side by side without one of them getting wet feet. July was excellent for swimming. Actually late July and the first half of August were almost the only time for swimming in the mountain lakes. The water had finally warmed up, but it wouldn't stay warm for long.

All the buildings and signage were in shades of brown with green accents, using the colors of the surrounding mountains as the theme. The exception was the umbrellas at the patio tables and beside the pool, which were bright blue with narrow white stripes. The entire property was rustic, but if you looked beyond the fresh coat of paint that was applied every May, the place barely lived up to its four-star reviews.

Kelsey made her way to the patio where she'd met Millie the day before. She passed the building and the main office, then turned left and settled into a chair at one of the small patio tables. A server came over and set a coaster on the table.

"Welcome. What may I get for you?"

"Just an iced tea, thank you."

The young man returned with her drink and asked if she wanted something to eat.

"Maybe later," she said. "I'll enjoy the view for now."

She sipped her tea, thinking about the housekeeper from the day before, but after almost half an hour, Kelsey hadn't seen her or many other staff. She declined lunch, left some money on the table, and wandered toward the pool and beach. She worked her way to the guest buildings. Glancing around and seeing no one, Kelsey stepped inside.

The hallway was long and narrow, the light low, the smell musty. There wasn't any housekeeping staff on the floor, but there might be a dogleg at the end of the hallway with more rooms around the corner.

The stairs were on her left. Kelsey opened the door and climbed to the second floor. She still didn't see any staff and wondered if housekeepers were working in the other building. How many housekeepers did the inn employ? There had to be more than a hundred rooms in the two buildings. Cleaning them must require several housekeepers.

Kelsey let the door close behind her and went up the last flight of stairs. This building, Lakeside Two, had three floors.

Lakeside One had two. It would be difficult to walk down each hallway and explore every floor without raising suspicions.

She stopped. Cameras. Did the inn have cameras in the hallways to monitor guests' comings and goings, to make sure no intruders entered the building? She took the last step to the third floor, a little out of breath, and eased the door open. She looked up over the stairwell doorway. No cameras. That was good. She was clear to approach the housekeeping cart halfway down the hall. Kelsey moved forward cautiously, not wanting to intimidate the staff, especially if it was the same woman from yesterday.

She knocked on the door frame and peeked into the room. The housekeeper making the bed glanced up, and when she saw Kelsey, her face went white. She shook her head.

Kelsey stepped into the room. "I overheard you speaking to someone while I was having lunch on the patio yesterday. Remember, I saw you in the ladies' room?"

The housekeeper froze.

"Something's wrong and I want to help. I think someone may be mistreating you and your family. I work for a lawyer. We can protect you."

The woman shook her head. "You no can help. Please go. Leave me alone."

"Sofia?"

The housekeeper's head snapped toward the voice in the hallway, and her body tensed, eyes widened.

"Please go. Ahora," she whispered.

As Kelsey hurried out of the guest room, she almost bumped into the man she'd seen ordering the women back to work the other day. She read his nametag. Juan. Security. Kelsey backed up against the hallway wall.

"What are you doing here?" He crossed his arms and

stared at Kelsey with deep black eyes, then a flicker of recognition. "You were here yesterday."

"I had lunch with a friend who was staying here. I came back to look over the property." She worked up a smile. "It's a beautiful space. My family is coming to visit in a couple of months, and we might have people stay here."

"You don't need to talk with a housekeeper to do that. You shouldn't disturb the staff while they are working. They have much to do."

The security guard took Kelsey's elbow and walked her down the hall to the elevator. She tensed at his touch and tried to block the memory of Hal's firm grasp when he'd yank her arm and scream at her for doing something like not screwing the top back on the peanut butter jar.

She didn't move until the elevator door opened. The man motioned for her to get in, then stepped in after her. He stood closer than necessary and pressed the button to the lobby. Kelsey watched the numbers over the door change from three to two to one. The security guard stared at her, and he asked if she wanted a staff member to show her around the property.

"It's fine," Kelsey said. "I've seen enough."

"Yes, I believe you have." He walked her to her car and watched her drive away.

Kelsey's fingers started cramping on the steering wheel, but she was too afraid to loosen her grip. Her throat closed as she thought of the security guard's steely glare, a look he might use to keep his staff in line. His eyes had bulged with anger the same way Hal's did when he came looking for a fight. And Kelsey was never fast enough to get out of his way.

A little south of Six Flags, she stopped at Panera for a dark roast iced coffee and a scone. Her nerves didn't need the caffeine, but her brain did. She shivered, dropped the scone onto the napkin, and took a long sip of coffee through the straw. Hard as she tried, she couldn't clear her mind of the security guard's threatening look.

"Yes, I believe you have seen enough," he'd repeated as he stood next to her vehicle. "If you're smart, you won't come here again." He'd held her door while she got in and then closed it with such force, the vehicle rocked from side to side.

Kelsey didn't know what the man was hiding, but he'd made it clear she was not welcome there. Which only made her eager to go back as soon as she could.

Chapter Five
Present Day

Maxi helped Rose clean up but declined her offer of coffee.

"I'm sorry I can't stay longer. I'm bushed. You know, this is just the beginning of our conversations, right? Keep that in mind. Thanks for dinner. It was delicious. I'm going to go home, spend a little time in the yard with the dogs, then hit the sack."

Rose walked Maxi to her car. The sun was already dropping behind the mountains, casting shadows over the stately pine trees lining the street and squeezing the lingering light from the woods. The air was still humid from the sunny August afternoon. On many summer days, it was too hot and humid to walk Gladys more than once in the morning. Her little body could overheat, and the sidewalks could burn the pads of her paws. Rose would try to keep the dog on the cooler grass beside the concrete sidewalk, but of course Gladys pulled on the leash and walked wherever she pleased. On the way back into the house, Rose decided it had cooled down enough for Gladys.

She leashed up the ten-pound bundle of energy dancing

around her feet. When her mother's life was slipping away, Rose had become Gladys's caretaker too. Although she never had a dog of her own, some of Rose's friends did, and she preferred their larger dogs who tolerated longer walks and hikes in the woods. Gladys was a sidewalk strutter, not a hiker. But she was a warm bundle of love. Her ability to sense Rose's moods, especially her sadness, surprised Rose. When Rose's grief brought her to tears, Gladys would often jump up on her lap and climb into her arms, trying to lick the tears away. Rose wasn't used to that kind of unconditional love, and she'd learned to appreciate it.

Rose walked with purpose and energy to burn while Gladys pranced. They went out the side door, down the driveway, took a right on Cedar, then another right on Pine and headed for Main Street. Gladys paused at every mailbox post, fire hydrant, or street sign along the way and left her mark. They walked up one side of Main Street, then headed down the other. Rose's thoughts swirled: the death of her mother, discovering her sister, and her childhood home now belonging to her and Kirk. And Maxi.

Her mother's will, with instructions spelled out by Randall, gave Maxi one third of the family's assets, including partial ownership in the house. Maxi had objected. Said she wasn't owed anything by a man who didn't acknowledge her as his daughter while he lived and wanted nothing from him now. The lawyers were still figuring it out. On the surface, Rose seemed to juggle everything fine, but she had a lot of processing to do and walls of her own to break down. Years as a photojournalist had strengthened her defenses to protect herself and keep her emotions in check. Mostly when she needed to. Sometimes when she couldn't help it.

Tonight, Rose's defenses were not strong enough to handle all the people enjoying the evening as it cooled. As she and Gladys looped back along Main Street, the crowds grew bigger and louder. Families with energetic children passed older couples holding hands. Nearly everyone licked an ice cream cone or dipped a plastic spoon into a sundae. Rose considered heading over to the Lake Amelia Creamery, but the last thing she wanted was to be around people, especially impatient and squirming children. A block later, Rose turned away from Main Street and the lake, eager to get home.

She had so many questions and too few answers. How long should she stay in Lake Amelia? How long could she stay on the sidelines before her freelance contacts gave her assignments to other photojournalists? After the rally in Philadelphia, when she could barely breathe or hold a cup of coffee, Rose worried her career was over. Would she regain enough strength to chase after reluctant newsmakers with a gear bag over her left shoulder and her camera held steady in her right hand taking photos? Or had she done that for the last time?

Over the years Rose had seen older photographers and videographers at events, their bodies slow to react when a newsmaker took off running, or the way they struggled to bend down for a better angle. She'd sympathized. It was difficult to quit doing what you loved when you'd been doing it for so long, even when your body demanded you find something else. But, for Rose, what else was there? Sitting in a newsroom, monitoring images coming in over the feeds to help decide which ones to use? Sure, people hung up their cameras and sat behind a computer to stay in the news business, but you could tell by the slouch of their shoulders or lack of sparkle in their eyes how much it pained them.

Gladys tugged on the leash, and as soon as Rose unlocked the front door, the dog ran into the kitchen and lapped from her bowl of water. Then she ran down the hall and disappeared into her mother's bedroom. When Rose walked in, Gladys was pawing the bed, a low rumble of sadness coming from her belly. Rose's eyes filled with tears. She picked up Gladys and lay beside her on the bed, pulling the pooch close. Gladys licked the tears falling down Rose's face onto her mother's favorite powder blue bedspread.

"I miss her too, Gladys. I miss her too."

Rose always pushed Gladys out of her mind when she thought about returning to Philly. Her life there did not include taking care of a dog, especially when an assignment could send Rose anywhere from Washington to New York City at a moment's notice. What would she do with the little dog if she went back to Philly? Give her up? As if Rose could look Gladys in the eyes and hand her off to a stranger. Rose teared up again at that thought.

Gladys. Maxi. Lake Amelia. The house that was becoming a home. Add a mysterious stash of money hidden in Dad's den. Was Rose wrong to want to find out who wrote the note and why they gave her father ten thousand dollars? If she didn't solve this mystery, who would?

Chapter Six
July 2010

Kelsey showered, dried off, then looked through her closet. She focused on getting ready, but her thoughts never drifted far from the man at the Western Inlet Inn and the way he'd glared at her. She didn't know anything about the inn or the owners, but she was determined to find out. Had the health department cited the inn for any violations? Had any workers filed complaints? She shot that second idea down almost immediately. Immigrant workers rarely complained about their employers. Most were grateful for the work and wouldn't risk causing problems. They might complain to one another, but none of them would ask the authorities to intervene. Still, Kelsey would do a thorough search and find out what she could.

Today was an in-office day with no court appearances or important client meetings on the schedule. She dressed in nice jeans and a navy cotton blouse, which could be dressed up with a blazer she kept in the office. Kelsey poured coffee into her tumbler, locked her apartment door, and got into her car. With no school buses—yay, summer!—and most tourists still asleep, Kelsey had the road to herself. She headed south, the sun peeking above the horizon and softened by a layer of cirrus clouds. Soft music played from the music app on her phone. While her mind reviewed what had happened at the inn, her body relaxed with the music.

Kelsey stopped at a four-way stop and was so lost in thought she didn't notice a vehicle pulling up behind her until its bright lights bounced off her rearview mirror and almost blinded her. She crossed Route 197 and continued on, but the SUV stuck close. For a moment, she thought it was an unmarked police car, but then the SUV tapped the rear of her vehicle.

What the hell?

She pressed the gas pedal to put some distance between them, but her four-cylinder Crosstrek was no match for the hulking vehicle on her tail. She tried to recall the maneuvers she'd learned during a defensive driving course, but focusing on two things at once was impossible. Her pulse raced. Her heart thumped in her chest. Those evasive maneuvers looked so easy in the movies and in video games. It was nothing like that in real time with a real threat. She needed to trust her instincts and reflexes.

She couldn't outrace the big SUV, so she looked for an escape down a side road. The road ahead was straight as a ruler for about half a mile, with no yellow line down the middle or oncoming traffic. A field of young corn covered a wide expanse to her left. To her right was a pasture. There was open space all around her, and Kelsey felt very alone. And very scared.

The SUV pulled alongside her. She couldn't see the driver through the tinted windows, but she noticed a logo on the side with an image of a building on a lake and some words she didn't have time to read. Was that the logo for the Western Inlet Inn?

Her vehicle bounced like it had hit a pothole. Or the edge of the road. She straightened out, easing off the gas and tapping the brakes. Maybe if she slowed down, he would keep going.

Nope.

Kelsey had two choices, and she had to make one of them in a hurry. She needed to drive closer to the shoulder or get hit by the SUV. There wasn't much room on the shoulder before the pavement ended and the ground sloped down into muddy ruts at the edge of the pasture. She opted for the shoulder, but the SUV wasn't done. He inched closer, and Kelsey realized he wasn't going to stop until she did. On the road or in the ditch.

Kelsey caught sight of a yellow sign up ahead with a black curving line and 25 MPH on it. Kelsey tapped the brakes again. The SUV nudged a little closer as the tires of her vehicle hit the edge of the roadway. Her dashboard dinged, warning her that she was veering off the road. Like she didn't know . . .

The green pasture ended in a wall of trees where the road curved. That curve was getting closer. She considered moving over into his lane to force him away but dismissed the idea. His SUV was too large, and it was tapping her vehicle again.

He blasted his horn, and she jerked the wheel to the right. She hit the brakes and squeezed the steering wheel, her knuckles white, beads of sweat running down her cheeks and the middle of her back. The pavement disappeared. Her Crosstrek slid down the embankment, leaned to one side, bounced a few times, and stopped.

Kelsey craned her neck to see the SUV as it sped away, but all she could tell was that it was large—as in Secret-Service-sized large. She couldn't see the license plate number or get another look at the logo on the side of the door. Great. It seemed three quarters of the vehicles in upstate New York were SUVs, half of them dark blue or black and large. Tracking down whoever ran her off the road would be like looking for the proverbial needle in a haystack. But her bigger concern was getting her vehicle out of the ditch.

Chapter Seven
Present Day

A fitful night's sleep in her old bedroom on the second floor didn't bring Rose any closer to figuring out her future, but she knew the first task of the new day had to be telling Kirk about the note and the money.

Is this a good time to chat?

She texted, then stared at her phone. The little dots moved. Then stopped. Her phone rang.

"I figured I'd call since I have time," Kirk said. "What's up? Are you at the house?"

"Yes." Rose looked at the money on the table. "I need to talk with you about something I found."

He groaned, probably recalling how Rose had discovered the photo of their father, his former mistress, and Maxi. Kirk had been slow to accept Maxi as his half sister. But when Carly Webster's will had included instructions from Randall to designate one third of the family estate to Maxi, Kirk conceded Maxi was their sibling.

"Have you been uncovering secrets again?"

"Well," Rose began, "I did find something odd in Dad's den."

"Maria and I slept in there when we came for Mom's funeral. I don't remember anything in there except for Dad's desk. Everything else was gone." Kirk had made it to Lake Amelia the day before their mother died. His wife, Maria, and their two teenaged sons had flown in from Florida the next day.

"What I found was in the built-in bookcase behind his desk. In a hidden compartment."

"You really need to stop this Nancy Drew stuff," he said after a moment.

"I wasn't looking for trouble, Kirk." She told him about the button, the handwritten note, and ten thousand dollars.

"Ten grand?" He whistled. "What does the note say?"

She read it to him.

"So it seems this person was looking into something and got scared because they thought someone was trying to hurt them or warn them," Kirk said. "Then they left the money for Dad to hire a private investigator to find out who was harassing them. To stop it. Does that sound plausible?"

"That's as good a guess as any. But there's no date. No names. Not even initials this time," Rose said. When she'd found the books in the attic that Maxi's mom had given to their father, they were inscribed to RW from KNT.

"I wonder if Brandt knows anything."

"If he was aware of an investigation, especially one involving a cash payment, wouldn't he keep the money at the office, not at home?" Rose responded. "Wouldn't Dad have told Brandt about it? Unless . . ." Rose trailed off.

"Unless what? What are you thinking?" Kirk asked.

"What if the person didn't sign the note because she handed it to Dad in the office? And what if Dad took the note and money home because he didn't trust someone in the office? And," Rose continued, building a case, "What if someone in the office was the person making the threats?"

"Or what if she didn't hand it to him, but left it for him under his door at the office, or through the mail slot at home? That would explain why there was no address or stamp on the envelope," Kirk countered.

"What if Dad didn't know who left the money?" Rose said. The 'What Ifs' were adding up.

They both fell quiet.

"He had to know who left him the money or he wouldn't have kept it," Rose said. She stood up and paced from the kitchen to the family room, turning around in front of the fireplace, letting her mind explore the possibilities, and wandering back toward the kitchen.

"We need to ask Brandt," Kirk said.

"Brandt?" Rose laughed. "I can't see him involved in something like harassment or running another car off the road. Dad liked him and planned for Brandt to take over the practice. Brandt has that streak most lawyers do when they turn off the charm to grill and berate a witness."

"Hey, I think I resent that." They both laughed, knowing Kirk's style was more about cajoling a witness or backing them into a corner of their own lies than browbeating them. Their father, though reserved, bristled with intensity when he learned that someone was mistreating others. Kirk had the same passion for protecting people's rights.

"All kidding aside, I think I should talk to Brandt in person," Rose said. "I don't want to handle this over the phone. I'll make a copy of the note. I want to keep the original in a safe place."

"You make it sound so covert. You're making this into a much bigger deal than it is."

"Well, I think ten thousand dollars in a secret compartment in Dad's den is a big deal." Kirk was seven years older and sometimes took the older brother thing too far, telling her what to do, rarely trusting Rose to decide on her own. "We still have Mom's safe deposit box at the bank. I'll ask the bank to make a copy of the note. Then I'll put the original and the money in the box."

"Just don't lose the money on the way to the bank. And try not to alienate anybody at Dad's office. I still need a contact there once in a while."

"Relax. I know what I'm doing. I've done a few investigations of my own." Argh. Brothers.

"Okay, don't get defensive. Let me know what you learn from Brandt."

Her father's old office number was in her contacts list. Not that she needed to look it up. Home numbers and parents' contact numbers followed people through life, even when the parents were gone and the landline disconnected. She connected with Brandt's assistant and scheduled an appointment for the next morning.

Rose set her coffee cup and empty bowl in the sink and finished getting ready. Then she put the envelope with the note and cash in her handbag. She considered driving to the bank, her brother's comment about not losing the money chipping at her self-confidence. But the bank wasn't far, and Lake Amelia was a safe town. She let Gladys into the backyard to do her business, freshened the dog's water when she scurried inside, and set out for the bank. Gladys knew Rose was going out and danced around her legs, begging to go along, but Rose needed time alone and the walk would do her good.

Was Kirk right? Was she making too much of the note and cash? Fifteen years was a long time. The trail was cold. Should she try to find out if the cash involved one of her father's last cases? Why not? It wasn't Rose's nature to pocket the money and be done with it.

Chapter Eight
July 2010

Kelsey leaned back in her seat and lifted her trembling hands from the steering wheel. Her handbag was on the passenger seat, but she made no move to get her cell phone, too busy trying to process what had happened. A movement off to her right caught her eye. In the distance, a tractor kicking up dust alongside the pasture headed her way. She was about to get out of her Crosstrek and wave to him but realized that was absurd. She already had his attention. With any luck, he could get her vehicle out of the field and back on the road. She got out and took several deep breaths, watching the farmer as he stopped the tractor and shut off the motor.

"Got yourself in a bit of a fix," he said as he climbed down.

"Did you see the big SUV that ran me off the road?" she asked, her voice shaking as she tried to find solid footing in the mud.

"I was plowing the field going west. When I headed back in this direction, I spotted your car in the ditch. I didn't see anyone else."

"A big dark SUV hit my bumper several times, then forced me off the road."

He looked her over. "Are you okay? I'll have my wife call the sheriff and tow truck in case I can't get you out of there." He pulled a bright red paisley bandanna from his hip pocket and wiped his forehead, then unbuttoned the pocket on his right thigh and pulled out a two-way radio. "Yesterday's rain turned this section of the pasture into mud, and you're in a pretty deep rut," the farmer said, studying her tires. "I'll do what I can. By the way, name's Charlie."

She introduced herself and reached for a handshake. But he'd already turned away. After speaking to his wife on the two-way, Charlie retrieved a chain on his tractor, hooked it under Kelsey's Crosstrek, and climbed up. Ten minutes later, after his tires had spun and sprayed mud in every direction, her vehicle hadn't moved. Charlie hopped down again. "I'm glad the tow truck is coming. They'll have better luck. Hang tight." The farmer wiped his hands on his hips.

A siren sounded and a county sheriff's cruiser pulled up. The deputy frowned when he saw her car, then sidestepped down the slope. He touched the tip of his cap and nodded at the farmer, then looked at Kelsey.

"I'm Deputy Farris. How did you end up here? Were you texting?"

"No," Kelsey said. "Another vehicle ran me off the road."

"Did you and the driver of another vehicle have an altercation?"

"You mean, did I try to pass him or flip him off?" She stared at the deputy. He looked fifteen. The ink on his academy certificate was probably still damp.

"I mean what happened, ma'am?"

Great, she wasn't even thirty, and she was getting the ma'am treatment. Not miss. Ma'am. Maybe it was a respect thing. Or maybe he intended to belittle her. If they were in the deep South, she'd say it was respect. Here, not so much.

"A guy in a big SUV tried to run me off the road. He came up behind me and hit my bumper. I sped up. He hit my bumper again, then he pulled up alongside me and kept moving closer until I lost control and landed in this muddy pasture."

Deputy Farris nodded. "I understand Charlie's wife called a tow truck?"

"Yep."

"Why don't you let me see your driver's license and registration?"

Kelsey got her wallet out of her handbag. She slid the driver's license out of its protective sleeve, found the registration tucked behind it, and handed both to the deputy.

"You're not the first driver to end up in Charlie's pasture. This curve has claimed more than its share of vehicles." He glanced at her documents. "You're lucky the mud slowed you down. A couple of drivers didn't have it so good. They hit the row of trees right over there." He shook his head. "Wasn't pretty what happened to those cars. Those people. I'll right be back." He navigated the muddy ground and walked toward the farmer.

A big engine roared as the tow truck pulled up. The driver called out to the farmer, "Is that road that goes behind your barn clear enough for me to get to the pasture?"

Charlie nodded and the tow truck turned around and disappeared behind the farmer's house and barn. The deputy returned to Kelsey's side.

"Charlie didn't see any other vehicle."

"Yeah, he told me."

"I'm not going to cite you for reckless driving because there are no witnesses, and I don't know how you ended up in this predicament."

"I told you. A guy in a big SUV ran me off the road. There was a logo on the passenger door. A building alongside a lake and some words."

"That describes a whole lot of vehicles around here and an equal number of logos. Lots of businesses near Lake George. Unless you can identify the logo, there's not much I can do." He tapped his pen on the pad beneath her documents. "I suggest you thank Charlie for his help, then have the tow truck take your car to the garage. Tell the mechanic what happened and ask him to make sure there's no damage to the drivetrain."

"But what if I want to report being run off the road? What if there's damage to my vehicle and I want to file an insurance claim?"

"I would think long and hard before doing that," Deputy Farris said. "It would go on your record and your insurance rates would likely go up."

Kelsey stared at him. "That's so unfair."

"Like I said, if you don't have a witness, I can't help you much. Take my advice. Put this momentary lapse of judgment behind you and move on."

With that, the deputy handed over her registration and driver's license. He got halfway up the slope when he reached out his hand. "Do you need help, ma'am?"

As she accepted the deputy's help, the tow truck came around from behind the barn and headed in their direction. Without another word, the deputy tipped his hat, got into his vehicle, and drove away.

Kelsey glared at the deputy's departing vehicle, swallowing the insult on the tip of her tongue.

Chapter Nine

Present Day

Rose stood in front of the bank and looked around. Her visit hadn't taken long. The office manager had made a copy of the note, then helped Rose retrieve the safe deposit box. Rose tucked the copy of the note in her bag and put the original, along with the ten thousand dollars, in the box.

It was hotter than normal for early August, and it wasn't even ten o'clock. Forecasters and scientists pointed to climate change for soaring summer temperatures around the globe, and Rose knew their data was compelling. As if people didn't get it when the temperature reached one hundred five degrees in Minnesota. In May. In the shade.

Bill wouldn't be at the newspaper this early in the day. Getting reacquainted with her former mentor at the *Lake Amelia Dispatch* had been one of the best parts of being back in town. He'd brought her in as an intern when she was in high school, then hired her every summer through college. Bill was disappointed she didn't come to work for him after she graduated, although he knew she wanted the excitement of a big city newspaper. He was always ready to bounce ideas around, whether she walked into the newspaper unannounced, or called from an assignment a thousand miles away.

Well, if she couldn't visit the paper, what about the library? It was open and she hadn't been there in a while. Plus, it was an easy walk from the bank. She might even get there without sweating through her shirt.

She trudged up the wide stairs and gulped in the cool air the moment she stepped inside. Carter Paxton, the library's director, looked up and smiled. Rose returned his grin and fanned her face as she strolled to the desk. Librarians were some of her favorite people.

"I haven't seen you since your mother's funeral. How are you doing?"

She sighed. "I'm okay. Good days and bad, as you know." Carter's wife had died in a car accident several months earlier, leaving behind her husband and eight-year-old daughter. "How's Ellie doing?"

"She's fine. At a friend's house this morning. They have a pool and Ellie swims like a mermaid now. I'm going to pick her up after lunch." He looked down and swallowed hard. "I was surprised when she asked to attend your mother's funeral and to stop by your house afterwards." He looked up, tears in his eyes. "I thought it would trigger too many memories for her, but I was the one who struggled."

"I haven't lost many people in my life," Rose said. "Both of my parents' deaths were unexpected. Mom's cancer was already in stage four when it was diagnosed. Dad's heart attack was a shock for all of us. But they were older. Your wife was still young. I can't imagine how you and Ellie handle it, although she is mature beyond her years. Must be all those books she reads above her grade level." Rose smiled.

Carter nodded and wiped a tear off his cheek.

"Kids are more resilient than we adults are," she added.

"Ellie used to sing with her mom all the time. They'd challenge each other to make up new verses to their favorite songs. Those sessions always ended with them collapsing onto the couch, laughing so hard they'd cry." He smiled at the memory. "I've tried to get her to sing with me. I know it's not the same, but I thought it would cheer her up. So far, she's resisted, but a few days ago I heard Ellie singing while she was making her bed. She didn't sing for long, but it's a good beginning."

Rose knew little about grieving and even less about parenting. She nodded and glanced down.

"Did you come in looking for a book, in addition to cooling off?" Carter switched to an easier topic, and Rose was grateful.

"No, I didn't. I'm still reading *The Lost Bookshop*, which I love, by the way. I wanted to revisit our conversation about taking photos of the library and updating your website."

Carter's wide smile pushed away his sadness. "That's great. Are you ready to get to work?"

"I've been picking up the camera a few times every day. My ribs are fine, unless I twist too far, but my shoulder muscles still scream if I lift my arm too high." She pointed to her wrist. "And my arm is still in a cast. I think I can take photos of an empty room or a well-manicured lawn." She laughed. "Of course, the doc still has to sign off."

"Rose, that's such good progress. When do you think you'd be ready?"

"As I recall, you wanted to bring in the cleaning crew and a lawn care company to spruce up the place. If you want to schedule those, I think I'll be ready after next week."

"I'll check with them today." Carter picked up a pen and made a note.

"I'd also like to stop in later this week to check the best angles in the different rooms, the light coming in from the windows, those sorts of things, so when I do come in to take photos I can work more efficiently."

"Sounds good. I've mentioned it to the board of directors, and they agreed it was time to update the website. As soon as you send me the estimate, I'll forward it to them. Approval should be a formality, unless it's going to cost more than I'm thinking."

"I doubt it," Rose assured him. "I'm grateful for the opportunity and you'll get my best price." When Carter had first asked Rose whether she'd be interested in taking photos to update the library's website, she wondered how many clients she could generate in town. Bill said he could use her on assignments sometimes, but she was sure he wouldn't have enough work to keep her busy full time. Perhaps she could find freelance work with businesses in town, updating their website photos. She should look into that, especially if she decided to stick around. And adding images of the Lake Amelia library assignment would broaden her portfolio.

"Does your best price mean a friends-and-family price?" Carter asked.

"Something like that." Her smile lingered until she realized she was staring at Carter. "Okay, then. I'm off. I have a meeting, and I don't want to be late. Talk to you soon."

She hurried home, showered, put on a nice pair of slacks, and a top with sleeves she could unroll in case the air conditioning in the office was too cool.

She made the trip to her father's old law office east of Saratoga Springs and just off Route 29 in half an hour. Tall pines, oak, and maple trees passed by the window, and she hummed one of her favorite songs. When she turned into the parking lot, she fell silent.

The law office was in a small building that also housed a hair salon and a real estate agent. She'd often driven by the building on her way to Saratoga Springs, especially when she first came back to Lake Amelia to care for her mother and take her to appointments at the hospital. The occupational therapist Rose worked with a couple of times a week was at the hospital. So was the surgeon who'd been monitoring her injuries. But all those times, Rose had kept her eyes straight ahead. Now that she was here again, the death of her father tugged at her heart and brought up those complicated feelings.

"Stop!" she ordered herself. She got out of the car, walked up to the doors, and went in.

Chapter Ten
Present Day

Cate, a little fuller in the face with a little more gray in her dark brown hair, presided over the reception desk just as she had since Rose was a teenager. Rose was grateful some things remained the same.

"We heard you were coming into the office today. It's nice to see you."

"Hi, Cate. Thanks for coming to Mom's funeral."

"I'm so sorry she's gone. Like your father, she left us too soon."

Rose nodded in place of the words she couldn't find.

Brandt must have heard Rose arrive. He strolled out of his office and wrapped Rose in a bear hug. It had taken her a while to get comfortable with Brandt's warm demeanor, so different from her father's formal way of interacting with people. She'd always enjoyed talking with Brandt and others in the office, and hoped today would be no different.

"Come on in," Brandt said as he stepped back. He led her into his office and sat in an overstuffed office chair behind his desk.

She took the chair across from him and pulled the note

out of her handbag. "Thanks for making time to see me this morning."

"I always have time for you, Rose. What can I help you with?"

She explained how she'd found the secret compartment in her father's den, revealing an envelope containing a handwritten note and ten thousand dollars in cash. "I hoped you might know what this is about."

"You brought the note?"

She slid the piece of paper across his desk.

His face gave no hint of any feelings as he read.

"This is mysterious." He looked up at her. "The person is scared of something, someone. They're asking your father to look into it, and I'm guessing the money is for a private investigator. But she must have given him some information in another document or letter, or in person. This isn't much to go on."

"I agree. I didn't know where to begin, except here. Does this ring any bells? Does this sound like anything my father discussed with you?"

Brandt hesitated and shifted in his chair. Rose's gaze didn't leave his face.

"This was fifteen years ago, but I don't recall your father consulting with me on any case involving someone who thought they were being harassed, their apartment broken into, their car run off the road. Those are events I would remember, and I don't."

"What about anyone else in the practice? Would they remember something about this?"

"You know this is a small firm, Rose. If it was important, your father or I would have been involved." He looked off to the side. "Until a couple of years ago, Mary had been here the longest. She was your father's top paralegal for more than twenty years. Cate's been here a long time, but she doesn't get involved in cases."

Rose glanced out the window behind him. Mary. Of course. She would ask Mary next.

"Do you recognize the handwriting?"

Brandt picked up the note again.

Was he studying it or pretending to?

"It doesn't look familiar, no."

"Is it Mary's handwriting?"

"No, it isn't." He answered her almost before she finished speaking, as if he expected her question. "Most people highlight a digital document, but Mary loved her sticky notes and said she couldn't stare at a computer all day. She'd print copies of documents she was reviewing and cover them with sticky notes and red pen edits. She was also a prodigious memo writer. I'd recognize her handwriting."

"Do you mind if I see one of her memos? Maybe a few sticky notes to compare?"

"Don't believe me, huh?" He had a hollow laugh like a politician who'd just been indicted. She kept her gaze steady, without a hint of a smile.

"I just want to be thorough."

He slid open a drawer on the right side of his desk. "Almost everything is digital now, but like I said, Mary wrote a lot of notes." He thumbed through the drawer, then pulled out a blue folder. He opened the folder on his desk and scanned a few of the documents. Then he pulled out a piece of paper and pushed it across her desk for her to see.

"Here's a perfect example, and it should be long enough to satisfy your curiosity. Please remember, this is confidential."

Rose nodded and motioned for him to give her back the note she'd brought in so she could compare them. She held them side by side and it was obvious that the same person did not write both documents. She gave him back the one with Mary's writing.

"Okay. Mary didn't write this," Rose said, "but she might know who did. She worked with my father for so many years."

He shrugged. "It's possible." He glanced over her shoulder at the door, then back at her. "Look, Rose, I'm not trying to be difficult." His voice was tighter than when she'd arrived, like he was trying to swallow his annoyance. "It wouldn't be like your dad to keep work at home. I know he died suddenly, and perhaps he stored the note and money until he could put them in the office safe. We can't know what he intended. If Mary has any insights, please let me know."

"Sure, Brandt," she replied, not altogether sure she would. Something was off about the way he reacted to her request. Did Brandt know more than he was letting on?

Chapter Eleven
July 2010

Kelsey thanked the tow truck driver for the lift and walked into the law firm. She hurried to Randall's office and knocked on the door. He was meeting with a client, but when he saw her face, he told her to wait for him in the conference room.

Kelsey stared out the window in the conference room and tried to think. Her hands were shaking so much that the water splashed out of the bottle when she opened it. She set it on the table. Why had that big SUV run her off the road? Could this be about the housekeeper at the Western Inlet Inn? The security guy had glared at Kelsey both times, like he wished his stare alone could cut her down. What was he trying to protect? *Who* was he trying to protect?

Those eyes, the way he'd glared at her—she knew that look. She had lived with a man who looked at her that way just before he'd pulled back his arm and slugged her. Hal. Mean and angry Hal. He'd apologize and promise to never hit her again and she believed him, wanted to believe that he could change. Until the abuse almost killed her. She'd escaped the pain and suffering, but not the vivid memories.

"I've never seen your face so pale," Randall said when he walked into the room. He looked her over again, then sat in the chair next to her and faced her. "Tell me what's going on."

Kelsey took a drink of water. She told Randall about the SUV and the two times she'd been to the inn on Lake George, though she did not mention the name of the inn. "One of the immigrant workers was distraught. She was worried about her daughter's safety if she cleaned the doctor's office because of what happened to another woman's daughter." Kelsey squeezed her eyes closed. "The security guard glared at Millie and me when he walked by."

Kelsey sipped her water, swallowed hard. "Millie had her back to him, so she didn't see the way he stared at us, but it was unnerving. His look was equally threatening when I visited the inn the next day and tried to speak with the housekeeper."

"And she didn't tell you what was going on?"

"She was too frightened, and the security guard interrupted us." She paused. "He could have been following me. I wasn't in the room long when he called out to the housekeeper. Whether the security guy is just flexing his power to intimidate the workers and me, or whether he's a genuine threat, I don't know. But I sure don't understand how what I heard warranted running me off the road."

"What's the name of the inn?"

Kelsey hesitated. "I don't want to pull you into this if knowing what I know could be dangerous. I want to figure out what's going on there without putting anyone else in harm's way."

"I'm not concerned about my safety. I think it would be best if you told me everything you know, including the name of the inn."

She paused, then told him.

His head tilted just enough for her to notice.

"What?"

"The owner of the Western Inlet Inn," Randall said. "His name is Leonard Browning. A couple of weeks ago, Brandt told me that Browning had reached out to him about handling some of his business. Browning has high-priced lawyers. I've met some of them. Why would he engage our services?"

"And why wouldn't Browning ask you, the head of the firm? Why go through Brandt?"

Randall nodded. "I've thought about that as well." He tapped his fingers on the table. "I'd like you to do more research—online only—about Leonard Browning and his properties. Broaden the search to include immigrant issues in upstate New York. See whether any of those articles mention Browning. I'll pull together a list of the men and women we've assisted with their documentation or other issues and find out whether any of them work for or live in any of Browning's properties. I'll choose people who are comfortable talking with one of us. We'll reach out by phone first. If we need to visit one of Browning's properties, I'll do it."

Randall held Kelsey's eyes and his jaw tensed. "We must keep this between you and me. If we need help, I'll find it outside of the office. I don't want to say anything more, but please come to me if you have questions. Ask me in person. No emails. Understood?"

Kelsey nodded.

They both stood. Kelsey picked up her water bottle and turned to leave, but Randall put his hand on her shoulder.

"Don't treat this lightly, okay?" he said. "I'd hate to see anything happen to you. Anything *worse* happen to you," he added.

"I promise I won't do anything irrational, like going back to the inn and pointing my finger at the security guy and accusing him of running me off the road." She offered a weak smile. "I want to, but I won't." She told him the deputy sheriff had advised her to not report the incident to police or her insurance company. "Don't you think I should in case something else happens?"

"I don't think anything else is going to happen," he said. "But to make sure, you're going to stop working in the field. If something is going on and people need our help, we'll find the problem and we'll fix it. I promise."

Later that afternoon, the tow truck company called and told Kelsey her vehicle was ready.

"There's no damage to the drivetrain, but you've got a couple dents, including a spot on the rear bumper," the man said. "You can pick it up when you're ready. I'll be here till six."

The dents might confirm someone had tapped her bumper, but she would let it go. For now. Mary dropped her off at the garage after work and Kelsey drove home, constantly looking back and forth between the road ahead and the road behind her.

Chapter Twelve

Present Day

Rose hopped into her SUV, cranked up the air conditioning, then pulled out of the parking lot. Her mind kept replaying the meeting with Brandt. He'd been so friendly when she walked in with that big smile and smothering hug. When she left, he'd shaken her hand like she had a communicable disease. She wanted to call Mary right away and see if she knew who'd written the note, but she didn't want to do that from the parking lot, so she headed toward Lake Amelia and turned into a gas station on the edge of Schuylerville. She called Mary with the car idling and turned down the AC.

"Hi, Rose," Mary said.

"Thanks for coming to Mom's funeral. I was hoping to chat with you at the luncheon, but I must have missed you."

"I had a doctor's appointment," Mary explained. "And you know how much they charge for last-minute cancellations. I'm sorry I couldn't attend the lunch. Your mother was a wonderful woman."

"I'm calling to see if I could stop by and talk with you in

person. I don't know if you still live in Schuylerville, but I'm outside of town."

Mary was slow to respond. "Of course you can come by, Rose, but it sounds like there's something specific on your mind. What's this about?"

Rose explained her discovery and said she wanted Mary to look at the note.

"I'm not sure how much I can help," Mary said, "but come on over." She told Rose she had moved to a development of modest homes on the other side of Schuylerville a few years ago and gave Rose the address. Like many developments in this part of upstate, the lots were about half an acre with pine, oak, cedar, and maple trees in most yards. Some homes had basketball hoops in the driveway and kids' bikes on the lawn. Others were more landscaped, with annuals and perennial bushes bursting with new growth and vibrant blooms struggling to hold on as the summer heat intensified. Mary's home fell into the latter category. Rose complimented Mary on her beautiful gardens when she greeted her at the door.

"I love the mix of colors and shades of grasses in your berm and the other garden out front here," Rose said as Mary gave her a quick hug. "Do you take care of the gardens yourself?"

"I do." Mary beamed. "It keeps me active and healthy, as long as I get out there before the day heats up. Come on in. It's good to see you."

Mary led Rose to the couch and offered her a drink, disappearing down the hallway and returning a few minutes later with two tall glasses. She picked up a couple of coasters from the center of the coffee table, placing one on the table in front of the couch where Rose sat and one at the end of the coffee table, before settling into a side chair.

"Why don't you show me the note?"

Rose took a few sips and set her glass down. She reached

into her handbag, pulled out the piece of paper, and handed it to Mary.

Mary put on her reading glasses. After studying the note for a couple of minutes, she passed it back to Rose. "I don't know what this is about," she said. "And I've no idea why your father would have put this in a hidden place with so much cash."

A noisy truck rolled past the house. Mary looked out the window, then down at her hands folded together on her lap. "I'll keep thinking about it and let you know if anything comes to mind," Mary said. "I worked with your father on most of his cases, but I don't recognize that handwriting as belonging to anyone in the office."

"What kinds of cases did you and Dad work on?"

"You know he was always fighting for people's rights. He got involved in a few statewide cases involving conditions in prisons and jails, working with other attorneys to improve them. He also helped immigrants gain green cards and address their legal status. And he tried to improve their working conditions. But goodness, Rose, he had his hand in a lot of issues, almost everything except domestic cases and drug cases." Mary blinked, and Rose thought she saw a flash of memory in her eyes.

"I'm sorry. I can't recall anything helpful," Mary said. "It's clear whoever wrote this note was worried about her safety. You'd think I would have heard something, but I just can't remember. My memory isn't what it used to be. It's one of the reasons I retired. It was time to step aside. I'm sorry I can't be more help," she said again.

"It's fine," Rose said, getting to her feet. "I appreciate your time. And it's so nice to sit and talk with you again. I always enjoyed seeing you when I visited Dad's office."

"Let me know what you learn," Mary said, giving Rose a

hug. "I hope nothing bad happened to the person who wrote the letter."

Rose climbed into her vehicle and glanced at the clock on the dashboard. Lunchtime. Where was Maxi? Rose found a wide spot on the road and pulled over. She texted Maxi.

Are you working? Do you want to grab lunch?

I'm running errands and could use a break. Thom's?

Meet you there in twenty?

👍

"Remember the note and the ten thousand dollars?" Rose asked after Maxi sat down across the table and ordered a drink.

"I'm not likely to forget something like that," Maxi said.

"I visited the lawyer who bought Dad's practice after he passed. Brandt Statler. I think you've met him."

Maxi nodded once, motioning for Rose to continue.

She told Maxi about Brandt's demeanor, going from friendly to wary, how she'd stopped at Mary's, and how Mary didn't know who wrote the note.

"The money was in the envelope with the note, right? Not separate in that hidden space?" Maxi asked.

"Right. But that's a dead end, then. What am I supposed to do?"

"Call your brother with an update and ask him what to do. He's a lawyer. He'll have some ideas."

The server was back with their sandwiches and they both dug in. Rose decided Maxi was right. She'd call Kirk. Wait, Kirk knew Mary. He knew Brandt. Maybe he could talk with them and get more information than Rose could. Thinking about Kirk brought her back to Maxi.

"Have you and Kirk talked at all since, you know . . ." Rose's voice drifted off.

"Since your big reveal?" Maxi smiled. "Kirk, Maria, and I talked a little after the funeral, but not about your father or your mother's will." Maxi wiped her mouth with her napkin and took a drink. "I reiterated that I don't want a share of your mother's house. I don't want the money either, but the lawyer says it's going to end up in my bank account whether or not I want it."

"Do you have something against inheriting money?" Why would anyone turn down a windfall of cash? A lot of cash. Rose never struggled to pay her bills, but she didn't know anyone who would turn down a lump of money.

"Your father doesn't owe me anything."

"I'm not sure about that," Rose blurted. "I think he owes you a lot. Did he ever pay child support? Did he ever spend a dime on you? What does your mother say?"

"What makes you think I told her you found out about me?" Maxi set her sandwich on the plate, her eyes laser-focused on Rose.

"I would have thought you'd tell her, that's all. Including you in my mother's will was my father's way of taking care of you."

A couple of guys at the bar shouted at the TV, which was showing highlights of the latest Yankees game. A busy bar was not the best place for a sensitive conversation. Maxi glanced at them, then back at Rose.

"I've managed on my own with my mom until now. Like I said, if I could refuse the money, I would. Maybe I'll give it away. Look, I don't want to talk about this today, okay? I want to enjoy lunch with you and not get into any serious topics."

"Sorry, I didn't mean to upset you." Then she thought about the letter, about how the woman said she'd been driven off the road and threatened. "How long have you been a deputy with the Washington County Sheriff's Office?"

Maxi picked up her sandwich. She tilted her head and raised her eyebrows. "Why?"

"I thought you might know someone who'd been there

fifteen years ago who might remember a woman calling the police about the incidents in the letter."

"I told you I couldn't get involved looking into this, and you have too little to go on." Maxi put down her sandwich again. "You don't know where she lived. You don't know where she allegedly was run off the road. You don't know if she dealt with local police or the county sheriff. Just let it go. If you don't want to keep the money, take a cue from me. Donate it."

Chapter Thirteen

July 2010

Kelsey stared as the door to her second-floor apartment inched open. Why wasn't the deadbolt engaged? When she'd left the apartment this morning, she'd locked the door and the deadbolt, hadn't she? She didn't remember leaving either lock undone, but when she'd inserted the key in the doorknob and began turning it, the door opened. Kelsey crept inside and flicked on the overhead light, followed by the lamp on the living room side table , and finally the kitchen light, even though the early evening sun still peeked through the windows.

The apartment was eerily quiet. Most of the tenants in the small complex were young professionals like her, and many of them didn't get home until after seven. Still, it seems there would be a little more noise somewhere. She walked through every room in her apartment, surveying the dishes on the counter and in the sink, the clothes on the chair in the bedroom, the towels hanging on the rack in the bathroom. Things looked just the way she'd left them this morning, but she couldn't shake the feeling that someone had been here. She looked at the bedroom window. The apartment had central air conditioning, so she didn't open the windows from late June through September. The window locks were in the open position. The window would only raise about four inches thanks to the safety mechanism, but who had opened them?

Her imagination started running in different directions, seeing danger where none might exist. Maybe she'd let in fresh air through the bedroom window the other morning when the overnight temperature had dropped, and she had forgotten to lock it. She'd left for work early that morning and may have been too sleepy to engage the deadbolt. Both were plausible answers. So why were the hairs on her arms standing on end? Why was something poking her brain that these were dangerous signs?

Kelsey changed into shorts and a T-shirt and returned to the kitchen. She pulled the ingredients for a salad out of the refrigerator and started chopping lettuce, but she was so distracted she stabbed her finger with the knife. Great. Just what she needed. She blotted the blood spouting from her finger with a paper towel, but it kept coming.

A memory flashed before her eyes, of blood on her fingers when she felt her swollen and bleeding lip where Hal had struck her. Hal was yelling and threatening to hit her again. She'd pushed him aside and grabbed her handbag, running out of the house to the temporary safety of her car.

Is that what this was about? Had the security guard triggered her memories of Hal's temper, which often ended with parts of her bloody and bruised? Had she seen threats in the guard's look because she was seeing Hal's face instead?

She washed her finger, sprayed it with an antiseptic, and covered it with a bandage. Then she rinsed the cutting board, leaving her unfinished salad on the counter. Kelsey walked from room to room, checking the locks on all the other windows. She turned out the overhead lights, then dropped onto the couch. She needed to talk with someone. Not Mary or Randall. Of course. Millie.

"Hey, Kelsey. Has work been keeping you busy?" Millie's bubbly laugh brought a smile to Kelsey's face but didn't connect with the rest of her tense body.

Kelsey opened her mouth but couldn't form any words. She stuttered. Then sobbed. Tears streamed down her cheeks.

"Girlfriend, what's wrong?" Millie asked.

Kelsey wiped her runny nose and tried again to speak. Nothing.

"I can't remember the last time you were so upset," Millie said. "No, wait. Yes, I can. That time Hal hit you so hard you called me from the ER. Is it about Hal? Has he come after you despite the protection order?"

"No, it's not about Hal. Last I heard, he moved to Florida. They can have him." Kelsey told Millie everything that had happened since their lunch at the Western Inlet Inn. The last piece was the deadbolt and unlocked window in the bedroom. "It's silly because I could have forgotten to lock them. But that security guard's look sent shivers from my toes to the top of my head and sent me back to those awful days with Hal. I can't calm down."

"Are you afraid the security guy's going to come after you again?"

"I don't know what to think. I'm almost too scared to think."

"You should get out of there for a while. A change of scene could help you. You're welcome here."

"Thanks, I appreciate that." Kelsey sniffed away her tears and shifted her thoughts to catch up with Millie about events in Kelsey's former hometown.

They chatted for half an hour. As the call neared an end, Kelsey felt stronger, safer, and she thanked Millie for listening to her.

"Remember what I said about coming to visit."

"I will."

Kelsey spotted a dining room chair and decided to take one more step to protect herself. She slid it under the front door doorknob, then went up to bed.

* * *

Morning came early and without a restful night's sleep. Kelsey showered, dressed, and ate breakfast focusing on the present moment and not yesterday's fears. Her drive to the office was the best kind—light traffic and uneventful.

Mary stepped into Kelsey's office, laptop in hand, and motioned to Kelsey to join her at the small conference table in the corner.

"Randall asked me to collect some information for you because he has something else that needs his immediate attention. He said he wants this completed as soon as possible. He didn't say why and asked me to keep it between us." She turned her laptop so Kelsey could see it. "I just emailed you the list of clients we've helped with issues around their immigration status, their ability to stay with family in the area and find jobs. Some of them, however, do not have family in the area." She pointed to two names on the list. "And some of them are living at the Queensbury Motel."

"Do we know where they work?"

"Only a few names include where they work. I'd offer to help you track down anything else you need, but I got the distinct impression Randall wants to keep whatever this is about to just the two of you. This is as far as I should be involved."

"Thanks, Mary. This is helpful."

"I'm deleting this email to you in five minutes, so you should download the list now and also delete the email.

Randall's instructions." Mary closed her laptop and left Kelsey's office without another word.

Kelsey returned to her desk, found Mary's email, and saved the list in a folder with the articles she'd found about immigrants in upstate New York. Then she deleted the email message. She thought about what Randall had said about keeping this investigation between the two of them, so she hid the folder inside another folder and saved it to her computer. Not the cloud. She was studying the information when her phone rang.

"This is Kelsey Jacobs. How can I help you?"

No one responded. She picked up a pen with her left hand and twirled it. "Hello? Is anyone there?" She thought she heard someone breathing, then a sharp crack exploded in her right ear. It sounded like someone banged the phone against a desk. Or wall. Something hard. She was about to hang up when a deep voice resonated over the phone line.

"Stop snooping or you'll regret it."

The caller sounded like a robot, words spoken slowly, without inflection. Until the last words:

"This is your last warning!" the person screamed.

Kelsey dropped the phone onto her desk and grabbed her chest, trying to slow her breathing. Should she tell Randall about the call, about the deadbolt and window lock in her apartment? Would he believe her? Or would he question her like the deputy sheriff did, think she'd exaggerated it, blown it out of proportion? She realized she couldn't prove any of these things had happened, and that only added to Kelsey's fears and insecurity.

Chapter Fourteen

Present Day

Rose let Gladys out into the yard as soon as she got home and watched the dog go about her business as she determined what to do next in her search for the owner of the money.

The coffee pot beckoned. Something needed to kick her brain into a higher gear, or another more productive one. While her coffee dripped, she cleaned up the kitchen.

When Rose let Gladys back inside, she looked out at the yard. The flowers looked tired, like they'd had enough of summer. She should do some gardening, water the plants, mow the yard. She looked at her right arm, which was still in a cast. Her shoulder still hurt some days, especially when she slept wrong. She was doing the exercises her occupational therapist suggested and was getting stronger, but Rose knew her limitations. It'd be better to hire a high school kid. She'd ask Aunt Tess or Mrs. Shaw, her next-door neighbor, if they could recommend someone.

She returned to the task at hand. Where else could she find information that could lead to the identity of the note writer?

Kirk was clear he thought she was wasting time. Their phone call yesterday had not been helpful.

"You need to find something to do," he'd said. "Maybe pick up the camera again and take photos. Find freelance work. You're on this wild hunt for information that's fifteen years old, with little hope of figuring it out. It's sending you on one wild goose chase after another. Don't you have better things to do with your time?"

She hadn't wanted to admit it—older brothers loved to be told when they were right—but she knew the search had little promise of turning up any leads. And no, right now she was still biding her time until she could work again. She also knew it was up to her to figure out who left the money and why. Kirk wouldn't. She'd go over all those papers until she was sure they contained no clues.

Her father had stashed money and a note in a hidden compartment in his den. Did he keep any other documents at home? She knew he liked to linger over a physical document while smoking a pipe in his brown leather chair in the den. Where were those papers? She didn't remember finding any when she and Aunt Tess cleaned out the office. But that was fifteen years ago, and Rose had been in shock over her father's sudden death. There were many things she didn't remember about those weeks after his passing.

Rose thought back to when she'd searched through the boxes of books in the attic a couple of months ago. She recalled another box with manilla file folders, filled with research he'd conducted into different issues. It called for a second look.

She went upstairs, into the main bedroom, and slid open the closet door. The small stepladder was leaning against the wall, right where she'd left it. Climbing into the attic was easier with her arm more healed, but it was still slow going. She slid over the piece of plywood to open the space above her head, climbed through the opening, and turned on the overhead light. As she looked around, she realized she needed to take care of everything in the house. Kirk wouldn't be much help. Aunt Tess would give a hand if Rose asked, but her mother's sister wouldn't care that much about any of this stuff unless Rose found a memento of Aunt Tess and her mother from childhood.

Cleaning out the attic could wait. She had a mystery to solve. Rose scanned the boxes as she walked to the side where the books were stored. Next to the books was the box of file folders. Potential clients? Important issues he followed? Time to find out.

She slid the box across the floor to the opening, climbed onto the ladder, and tried to lift the box with both arms. Nope. There was no way she could carry it down the ladder. She could remove some folders and take them down a few at a time, but that would be tedious. She leaned against the ladder as best she could and slid the box closer to the opening. Slid the box a little farther and leaned back as the box fell to the closet floor.

Boom. Yikes. That was louder than she thought it would be.

Then she slid the plywood back over the opening, worked her way down the ladder, and leaned it against the wall. She didn't need to take the entire box downstairs, only an armful of folders at a time. She'd be up and down several times to get through the box, but the regular stairs wouldn't tax her arm and shoulder the way the stepladder would. She grabbed the first few folders and returned to the first floor.

Almost two hours later, after three more trips to retrieve folders, printouts, and legal-sized papers filled with notes, the dining room table was covered. Rose sighed. She was no closer to knowing any more than she'd been before. The file folders covered topics like illegal betting on horses, land grants preserving farmland and natural habitats of endangered species, and the undocumented immigrant population in upstate New York. The largest folder was dedicated to the cleanup of toxins in the Hudson River. It might be worth it to go through all the folders again, but her brain wasn't up to it. She shoved the stack of folders across the table and went into the kitchen for something to eat.

Chapter Fifteen
July 2010

Kelsey wrote up her report for Randall, attached the most relevant articles she'd found on the internet, and slid them under his office door. Although he was in court, no one else would go in while he was out. Then she went back to her office, sat back in her chair, and considered what to do next.

The threatening phone call only increased Kelsey's determination to find out whether the immigrants the firm had assisted were being mistreated, or if any immigrants working in upstate New York were being abused or coerced. She was restless waiting for Randall to send her the other list they'd talked about—of clients who were connected to Browning's inns or apartment complexes. It was a task Randall said he didn't want anyone else to handle. Kelsey's research hadn't turned up any incidents of human trafficking of immigrants in the area. She found one article about the arrest of a group of men several months ago for forcing women into sexual liaisons with men. But that was downstate and there was no mention of Browning. She pushed her brain to think of what else she could do.

Kelsey thought again of the conversation she'd overheard with Millie. The housekeeper said another woman had allowed their daughter to clean the doctor's office and that when the girl had come home, she'd gone straight to her room, didn't even eat dinner. Did something happen between the doctor and the daughter? Is that what was going on? Did the owner of the Western Inlet Inn and his friend, the doctor, force young immigrant women to go out with men, to have sex with them? Or were the owner and doctor taking sexual liberties with the young women and threatening them if they told anyone?

She may have just hit on something that would prompt a security guard to run someone off the road, break into their apartment, threaten them. Yes, the threats were real. Kelsey needed to find out if her theory about what was going on at the Western Inlet Inn was correct, but she couldn't go back there. That would be asking for more trouble. There was only one other place to go, and it was a short hop up the Northway.

* * *

What a dump. The Queensbury Motel Complex, as it was grandly called, wasn't for tourists. No one in their right mind would stay here if they didn't have to. Only a couple of cars were in the parking lot. Kelsey studied the buildings. Someone had renovated the old motel into an apartment complex, a low-income apartment complex. No one sat in the chairs next to the unit's front doors, even though it appeared none of the units had window air conditioners. Not in the front windows. At least one front door on the second floor was open, probably to help move air through the unit. People were putting up with the heat in their rooms, or they were at work.

Kelsey checked the clock on the dashboard. It was late

afternoon. Too early for most people to be home from work, and those working evenings in restaurants or bars may have just gone into work. She parked as far away from the office as she could and climbed the stairs to the second floor. Cigarette butts and pieces of plastic collected in the corners of the stairwell. Layers of dirt covered the floor and cigarette smoke was embedded in the brick walls.

At the top of the stairs, Kelsey turned right. Noisy voices on the television poured from a unit with the door open. Her soft-soled shoes kept her approach quiet until she reached the door and glanced inside. A man stretched out on the bed, propped up by pillows. His eyes moved from the TV screen to Kelsey, and he whistled.

"You here to clean my room or what?" he asked, looking her up and down with eyes that made it clear it wasn't his room he wanted her to tend to.

"I'm looking for someone who works at the Western Inlet Inn," she said. That was true, more or less.

He stared at her. "Why?"

"A friend told me some of the women who work there might be interested in additional work," she said.

"Now why would they want that?"

"To earn a little money. I know the money can be tight and people around here don't pay enough to live on. Who wouldn't want a chance to make more money?"

He looked at her and laughed. She needed to sound more convincing.

"I work for an agency that helps immigrants find work," Kelsey said. "I know people are not paid much for working at the inns and restaurants in the area, so we try to find additional work for them. If they're interested. I heard Sofia might be interested. Is she here?"

He pushed himself up off the bed and came toward her.

Kelsey's survival instincts kicked in, and she took a step back onto the terraced area in front of the units. Someone might spot her on the second-floor balcony, but that was preferable to being dragged into a room.

"Back to my question," Kelsey said. "Do you know if Sofia is around?"

"I'm sure she's working, and I don't think she'll be interested in any of your offers."

"Okay, then. I'll be going." Kelsey turned back toward the stairs and felt the man's eyes on her. She sped down the stairs and out into the open. But the man in the second-floor unit was no longer the problem. The person in the motel office was. He walked across the parking lot and was alongside her car before she could hop in.

"Can I help you?" he asked.

"No, thanks. I'm just leaving."

"Why are you here?"

"I just told the man upstairs. I work for a nonprofit that helps find work for people, especially immigrant women. I stopped by to see if anyone could use my help."

"And what did the man upstairs tell you?"

"He said no one needed my help, so I'm leaving."

"Good," he said, opening the driver's door for her.

Just before Kelsey got into her car, she thought the man next to her looked up and nodded to the man she'd been speaking with on the second floor.

Kelsey put the car in reverse and pulled out of the parking lot. Randall was right. She wouldn't tell him about her visit to the Queensbury Motel. Kelsey wouldn't call her actions stupid, maybe ill-advised. Okay, maybe stupid. She drove east and was about to get back onto the Northway but opted for secondary roads instead. Even then, she made it home in less than half an hour. Her body still tense, she went for a walk in the surrounding park instead of drinking a glass of wine.

The sun was disappearing faster than she'd expected, lengthening the shadows where daylight had peeked through the trees less than thirty minutes ago. She usually stuck to the main trail on her walks, especially in the early morning or late evening. The paved trail was popular with hikers or casual walkers who lived in the neighborhood. But this evening, lost in her thoughts, she'd veered off onto a side trail, where brush and tree limbs encroached. She'd reached a point where the path was difficult to track. When she realized how quickly darkness was closing in, she turned around and picked up her pace. This was not a good time to get lost in the woods.

A twig snapped. Then another. Was someone else also hurrying to get out of the woods before daylight faded? Or had a bear picked up her scent? Last spring, a bear had been standing in the middle of the trail when she rounded a corner. Someone once told her to shake her keys or sing at the top of her lungs if she ever encountered a bear. Kelsey's brain shut down as she and the bear stared at each other. The bear twitched. Kelsey started singing the one song that came to mind, "God Bless America," as loud as she could. The bear lumbered away.

Snap. Again. Closer. She kept speed walking. Then she heard footsteps behind her. Two feet, not four. Her heart jumped into her throat. She could barely make out the main trail up ahead. She moved so quickly she didn't see the tree root jutting out of the ground. Kelsey almost lost her footing, but fear kept her upright and propelled her forward. Then she was jogging, gulping in shallow breaths with minimal oxygen. She launched herself onto the trail, veered right, and ran as fast as she could with her heart pounding in her chest. Streams of sweat soaked her shirt and dripped off her nose.

The other footsteps faded away, but she didn't quit running until she closed the apartment door behind her and locked it, heart pounding like a drum beat in her ears. She peeked through the curtains. A figure stood in the shadows cast by the trees on the edge of the parking lot. He strolled behind her car, paused, then disappeared. She dropped onto the couch, sure she had stumbled onto something during her investigation, and not at all sure whether someone was trying to scare her or hurt her.

Chapter Sixteen

Present Day

Eye drops. Rose needed eye drops and another glass of wine. Okay, not wine. That would put her to sleep. After Rose grabbed a bite to eat, she returned to the dining room table.

She had only two more folders to go through before she exhausted the papers on the table. She reviewed the thickest file again first—the one about toxins in the Hudson River—skimming articles. It was a major issue over the last several decades, and Rose couldn't imagine someone giving her father ten thousand dollars to help with something connected to it. Of course, if the woman had uncovered the history of someone's illegal dumping, that person could have run her off the road. But the investigations had already determined the businesses responsible for the contamination. Nope, that was a dead end.

The other folder required a closer look. Then she would be done. It was about the influx of illegal immigrants into upstate New York. She knew her father had done some pro bono work to protect immigrants' rights. Mary had even mentioned the work he did to help immigrants obtain green cards, find jobs, and locate apartments in a tourist area where cheap living space was difficult to come by.

Her journalistic juices were running hot again on the search for information. She was close to something. Her weary eyes swept over the folders spread over the table as she thought about the folders still left in the box upstairs. Since she hadn't found any leads yet, it was time to make one more trip and see if she might have missed something.

She sat on the floor next to the box in her parents' old bedroom and removed the remaining folders—almost a dozen of them—all with no more than a few documents inside. She read each folder label, then opened it to confirm the contents matched and none were relevant to her search. Her hopes were fading when she saw only a few folders remaining. Then she found a folder without a label. It was so thin it was easy to miss.

She opened the folder and stared at the headline on a newspaper article: POLICE SHUT DOWN ESCORT SERVICE, and the subheadline, DOZENS OF UNDOCU-MENTED IMMIGRANTS INVOLVED. Rose read the first paragraph of the article twice.

Police in Newburgh, working with the FBI and other agencies, have shut down a human trafficking ring that forced female immigrants to perform sexual acts under threat of deportation. Most of the victims were of age and forced into prostitution in return for their safety, but some of the victims were as young as fourteen.

Rose massaged her eyes. Fourteen. What kind of evil person would do that to a fourteen-year-old and ruin her life? To any woman of any age, but girls were so vulnerable.

As she lowered the folder to her lap, a piece of paper brushed against her. The paper was taped on the inside of the file folder. Her heart skipped a beat as she stared at the hand-written note. Then she raced down the stairs to the den. Rose sat at the desk and tried to slow her breathing. She opened the center drawer and pulled out the copy of the note she'd found in the secret compartment. She set that one on the desk, then put the piece of paper she'd just discovered next to it. Her breath caught in her throat. She was no expert, but you didn't need training to spot the similarities in the handwriting.

Randall:

FYI: Here's a story I found that could be connected to our ongoing work around immigrant issues. I'm not sure whether the ringleaders of this sex trafficking ring have any ties to our area, but I think we should look into it. At the very least, we need to be aware of this issue.

This note wasn't signed. It was on the letterhead of her father's law firm. Rose was sure it was written by the woman who'd left the note with the ten thousand dollars.

Finally, she had a lead, and it went straight back to her father's law office.

Chapter Seventeen

Present Day

Rose finished her breakfast, leashed up Gladys, and took her for a long walk to release the nervous energy bouncing around her body. Rose's body. Gladys seemed pretty chill lately. When her mother was dying and Rose realized she'd be responsible for Gladys, she'd leaned toward finding the Maltese mix a new home. But then she fell in love and couldn't imagine not having Gladys in her life.

They walked to the park at the southern end of Lake Amelia and sat on a bench. Rose watched the gentle waves on the surface of the lake with birds soaring overhead while Gladys sniffed around and left her mark. Ten minutes of quiet time for both of them, and Rose was ready to return home.

What could she do next? Rose stared at the two pieces of paper sitting on the table in front of her. She could reach out to Mary again and show her the new document. She could reach out to Brandt and push him for information because she suspected he wasn't telling her everything he knew. Or . . she drummed her fingers on the table and looked out onto the patio. Or she could reach out to Bill Poole at the *Lake Amelia Dispatch* and see if he could help. The woman claimed she'd been run off the road one day and another time someone had broken into her apartment. She would have contacted the police, wouldn't she? In her note, the woman sounded scared. Maybe she didn't want to involve the police. Rose needed to find out whether there were any official reports.

It was a little early for Bill to be in the office, but she called anyway.

"Oh, hi," Rose stammered. "I didn't expect to find you in."

"I came in early for a meeting. What's up?" The intensity in his voice softened. "And how are you doing? You've had a rough couple of months."

"I'm pretty good, you know, a little less sad every day except for when a wave of missing Mom hits me. I keep focusing on all the good memories. I'm also focusing on something else I want to tell you about. Do you have time for a quick chat this morning?"

"Sure. My meeting will be over by ten."

"I'll see you then."

Rose ended the call and set her phone on the table. She glanced down at her feet where Gladys sat staring at her.

"Oops, did I forget to feed you?" Rose refreshed the dog's water dish and fed her the raw beef mixture she loved so much. Then it was time for a shower. For Rose. Gladys always smelled sweet.

Rose slept in her childhood bedroom on the second floor, across the hall from the main bedroom. Rose had considered moving into the larger bedroom because the view of the woods was better—the old oak tree didn't block the window the way it did in her bedroom. But it was too soon. And her parents' bedroom might always be her parents' bedroom. After getting ready, she kissed Gladys and left her on the couch in the living room.

* * *

Bill greeted her with a big hug and a small cup of coffee.

Rose looked at the cup, which was somewhere between the size of a bathroom Dixie cup and the smallest paper cup available local convenience store. She frowned. "Has rationing been imposed?" Rose asked as she followed him into his office.

"Someone forgot to order cups and most of the mugs in the kitchen are broken. We've been making do with these cups someone got at the dollar store. Not a coffee drinker, obviously." He walked behind his desk and motioned her to take the familiar chair across from him. "What have you been doing? Are you here to tell me you're ready for an assignment?" He picked up his mug and took a big drink.

"I think I'm ready, as long as it's not too taxing," Rose said, staring at his mug.

"That's great. I'll tell Earl."

Earl and Bill, the two men who'd been her mentors beginning in her sophomore year in high school, then her friends and colleagues since she graduated from Ithaca College. Their recommendations, and some excellent articles she'd written as an intern for the *Dispatch* had led to her first full-time job at the *Times Union* in Albany.

"What can I do for you?"

She gave him the short version of the letter and money, her meetings with Mary, and her efforts to find out who the woman was.

"Ten grand, huh?" Bill whistled. "But that was a long time ago."

She nodded. "I know finding the owner of the money won't be easy, but I thought I could search the database for articles about a vehicle run off the road, an apartment broken into. You know, something to connect to the woman."

"That's going to be difficult, even with the published police blotters."

"I have time," she said. "And I thought you could help me another way." She smiled.

He raised his eyebrows a half inch closer to his receding hairline.

Then she gave him her best 100-watt smile. Or was it a 14-watt LED bulb smile? Only that didn't sound as powerful.

He looked at her. Again with the eyebrows.

"You've been here, like, forever—"

"Thank you for that—"

"And you have lots of sources in the police department. Maybe someone remembers something. Cops often remember the smallest details. They review information repeatedly as they try to crack a case or track down a perpetrator. It's no wonder so much sticks in their brains."

"But really, fifteen years ago? About a car running off the road or an apartment break-in?" He stared at her. "You could deposit the money and let this go," Bill finally said, raising his mug to his mouth and frowning when he realized it was empty. He set it down without taking his eyes off her. "Why is this so important? Why are you determined to find this woman? It can't be just about returning the money."

There he was, asking pointed questions again. After all, Rose had learned from the best. This wasn't about the money, of course. And if she was going to get his help, she needed to tell him what had happened.

Chapter Eighteen
Present Day

"I visited one of my favorite farmer's markets around Philly," Rose began. "I stopped in almost every Saturday. It was a year-round, indoor market with all kinds of fresh produce, more beef and chicken cuts than you've ever seen, homemade jellies, breads, coffee beans, soaps. And prepared foods galore. My favorite stall had the best Mexican food. I mean, you could feel the sand between your toes at Cancun and practically taste the poblano and chorizo and beef whose aromas hung in the air. It was that strong, savory, and mouthwatering.

"Lucia always greeted me with a big smile. She often wore a huipil—a sleeveless tunic—with bright flowers on a dark brown background. Lucia would fill a large container with four chicken and cheese enchiladas and another container piled high with rice and beans. That would last me all weekend. Then she'd add guacamole and chips, whether I asked for them or not. While she put my containers into a takeaway bag, she'd ask about my family, my work, when I was going to get a boyfriend. But when I asked about her family, her face darkened, her smile disappeared, and she moved on to another topic. Eventually, I stopped asking about anything personal.

"One Saturday morning when I walked up to her stall, she looked close to tears. I asked her what was wrong, and if I could help. She hesitated, then said her landlord at the apartment she was renting—in the Germantown section of the city—was threatening to raise her rent, even though he knew she couldn't pay more. The same man held her lease at the farmer's market, and he said he could raise her rent there as well if he wanted to. She was afraid he would evict her. To make matters worse, the man had made threatening comments, even suggesting she could pay the rent in other ways. She didn't know what to do.

"Two weeks later, she had a bruise the size of a small lemon on her left cheek and jaw. When she handed me my bag, I spotted red welts and bruises on her right wrist. Again, I asked what was wrong. She brushed me off. Everything was fine, she said. I lingered to see if she wanted to talk because, despite what she said, something was wrong. But another customer walked up. She waved goodbye to me and went over to help them.

"I stopped by some other vendors and was on my way back to my car, but I couldn't get the images of Lucia's bruised face out of my mind. So, I wandered back over to her stall. She was on her the phone with her back to me, her head down, her shoulders hunched. When she heard me approach, she ended the call. When she saw it was me, she said, 'Oh, Rose.' I begged her to let me help, and she reluctantly agreed. She said she would tell me more when she saw me the following week."

Rose reached for her empty cup on Bill's desk.

"Would you like some water?" he asked.

She nodded, unable to find her voice.

Bill twisted the cap off the bottle of water as he walked

back into his office and handed it to her. She took a couple of swallows as he sat back behind his desk.

"Two days later, just as the sun was coming up on Monday morning, I got a tip about a body in the Schuylkill River about two hundred feet above where the Wissahickon Creek flows into the Schuylkill near Kelly Drive. Sorry, I know these names don't mean much to you. I'm just remembering the details as they pop into my mind. A man jogging along the bike trail had spotted what he thought was clothing in the water. He was concerned that it could be a body and called the police. I was one of the first media on the scene, thanks to being an early riser and living nearby."

Rose's eyes softened. She pressed her lips together so hard they turned white. She sucked in a breath through her nose and let it out through her mouth. Bill's eyes never left her face. She shrugged and gave him the hint of a smile.

"Being the first news reporter or photographer on the scene of an accident or a crime isn't all it's cracked up to be, you know? The body was . . ." She swallowed hard. "I couldn't use any of my first shots. They were too graphic even though the body was stuck in some branches and in the early-morning shadows. I stared at the clothes. The material was dark and covered with bright flowers. My heart stopped. I thought it was Lucia. The start of a scream pounded in my lungs and pushed to get out. I shoved it down and kept shooting photos as tears filled my eyes. Then a small wave washed over the body and exposed more of the woman's face. It wasn't Lucia. The woman was younger, but the clothes, the dark hair, the color of her skin were so close. I was relieved, then felt terrible. Someone had lost their life, perhaps in a violent way."

Rose walked over to the conference table in front of a bookcase and grabbed a couple of tissues. She fell back into her chair.

"I saw Lucia the following week and gave her the name of

an attorney friend in Community Legal Services and another attorney I knew at the ACLU. I told her one of them could help her with the landlord, and I could go with her if she wanted me to. She told me a couple of weeks later that she and her daughter had met with a lawyer, and he pressured the landlord to stop making threats. The lawyer persuaded him to honor her current leases for the apartment and the farmer's market stand. She was so appreciative.

"Even though it wasn't Lucia in the river, the face of the woman still haunts me, Bill. I learned later that the victim was a legal immigrant who was assaulted by the man she worked for. He was arrested and sent back to South America. I've always wished I could have helped that woman. I couldn't have, didn't know who she was, but . . ."

Rose raised the bottle of water and took a swig.

"When I connected the handwriting in the letter with the money that I found in Dad's bookcase to the note with the articles he had on immigrant issues in upstate New York, I immediately thought of Lucia and the woman's body in the Schuylkill River. If the woman who worked for my father and alerted him to possible abuse of immigrants went into hiding because she feared for her safety, I can't look away. I have to find out if she's okay. I have to find out what she knew. And if something illegal is or was going on, I have to expose it."

Chapter Nineteen
July 2010

Kelsey didn't sleep well again, even after double-checking the locks and sliding a chair under the front doorknob. She shuffled into the kitchen and picked up the pile of mail she'd left on the counter. All advertisements. She went to put the recyclable pieces in the recycling bin in her spare bedroom where she had a desk, but the bin was full. She pressed the flyers and catalogues into the bin, picked it up, and headed into the kitchen. A quick look under the sink showed the trash bin was also full. Well, she'd begin the day with a trip to the dumpsters behind the building.

Kelsey wasn't self-conscious walking into the apartment's parking lot in her pajamas, even her summer-weight T-shirt and shorts. Plenty of women wore more revealing clothes, not just to sleep in but to run errands and shop for groceries. But today Kelsey dressed in jeans and threw a long-sleeved shirt over her nightshirt. She picked up the bag of trash in one hand and the recycling bin in the other. The apartments had walkways between the units, so no one was far from the dumpsters. Her apartment complex had security and motion-detector lights to light the path. A neighbor had just dropped his trash into the big dumpster when Kelsey started across the narrow lot, and he held up the heavy plastic top so she could toss in her bag. They strolled back through the walkway together. As they wished each other a good day, Kelsey felt the tension in her body ease.

The tantalizing aroma of fresh coffee drifted out of a neighbor's window. Kelsey hurried into her apartment, made her own coffee, then showered. As she sipped her coffee, she thought about whether she should tell Randall about her trip to Queensbury. Randall had asked her not to do any more investigating in the field and Kelsey didn't think going to the Queensbury Motel would be a big deal. Until she'd been chased through the woods. Her hand gripped her coffee cup tighter, recalling her panicked breathing as she'd run toward her apartment. It was the same panic she experienced the nights Hal had come home late, drunk, and angry.

Now, someone was following her. In her car. In the woods. They may have broken into her apartment. They'd called her office phone and threatened her. No one had hurt her. Yet.

She thought about how much she wanted to help the women working at the Western Inlet Inn. Yes, it was because she was only a second-generation American, whose grandparents had come to the United States seeking a better life. She was in favor of immigration, limited immigration, so everyone who migrated here could find productive work with a decent standard of living. But she also wanted to help them because she worried that someone connected to the inn was abusing the teenaged daughters and maybe some older women as well. But it was clear she could not participate in any investigation. She realized that now.

Okay. She was going to tell Randall and accept his criticism for not following his request to stay away from Browning's properties. She dressed and hurried out of her apartment, resigned to face his disappointment.

Except something was wrong.

The driver's side door of her SUV was unlocked. She reached for the passenger door. It too, was unlocked. A quick walk around the other side of the vehicle showed all four doors were unlocked. Come on. Someone was playing games. She'd locked the vehicle. She was sure of it. Her head swung around. Had someone just been here and unlocked it? Was the person still here? Did they tamper with her car?

She opened the front door and noticed, for the first time, the papers on the driver's seat. She'd been too focused on the unlocked doors to spot them. Some were brochures for the Queensbury Motel. Others looked like articles from an online source or a printed newspaper. Kelsey picked up one of the articles. The headline screamed out in a large bold font:

"INVESTIGATOR FOUND DEAD IN MOTEL."

She probably shouldn't read the article, but she did:

"Police responded to a call at 6:45 a.m. They found the beaten and mangled body of an investigator who'd been looking into allegations of human trafficking in the Hudson Valley."

Damn. She'd done it now. Her impromptu visit had angered the owner of the Queensbury Motel and the Western Inlet Inn. Was this a threat from the inn's security guard or that guy from the motel? She didn't think one of them had followed her home yesterday, but if this was the work of the security guard, why would there be brochures for a motel that didn't take guests?

Kelsey ran back into her apartment. She called Randall and left a message that she didn't feel well and wouldn't be in, that she was going to the drugstore and would be online by lunchtime.

How could she be sure no one got into her apartment while she was gone? What did they do in the movies? They put a string, a piece of hair, or thin thread between the door and the frame. Did that really work? She'd find out. If it wasn't in the same place when she got home, she'd turn right around and go to the police.

Should she go to the police or the county sheriff now? Or was she overreacting? What would she tell them? That someone had left brochures and some printed articles in her car? She could hear that Deputy Farris, who'd come to the scene where she'd been run off the road, laughing. Would he take her seriously now? The articles hinted at a threat, didn't they? And what about the phone call yesterday? That was a real threat.

She willed herself to calm down and found a spool of white thread. Picking up the scissors, she snipped about a ten-inch piece of thread and placed it between the door and the frame a few inches below the doorknob. She closed the door and said a small prayer. Then she climbed into her Crosstrek, put the brochures and printed articles in a reusable shopping bag, and drove away. Just over an hour later, after stopping at the bank and grocery store, she returned home to find the white thread still intact. Finally, a bit of good news.

Kelsey spent the rest of the afternoon packing clothes, computer supplies, and communicating with others in the office via email, telling them her throat was too sore to speak on the phone. The chair remained in front of the front door, and she kept all the curtains closed. That night she caught a few hours' sleep, alert to any sounds. At four in the morning, she took a quick shower, then made two trips to her vehicle with all her stuff. She was less nervous than she'd expected to be as her eyes kept sweeping the area, but she didn't think someone would be watching her apartment at that hour. With one last glance around her apartment, Kelsey closed the door, hopped into her Crosstrek, and drove away.

She had one last task. Less than twenty minutes later, she

eased into the curve and down the hill onto Main Street. A few blocks later, she turned onto Pine, then Cedar. Kelsey parked across the street from Randall's home, holding the envelope in her hand and wondering if she should ring the bell. A vehicle's headlights flashed in her rearview mirror. She slid down in her seat, out of sight. As soon as the car passed, she got out, ran across the street, and slipped the envelope through the mail slot. Then she scurried back to her vehicle and headed for the highway.

Chapter Twenty

Present Day

Bill looked at Rose with a tenderness she'd rarely seen, and he struggled to find words. "We cover these stories hoping they'll expose injustice, especially among poorer populations, and improve conditions in people's lives. Before anything bad happens." He stretched his arms out on his desk. "Sometimes we learn something in time to avert a tragedy, but too often we don't. It sounds sort of asinine to state the obvious, but we can't report on what we don't know."

"I know it comes with the territory," Rose said. "We're journalists, not activists, but that woman's death haunted me. Without warning, the image of her battered and swollen face would pop into my head and tear at my soul. A few times I woke up from a deep sleep, seeing Lucia's face on the body. I didn't sleep well for weeks."

"Give me a few minutes to create a new account for you in our system," Bill finally said. "If you're going to do some free-lance work for the *Dispatch* while you're in Lake Amelia, you'll need an email address, log-in info, and you'll have to fill out a W-9. You'll have as much access as an employee. Then you can spend all the time you want searching the files. Do you have time today?"

She smiled. "Just like old times, huh?"

He smiled too. "You tell me a story like that, and you think I won't help?"

"And your contacts in the police department?"

"I'll do that later today. The cops will think I've been smoking something, but I'll make some calls. Now, go wander around the newsroom and pick out an empty desk. We've reduced employees over the years. You'll have lots of choices. I'll have you up on LexisNexis shortly." He snapped his fingers. "We might not have any extra computers. Do you have your laptop?"

She shook her head.

"Go home and get it." He waved his hand toward the open door. "By the time you get back, you'll be all set."

Rose stood. "Thanks, Bill. I owe you."

"Yeah, I'll add it to your tab." He waved his hand again, and she scooted out the door.

She chose a desk close to Bill's office and put her notepad on it, so he'd know which one, then hurried back home for her laptop. When she returned, the documents he promised were on her desk, including log-in information and instructions on where to find the other documents online. She fired up her laptop and went to work.

The secret to successful research was often to provide less information, not more. Just as a person's brain can shut down if overloaded with too much information, a search engine can spin its wheels trying to connect too many search words. Give it less, get more back.

Apartment break-in. Rose typed into the LexisNexis search window. Should she change it to *Washington County break-in*? Yeah. She retyped her search parameters and hit enter. She scanned the articles that populated her screen and checked when they'd been published. Should she add dates to narrow the search more? Her father died July 25, 2010. She went on the assumption that he received the envelope with the money shortly before he died. She added *January 2010-July 2010*. The spinning started. Oops, too much. Start with just *January 2010* and the other parameters. Rose hit enter and was rewarded with a short list of articles. None of them looked relevant. She changed January to February, kept everything else in her search words the same, and hit the return button.

Rose was impatient in many ways, but not when it came to research. Still, she was getting antsy at not finding any mentions of an apartment break-in during the first seven months of 2010. Okay, time to try tracking down the woman's claim that someone ran her off the road. Should she use those exact words? She shrugged and typed *car run off road* along with *January 2010* and hit enter. This was more productive. And time consuming. Maxi had told Rose it wasn't unusual for drivers to get stuck in a rut or heavy grass and require help getting their vehicle back on the pavement. It was quite another to swerve so far off that your vehicle landed in a ditch. That required a call to a towing company and might bring the police or the county sheriff to make sure the driver wasn't under the influence.

Rose kept searching by month and different terms, including *vehicle in ditch, car in ditch* to see if that helped. She was breaking her rule and using longer terms, but she wasn't getting enough with shorter search items.

By the time she entered the month of May, she realized Bill was right and this search could be futile. She continued searching with *vehicle run off road* through June and July 2010 and was thinking Bill and Maxi might be correct that the woman didn't report either incident.

Rose looked at the clock over the newsroom door. She had another hour before her occupational therapy session at

Saratoga Hospital and she should spend a few minutes with Gladys, but she wanted to squeeze in one more search.

She typed *immigrant workers* into the search bar and sat back. Ouch. She'd been leaning forward for a while and her lower back complained. Rose stood and stretched from side to side with her arms out. Then she raised her arms over her head and turned from side to side again. That was better. She'd loosened up and could tell her therapist she'd been stretching.

She glanced at her laptop, at the long list of articles her search had returned. Pay dirt! This was better, although she realized some were the same articles her father had kept in his folder on immigrants in upstate New York. She saved the new articles in a digital folder on her laptop, watching the clock, and hoping she'd get to July 2010 before she had to leave.

Nope. There were so many articles on immigrants, illegal immigrants and immigrant housing and working conditions that her folder now had more than a dozen articles and she needed to search May, June, and July. She was about to close out another article when she spotted her father's name in a story dated April 18, 2010. The topic was immigrant working conditions. Her father was quoted in a short paragraph near the end.

According to attorney Randall Webster, immigrant condi-tions in upstate New York are deplorable, bordering on illegal. "We've been at the forefront of growing concerns over immigra-tion rights and living conditions for more than a year now. These are important issues, and we seek to address and find solu-tions to them, through the courts if necessary."

Rose printed the story and saved it to her laptop's folder, then sprinted out the door.

Chapter Twenty-One
Present Day

What a lousy time to be pulled away from her research, but Rose knew that without her occupational therapy sessions, she wouldn't be getting close to working again. She and Carter were ready to schedule the photo-shoot at the library, and Rose wanted to make sure she was up to it. And, in fact, the surgeon needed the OT's approval before agreeing that Rose could work again. Since the drive to Saratoga Springs would take less than an hour, Rose called Mary.

"I found a folder in the box from the attic," she told her, then filled Mary in about the article on immigrants and sex trafficking in Newburgh. "But the most important thing is a handwritten note that was in the folder with the article. I think it was in the same handwriting as the note with the ten thousand dollars."

"And the article was about sex trafficking?" Mary said. "Hold on a second. That rings a bell . . . But is that because of the stories and trials in recent years—the trafficking ring in Newburgh—or is it something else? Sorry, Rose. My memory isn't what it used to be. Give me a minute."

Rose told Mary to take her time. While she waited, her thoughts returned to her upcoming appointment and whether Debbye would clear her to work. The thought that she could soon pick up her camera and take photos lifted her spirits. She smiled. Then grew serious as another thought entered her mind. When would she have to decide whether to return to Philadelphia? Her condo was there. The base of her freelance work was there. Her friends were there. She pushed that complicated thought out of her mind.

Mary cleared her throat.

"A woman joined the firm for a while, maybe a year," Mary began. "She was a paralegal. Quite good, actually. She was from downstate and helped lighten my workload. We worked with your father on a few cases." Mary went quiet again. "I'm pretty sure there was something going on that Kelsey—yes, Kelsey, that's her name. That's the woman." Mary's voice rose as she recalled more information. "Kelsey Jacobs was looking into the mistreatment of immigrants in the tourism industry. Your father once asked me to compile a list of our immigrant clients for her, and I remember it was odd, because he told me not to mention it to anyone else in the office. I didn't ask him why. I gave Kelsey the list, and that's the last I heard of it."

"You don't have any idea—"

"Hang on, Rose."

Rose leaned closer to the dashboard to hear Mary, even though the volume was up all the way. A stab in her lower back told her this wasn't a great position, so she pushed her body back in the seat. Mary had recalled the woman's name. Kelsey Jacobs. That was huge. What other lead could Mary come up with?

"Kelsey disappeared," Mary said. "That's what happened. Kelsey disappeared, and it was right around the time your father died. I think we all sort of lost track of Kelsey at first because of the disruption in the firm. You know, Brandt taking over. I guess your mother had all those financial details. Brandt was going to buy out your father's practice when he retired, but I'm not sure how the transfer took place. I just remember it was chaotic. Your father was there one day, then gone. Kelsey was there one day, then gone. At about the same time." Mary almost whispered the last words.

Rose recalled the turmoil that followed her father's sudden death in her family and in his office. He'd brought Brandt on board a couple of years earlier with the understanding that Brandt would buy the practice—and pay Randall a fair price for it—when Randall was ready to retire. But her mom had worked out some deal, with Kirk's legal guidance, of course, and Brandt got the practice sooner than anyone had expected. Probably cheaper too.

"I wonder if Brandt would give us some handwriting samples from Kelsey," Mary said. "I'd love to know for sure if she left the note and money. And I would love to know what happened to her. Why she disappeared."

Mary said *us*. She wondered if Brandt would give *us* some handwriting samples. It sounded like she was interested enough to help Rose figure things out. Good. Rose needed all the help she could get.

"Brandt would also have Kelsey's employee records, wouldn't he?" Rose asked.

"Kelsey's been gone from the firm for fifteen years. If I remember correctly, the IRS only requires employers to keep employee records for four years. Something like that. Not long."

"That doesn't help us, even if Brandt is willing to share her info, which he probably isn't."

Rose crossed over the Northway and was minutes from the occupational therapy center. She was thrilled with the new information. She had the handwritten note on her father's letterhead. And now she had a name. Rose believed Kelsey Jacobs gave the money to her father. Some questions were being answered, but many more popped up in their place.

"Mary, I've got to go to my therapy session, but please give this some more thought. You've identified Kelsey. That gives us a new lead. I'll show you the article on the Newburgh sex trafficking ring and Kelsey's note about it the next time we get together."

Rose signed off, parked her SUV, and walked inside the center.

"How's that arm doing, Rose?" Debbye greeted her with a big smile.

Rose raised both her arms in a bodybuilder kind of pose, squeezing her fists and hoping her biceps showed a hint of muscle.

Debbye squeezed her arm. "You're not Rocky, but I believe your right arm is getting stronger. Let's get to work and increase your strength."

For the next forty minutes, Debbye led Rose through the familiar series of exercises they'd been doing for the past several weeks. Different exercises targeted her fingers, her wrist, and her shoulder. The shoulder ones still hurt the most.

"Why is my shoulder taking so long to heal?"

"That's a question for Dr. Levinson, but according to his notes, the damage to your rotator cuff wasn't just from the rally in Philadelphia. There was scar tissue." Debbye mimicked the motions as she described them to Rose. "Years of lifting your camera bag, slinging it over your shoulder like this, lifting the tripod, and some of those overhead shots you told me you like to take, holding your camera up high. All of those stressed your shoulder. I think the accident was the final straw. Your shoulder needs time to heal. It needs a rest." Debbye helped Rose finish the last few reps. "How are you feeling otherwise?"

"I'm a slug," Rose admitted. "I walk Gladys. Actually, I

take her for a casual stroll. Our walks will never register on the cardio scale. With my arm in a cast and my shoulder muscles still tender, I spend too much time sitting around." She felt the tears swell in her eyes. "Sometimes I think about how my father had a sudden heart attack and I worry it'll happen to me if I don't get my stamina back."

Debbye rubbed Rose's healthy shoulder. "Four to six months of inactivity will not make you a candidate for a heart attack. However, if you're concerned about whether you could have a heart attack like your father did, whether it's genetic, there's a test for that."

"Really? What's it called?"

"There may be more than one. You should ask Dr. Levinson the next time you see him. My father had a cardiac calcium scale test because his father had passed of a heart attack. My knowledge of this is limited," Debbye admitted. "You're the whiz at research. Look into it and ask Dr. Levinson."

"Thanks for the tip." Rose promised to continue exercising and said she'd be back soon, the same day she had an appointment with Dr. Levinson. She mentioned Carter's offer to have Rose photograph the library, and Bill's interest in giving her freelance assignments.

"Static photography, like rooms in the library or the exteriors, are probably fine," Debbye said. "Let's see what the doc says."

Rose agreed. The healing process was slower than she wanted, but she was making progress. And she could get back to work. She couldn't wait to tell Carter, and she'd update Bill and Earl. She'd continue learning more about immigrant issues, and now she had another subject. The cardiac calcium scale test. If she was a candidate for a heart attack, she wanted to know sooner than later.

Chapter Twenty-Two
July 2010

Millie wrapped Kelsey in a hug. Kelsey hung on tight.

"I don't mean to disrupt your life just because I'm disrupting mine," Kelsey said as tears fell from her eyes. "I didn't know where else to turn."

"Don't apologize." Mille released her from the hug but held Kelsey's shoulders tight and studied her face. "You look exhausted, and you must have left home early. It's not even lunchtime."

"I wanted to get an early start and make sure nobody could follow me. I stopped at two rest areas on the Thruway to make sure no one was on my trail."

"We'll get your bags in a minute. I'll bet you could use a cup of coffee and something to eat."

"Yeah, but before that I could use the bathroom."

"I thought you stopped at the rest areas," Millie said, her arm around Kelsey's waist as she led her up the walkway and through the door.

"I didn't get out of the car. I watched other vehicles pull

into the parking lot after me and waited until they left before I got back on the highway."

"I'm so sorry for what you've been going through," Millie said.

After Kelsey freshened up, she walked into the kitchen to find Millie scrambling eggs and pouring her a cup of coffee. Kelsey sat at the island and devoured the eggs. It had been a long time since the cup of coffee and piece of toast she'd had for breakfast.

"How's work at the firm?" Kelsey asked. "When we had lunch, you said you were still adjusting to the pace of fulltime work. I mean, I'm sure you had a taste of how crazy and long the hours could be during your summer internships."

"I knew what to expect from my dad and brother. It's nothing like when you're immersed in it sixty hours a week and you know you're not headed back to school."

"Do you ever have second thoughts about not joining the same firm as your dad and brother?"

"I still might join them one day, but I wanted to start off on my own. But enough about me," Millie said. "I've waited long enough. If you're done eating, let's sit in the living room and you can tell me what you stumbled onto."

Sitting on the couch, Kelsey told Millie about things that had occurred since their phone call, the additional events that convinced Kelsey someone was threatening her.

"And you think it all goes back to this guy, Browning, who owns the Western Inlet Inn and other inns or motels in the Adirondacks?"

Kelsey nodded. "Remember how upset the woman was when we overheard her on the patio? Then I learned about a sex trafficking ring in Newburgh, and I wondered if that's what Browning was—is—up to. Even if it's not, he's mistreating some of his employees."

"Are you close to having the evidence against Browning?"

"Not enough hard evidence." Kelsey blew out a deep breath. "I mean, I think I'm getting close because of how people are coming after me. But do I have someone who would testify against Browning if I persuaded the cops or the FBI that I could build a case?" She shook her head. She hated leaving in the midst of finding evidence against Browning, but it wouldn't do much good if she wasn't around to share the info with Randall. She shook her head again and stared out the window.

Millie lived in a two-story condo in a neighborhood on the outer edges of Bedford, Westchester County. Millie's parents had gifted her the condo when she graduated from Yale and Kelsey knew that Millie's boyfriend, whom she had begun dating in their last year at Yale, often stayed overnight. Kelsey had met Josh a few times and knew he was not threatened by Millie's career. Josh was nothing like Hal, who undermined Kelsey every time she tried to improve her education, improve her life. Every time she grew stronger, Hal felt more threatened. Kelsey shivered. She didn't know what would have become of her if she hadn't left him.

"You know," Kelsey said, "one of the worst things was when the deputy responded to the call about a vehicle off the road. You should have seen how he looked at me. He didn't believe me." Kelsey set her drink on the table and wrapped her arms around herself. "It was like when I first told people that Hal hit me. So many people didn't believe me. People liked him. He was funny, bought other people dinner, drinks. People only saw the pleasant side of him. I only saw that part of him too when we first got together, but then the anger he'd been hiding from me and everyone else came out."

Kelsey wiped a tear from her eye. "I'll never forget the first time I made him angry enough that he hit me. I was shocked and called you, crying. You told me to leave him. But I loved him. He promised he would change. For too long I believed him."

"But you got there," Millie said. "It took a while to convince you, but you realized your life was in danger."

"Yeah, and that's the way I felt when I thought someone was chasing me through the woods. When I found my apartment door unlocked. When I heard a threatening voice scream at me on the phone to stop poking into someone else's business." Kelsey looked at Millie. "I'm smarter now and I read the danger signs much faster. If I had stuck around upstate New York, there's no telling what could have happened to me."

Chapter Twenty-Three

Present Day

Rose kept thinking about her father during the drive home, about his heart attack and the way so many people had used the word "sudden" to describe when he'd passed. Kelsey worked for their father on immigration cases, and a handwritten note with an article about immigrant trafficking appeared to match the hand-written note with the ten grand. Was Kelsey the mystery woman? Rose sure thought so, and she was eager to talk it over with Kirk. She hoped he wasn't in court as she connected the call.

"Got a minute?" she asked as soon as he answered.

"What's up?"

She filled him in and waited while he processed the information.

"You and Mary think this Kelsey could be the link to the money in the bookcase?"

"Yep. Now the challenge is to find her and return her money."

"How are you going to do that?" Kirk asked.

"I'm thinking of starting with Brandt, even though he

wasn't exactly helpful the last time I asked. Now I have more information."

"And he has records about people who've worked at the firm."

"Yes, but he might not have Kelsey's records. Mary thinks employers only have to keep records for four years."

"I forgot about that. Sounds like another dead end." Rose heard him take a sip of whatever he was drinking. "Maybe you can find more documents in the attic."

Did she detect a note of contempt in his voice?

"You went back up and found the folders with his research. I was surprised they were at home, but he worked at the house sometimes and didn't do everything on his laptop. I remember him sitting in that chair in his office, reading the newspapers, and clipping articles for his files."

His laptop. Rose sat up straighter. "Whatever happened to Dad's laptop?"

"As I recall, Dad's laptop was at the firm. I went into the office with Mom to go through Dad's belongings and pack up his stuff so she wouldn't have to do it alone. The laptop was there. I checked with Brandt, and he said it was fine if I took it. Everything is backed up on the cloud and was fifteen years ago as well."

"So what happened to the laptop?"

"I think Mom got rid of it. She used it for a few years to FaceTime with me and Maria when the kids were young. She didn't use it for much else and she was having problems with it. I bought her a new one."

"What did she do with Dad's?" Rose pushed. Laptops were full of information and if she could locate her father's, who knew what she'd find?

"I told her ways she could safely recycle it, but I don't know whether she did."

"It could be here in the house somewhere."

Kirk laughed. "Rose, haven't you searched enough of the house by now to know what's there?"

"Not really," she said. "I've gone through some things in Mom's bedroom on the first floor, but there's stuff in the closet of their old bedroom upstairs I haven't touched." Rose got up from the couch in the family room and walked through the kitchen into the living room at the front of the house. She picked up the laptop on the lower shelf of the table next to her mother's recliner. "What kind of laptop did you buy her? A Lenovo?"

"Yep, that's it."

Rose turned it on. The screen came to life, filled with photos of Kirk's family and of Rose and her mother on vacations to the beach and the mountains. She scanned them and smiled, seeing her nephews mugging for the camera and Maria trying in vain to stop them. The largest photo on the screen was of Kirk, Maria, and the two boys laughing. It was obviously one of her mother's favorite photos, and it brought tears to Rose's eyes as she held her mother's memories in her hands.

"Rose?"

"I'm here." She told him about the photos on their mother's laptop and they both quieted.

Kirk coughed. "I've got a meeting coming up. Thanks for updating me and keep me posted."

"Wait, Kirk. I have to ask you something."

"Make it quick."

"Have you ever had a cardiac calcium scale test? Have you ever heard of it?"

"It sounds vaguely familiar. Why?"

"I mentioned to my occupational therapist that I was getting so little activity right now with all of my injuries that I didn't want to become a candidate for a sudden heart attack. Like Dad."

"You're not going to have a heart attack because you've

been inactive for a few months. You said you're taking Gladys for longer walks and your energy is picking up. Don't worry about a heart attack."

"But the cardiac calcium scale test will tell me if cardiac issues are hereditary. If I could have a sudden heart attack like Dad did. Not next week. Not next year. But, you know, one day sooner than expected. You should have the test done too. Just in case."

"If the kids haven't given me a heart attack yet, I think I'm pretty safe," Kirk laughed. "But okay, I'll look into it. I really have to go now."

Rose disconnected the call. Shut down her mother's laptop and thought about places she hadn't explored in her parents' home. Next chance she got, she'd poke around the closets, upstairs and on the first floor. Her childhood home kept revealing secrets. Rose hoped there was at least one more.

Chapter Twenty-Four
Present Day

Before Rose resumed searching for clues, she needed to push Brandt for information.

"Hi, Cate. Is Brandt in?"

"Sure. Just a minute."

It was Cate, not Brandt, who got back on the line. "Sorry. I didn't realize he's on another call. Can I have him get back to you?"

"That's okay. I'll hold."

Cate hesitated. "I don't know how long he'll be."

Cate's voice was laced with tension. Rose suspected Brandt was putting her off, but she wouldn't wait for a call that might not come. "No worries. I'll hold."

Brandt got on the line less than a minute later. And was all business. "What can I do for you, Rose?"

"I'm following up on another lead to the money in my dad's den. Mary mentioned that a woman named Kelsey Jacobs worked for Dad for about a year before she disappeared. Do you know anything about her? Can you give me her phone number or an email address so I can determine if the ten thousand dollars is hers?"

"I can't confirm whether someone worked for the firm, even if it was more than a decade ago. Besides, we don't keep records that long."

His voice was more tense than Cate's. Rose got the impression he would hang up if she didn't ask more questions. Quickly.

"But she worked there for more than a year. If Mary can remember the woman, why can't you?"

"I didn't say I didn't recall the woman," Brandt snapped. "I said I can't give you any information. And Mary should have checked with me before telling you."

"She's just as interested as I am in figuring out who left the money and getting it back to them. Clearly you aren't." Why was he so annoyed with Rose's questions?

"We're done, Rose. I hope you find what you're looking for, but I cannot help you."

She glared at her cellphone as it beeped. Brandt had gone from friendly when he'd first greeted her in his office, to defensive during the meeting that had followed, to downright hostile during their phone call. What was up with him?

She shook off Brandt's negative energy and headed for the closet in the first-floor bedroom. It was Kirk's room when they were growing up, and where her mother had settled in after the stairs to the second floor had become too much. Maybe Rose would have better luck finding her father's laptop than she'd had getting info from Brandt.

She pushed aside several boxes of shoes and a bag filled with handbags her mother stopped using but wasn't ready to part with. There was no sign of a laptop. She climbed the stairs and walked into the main bedroom. She'd left the closet door open the last time she'd gone into the attic, but she'd been looking up, not down.

A pile of blankets was crammed into the dark corner. She pulled them up and found some books, old magazines, and a soft black case. About the size of a laptop. Her heart skipped a beat as she picked it up.

It was tempting to drop to the floor and open the bag, but she slowed her racing mind. She took the bag downstairs, set it on the table, and unzipped it.

"Well, hello there," she said, smiling at the computer. "At last, a bit of luck."

Her mother had packed away her father's laptop with care. It was clean, with a shaft of sunlight bouncing off its silver surface. She found the power cable, pulled it out, and slid the laptop closer to the end of the table so she could plug it into the wall socket.

And then, nothing. Of course, the battery was dead after all this time, but perhaps it would recharge while she checked her email on her own laptop. An hour later, with no signs of life from her father's laptop, Rose located a computer repair place. Tapping the laptop's touch pad one more time and seeing nothing, she resigned herself to making a trip to Glens Falls. She packed up the computer and headed out.

* * *

"Let me take a look," Nasir said, pulling the laptop out of the bag, plugging it in, and turning it on. The screen was still black. She explained that it was her father's laptop and had sat in a closet for ten years. Nasir nodded as she talked, tapping keys and furrowing his brows. But he stopped working the moment she mentioned her father had been an attorney. He pulled his hands close to his body Bond took a step back.

"A lawyer? You said this belonged to your father."

"Yes, my father was a lawyer."

"Are you a lawyer?"

She shook her head.

"This could contain confidential information. Privileged

client attorney information. Do you have the password for this?"

She shook her head again.

"You need to find someone else to help you. I'm sorry." Nasir closed the lid and pulled the power cable from the outlet. He packed them both in the black case and handed it to her.

"But it's my father's," Rose said.

"I understand what you're saying, but all I have is your word. No offense, but I don't really know this is your father's laptop. I got into trouble once working on a computer that contained confidential information. The person who'd brought it in wasn't honest about who owned the laptop. I'm not going through that again. Sorry."

Rose grabbed the computer bag and shuffled to the door. She was in her SUV and headed back home, deflated. Her cell chirped with a call from Maxi.

"What have you been up to?" Maxi said.

Rose filled her in.

"I agree that the connection with Kelsey sounds plausible. I don't know what's up with Brandt. Maybe he's just being a jerk."

"I never knew Brandt well, but I had the impression he was nicer than he's been to me the past few days. And I trust my father's judgment about the people he hired."

"I only took one psychology course in college, so I can't help you figure out Brandt. Back to the laptop. Are you still in Glens Falls?"

"I'm just leaving."

"Okay, head southeast, and swing by my place," Maxi said. "I know a guy."

Chapter Twenty-Five
Present Day

Rose didn't know how long it would take Maxi to get back to her about the laptop, but she needed to keep busy and pursue any lead she could. When she got home, she picked up the folder on immigrant issues and pulled out the last article and Kelsey's note that quoted her father. The article mentioned a motel outside of Glens Falls that health officials had cited for blocked exits, intermittent hot water, and mold under some of the carpets. According to the article, the motel was converted into apartments and housed immigrant workers who cleaned the nicer motels and inns, maintained the grounds, and worked in the restaurants. The motel was about as far west as you could go in Glens Falls before stepping into the deep woods, in West Glens Falls in Queensbury Township. Okay, time to take a look.

She picked up her camera and notepad, gave Gladys a kiss, and headed out the door. Her last stop on the way out of Lake Amelia was for a cup of coffee from Stewart's. There was no direct route to her destination, and it took close to forty-five minutes, although Rose rarely complained about driving in an area with so much natural beauty.

The motel looked worse than she thought it would.

The sign at the entrance looked neglected, the paint was peeling, the two spotlights drooped into the sign like they were too tired to hold themselves up. The motel was a familiar layout, with the office on one end and two stories of rooms stretching out to the side. Another building was farther back. Few cars were in the cracked macadam lot, in front of doors displaying large numbers on their dark gray surface. The cars were old, smaller sedans, and one more rust patch away from being illegal.

Rose parked a few spaces away from the office. She left her camera and notepad on the floor of the passenger's side and walked to the main entrance. As she pulled the door open, a wave of smoke and dampness assaulted her senses. She covered her mouth and coughed, wishing she could cover her nose. A young man stepped through a doorway and up to the counter.

"¿Qué pasa? Can I help you?" Cigarette smoke polluted his breath and clung to his wrinkled T-shirt, which had a large coffee stain near his belly.

Wasn't indoor smoking prohibited in most places? She tried to inhale as little as possible. "The sign says you have mini suites. Do you have any available for rent?"

He looked at her like she was crazy. "We're booked."

"The sign says vacancy."

"It's broken."

"I'm trying to find someone who recently stayed here. Perhaps you can help me."

Now he looked at her like she was crazy *and* stupid. He scanned her clothes, her hair, her handbag. The smirk on his face showed he doubted her need for accommodations. "I thought you wanted a room."

Her interrogation skills were rusty, and she needed to get her story straight. Perhaps it would be best to stick to looking for someone who'd stayed here. "I'm just trying to find someone."

"I can't help you. We don't give out information about our guests."

"Guests? I thought this was housing for immigrants who worked in area hotels and restaurants." She looked around the office, then back at him with raised eyebrows.

"We don't have a room. I can't give out names of people staying here. Anything else?"

"Okay, last question," Rose pushed. "Can you give me the name and phone number for your boss, the owner?" She glanced at the counter, looking for a business card or a brochure, but found nothing.

"Are you a cop or something?"

"No, I'm not a cop or something. Like I said, I'm looking for someone."

"You can't look here unless you're a cop. Even then, you'd need a warrant." He started walking like he was going to come around the end of the counter and escort her out.

She thanked him and hurried out the door, thinking she should have worn shorts and a T-shirt to blend in. She stood out as someone who didn't belong: a white woman in what looked like a Latino community, judging by the people in the surrounding neighborhood, including the trailer homes she'd passed just before turning into the motel's parking lot.

As she strolled to her car, she glanced back at the office and didn't see the man at the counter. Perhaps he'd gone back into the office for a smoke. She walked to her car and acted like she was getting in, then circled around behind it and crossed the parking lot. A woman, about thirty years old or so, came out from one of the first-floor units, pulling a pack of cigarettes out of her pocket. Rose sauntered over.

"Good morning."

"Do I know you?"

"No. I'm looking for someone who can tell me about the man who owns this place. How long have you lived here?"

The woman took a long drag. "Mr. Browning—the owner—he doesn't like us talking to the police."

Mr. Browning. The owner. That was a nice nugget of information. Rose thought she might have seen Browning's name in some of the articles she'd been scanning. She'd double-check when she got back home.

Rose reassured the woman she wasn't a cop and explained she wanted to ask the owner about one of his properties. "What's your name?"

The woman shook her head.

"Mr. Browning. He owns a few motels and inns in upstate New York, doesn't he?" Rose didn't know that for a fact, but maybe the woman would. "Have you lived here long?"

"¿Mamá?" A girl with sleep in her eyes and hair shooting in every direction poked her head out the door.

"Vuelve a entrar en el apartamiento," the woman ordered. She flicked the ashes off her cigarette. "Mr. Browning has spies everywhere," she said under her breath. "It would not be good for me to be seen talking to you. I can't afford to lose my job." She turned and walked back into her room, closing the door behind her.

Rose understood that jobs were important. People couldn't afford to lose them, and she didn't want to be the reason anyone was fired. But she had to talk with more work-ers, had to see if this Mr. Browning was connected to Kelsey's abrupt departure from her father's law office.

And poking her nose into his businesses was the way to do it.

Chapter Twenty-Six
July 2010

"I'm going into the city for a couple of meetings," Millie said. "I don't have any other commitments after that. Do you want to come with me? We could have a late lunch, go to a museum."

Kelsey was finally beginning to relax on her third day at Millie's. She hadn't left the house, not even for a walk around the neighborhood to expend some of the tense energy running throughout her body. Millie's idea of an outing to New York City was an excellent one, but Kelsey wasn't ready for that hectic pace. She'd prefer another day hunkered down in the safety and comfort of the condo, reading books, and thinking about what to do, where to go next.

"Maybe next time," Kelsey said. "Is it okay if I hang out here?"

Millie reached across the table and squeezed Kelsey's hand. "Of course. I keep telling you, you can stay as long as you need. I'm going to run upstairs and get ready."

Kelsey nodded and flipped open her laptop. She'd avoided social media ever since she'd fled and hadn't even checked the news except for watching TV with Millie in the evening. Kelsey surfed a couple of news sites and sipped her coffee. Suddenly, she screamed and slapped her hand against her chest. Millie ran into the kitchen, her hair wrapped in a towel.

"What is it?"

Kelsey snapped her head toward Millie, then her eyes darted back to the laptop. "This article I found in the *Times Union*. It's the Albany newspaper. It says . . ."Kelsey swallowed as tears formed in her eyes. "He's dead." She stared at the computer screen.

"Who's dead?" Millie stepped closer to see what was on the screen.

"Mr. Randall. He's dead. The article says he died of a heart attack. He wasn't that old. I mean, he was in his sixties, but he wasn't overweight. No one ever mentioned that he had any health issues." Kelsey shook her head. She kept reading as Millie leaned over her shoulder.

"The article calls it a sudden heart attack," Millie said.

"They got to him." Kelsey's voice quivered.

"Who got to him? Kelsey, what do you mean?"

"The same people who threatened me to stop investigating must have gotten to him. I was working with him. He was my boss. And . . ." Kelsey's couldn't finish the sentence.

"And what?" Millie asked after a moment.

Kelsey rubbed her face with her hands, then looked at Millie. "And I gave him ten thousand dollars to continue looking into what Browning was doing. Maybe I put him in danger by asking him to investigate Browning. I went to that motel even after he asked me not to. He told me to continue my investigation but only online. He didn't want me to put myself in danger by visiting Browning's properties." Kelsey rambled on while Millie stared at the laptop. "I wasn't careful enough. And now my actions may have cost him his life."

"Don't you think that's going a bit too far?" Millie said as she placed her hand on Kelsey's forearm. "Do you really think people would murder someone to keep them silent about how they treat their workers?"

"All I know is Randall Webster is dead, and I might be next."

Chapter Twenty-Seven

Present Day

Rose was fired up to do more research about Leonard Browning, but first she had to get to the *Dispatch*. Bill had texted her and asked if she could handle an assignment that afternoon. Of course, she said yes and told him she'd be in the office within the hour.

"Argyle? You mean like the socks?" Rose had taken a seat in the usual spot across from Bill's desk.

"You've heard of Argyle, for crying out loud. You used to live in the area. Argyle, one of the last dry towns in the state. Active in the Underground Railroad and abolitionist movements. Home of the Cheese House. Surely you remember some of your local history?"

"I've heard of Argyle. I'm just pulling your leg. Haha. Get it? Leg. Sock."

He looked at her without comment, but she could tell he was struggling to control the upward turn of the corners of his mouth.

"Where are Earl and the other photographers?"

"Earl's on vacation, spending the next two weeks fishing

up around Speculator. He never tells me exactly where, likes to keep his fishing spots secret. Never mind that I don't fish and couldn't care less where he goes. Joey called in sick."

Rose rubbed the cast on her wounded right arm. She was ready to take photos of the library using a tripod. Empty rooms. Ideal lighting conditions she could control. Was she ready for a news assignment?

"What's going on in Argyle?"

"A picking party." Now he had her. Bill put his hands behind his head and leaned back, waiting for Rose's reaction. She may have gotten him with a sock joke, but he had her at picking party.

Rose's gaze was steady. "What are they picking? Apples? No, it's too early for apples. Too late for blueberries. Corn? Maybe. I read that local corn is now on the market." She sipped her coffee. "What kind of picking party are we talking about?"

"Mostly guitars. Some ukuleles. Probably a banjo or two. Maybe a mandolin."

"A. Music. Picking. Party. You do recall I've won a bunch of awards for my news photography, right? One photo for spot news, for capturing an image of an elderly Black woman, a shawl draped over her shoulders and hobbling with a cane, leading a little white boy from a burning building, tears streaming down both of their faces, creating streams through the ash that almost covered them."

"I remember. You sent me a framed copy, along with a photo of you holding the state AP awards. You had a big smile on your face."

"I might have won the Pulitzer and my smile would have been bigger if it weren't for the *New York Times'* coverage of the protests in the Middle East." She shrugged. A spot news award from the AP still looked good on the resume.

"So, back to Argyle. It's an easy assignment. You go to the big church in town where about forty people are going to sit in those uncomfortable folding chairs for a couple of hours and play songs together. I need three or four images for a feature article Ricky wrote a couple of weeks ago. He's been to three picking parties already. As soon as we get these last photos, we can run it."

"They have that many picking parties?"

"Yep. It's a thing, especially with older folks who like music and the companionship."

"Will Ricky be there?"

Bill nodded. "I know you're technically not supposed to be working yet, so Ricky will help. He can carry the tripod, set it up, and grab your gear bag. You take care of the camera."

"I won't need that much help. But if Ricky could carry the tripod, that'd be great. I've healed a lot over the past several weeks. If my next X-rays look good, the hard cast may come off." She fidgeted in her chair, rubbing her cast. It couldn't come off soon enough.

"You seem a little hesitant. Are you anxious about picking up the camera for an assignment again?"

Yep, he knew her well. "I've held the camera and taken some photos, but it's still a little awkward. I don't want to fumble around or, God forbid, drop it. It's the only camera I have until the insurance money comes through."

"You'll be fine, Rose. You're a pro. I wouldn't ask if I didn't think you could handle it. It's a picking party. You won't need to chase anyone. They'll all be sitting in chairs strumming their instruments." He grinned. "Heck, I could probably even take a good photo."

She stood. "Well, I'm glad you've set the bar so high. I'll leave you to your nice cozy office and your big mug of coffee."

* * *

Bill was right. Every chair in the church basement was taken. People held all sizes and makes of stringed instruments, their eyes shooting back and forth between their sheets of music and the man leading them in song, everyone strumming together. Or not. Some people had big smiles on their faces, others had serious looks of complete concentration. One man was so focused, he squeezed his tongue in and out between his teeth and moved his mouth from side to side. Rose thought it would make a great photo, but she didn't want to embarrass him. She pointed her camera in another direction.

The music bounced off the walls. Getting good photos was easy. She hummed along with the songs she knew and nodded to the beat of songs she didn't. And it turned out Ricky was full of information not related to stringed instruments.

"Do you know anything about Leonard Browning?" Rose asked Ricky during the intermission when the musicians used the facilities and then snacked on food everyone had brought. She'd looked Browning up online in the ten minutes she'd had between meeting with Bill and getting ready for the assignment.

"Leonard Browning," he repeated. "Yeah, I've heard of him. I think he had some legal issues with his properties a while back. Are you working on a story?"

"Sort of." Now that Ricky mentioned it, Rose might have a story for the *Dispatch,* depending on what her investigation turned up.

"I'll tell you what I know about him when we have enough photos from today's event. Let me see what you've got."

Rose scrolled through the photos and found some of her best images. She held the camera so Ricky could see the screen and clicked through them.

"Those are terrific, Rose. You have a great eye for composition. We'll have plenty of photos to work with, and I'm sure Bill will be pleased. We don't need to stick around any longer. Let's grab a bite to eat and I'll tell you what I know about Browning."

They stowed Rose's gear in her SUV and walked to a small diner a block away. The server greeted them, then led them to a red vinyl booth in front of the windows overlooking the quaint town. Rose ordered a grilled cheese and tomato sandwich with her coffee. Ricky ordered a cheeseburger and a Pepsi.

"Browning is a rich guy who treats his workers like dirt. The guy's got no respect for others." Ricky didn't sugarcoat his opinion. "They live where he tells them because they can't afford a decent apartment on the salary he pays. Most don't have health insurance, so they see the doctors he tells them to see. One doctor connected to Browning is a guy named Collins. I can't remember his first name.

"Browning has been cited by the health department for the conditions at the Queensbury property several times, and he always avoided major fines." He looked across the diner at a young mother and her daughter who were thumb wrestling and smiled at them. "These people need the jobs," he said, turning back to Rose. "They are so grateful they don't complain. But he takes advantage of them, plain and simple. Remind me again what sparked your interest?"

She repeated the bare-bones information she'd given him earlier about following up on an old article involving unhealthy living conditions for immigrant workers, legal and undocumented.

"He's the kind of guy who'll do just enough to clean up his act or his properties with the threat of fines. And from what I hear, he treats his adversaries the way he treats his workers." Ricky sipped his drink and looked at Rose with worried eyes. "If you go poking into Browning's businesses, be very careful."

Chapter Twenty-Eight
Present Day

Rose wanted to get an early start in the morning, so after dinner, she walked next door to Mrs. Shaw's with Gladys and a bag of dog food. Gladys had been a regular visitor to Mrs. Shaw's when her mother was alive, taking care of the dog whenever her mother went out of town. That wasn't often, but it was enough that Gladys was comfortable in the neighbor's house. She even had her own doggie bed there.

"Go have fun tomorrow and don't worry about this girl," Mrs. Shaw said as she stood on the porch with Gladys in her arms. Rose was halfway to the sidewalk when she turned, ran back up the steps, and kissed Gladys one more time. Then she went home, organized her camera gear, and went to bed.

She was up before the sun and headed for the Northway. She considered starting with the closest place in Lake George, but then the logistics part of her brain kicked in. She should go to Lake Placid and Saranac Lake first, then end her day in Lake George with a shorter drive home when she was sure to be exhausted.

Ricky had told her about a magazine profile on Leonard

Browning several years ago. It was easy to find in the Lexis-Nexis database. She had downloaded the article and read about his many properties in the Adirondacks, including the three she was on her way to visit. Browning was credited with bringing jobs to the Adirondack region. Many of his fellow business owners in the area praised his work with nonprofits. He was also criticized for not providing a living wage for his immigrant workers, most of them legally permitted to work in the US.

His critics blast Browning for charging high rates at his inns and restaurants, the article in the *Adirondack Business Sense* stated, *making him one of the wealthiest business owners in the Adirondacks. Yet he doesn't share his profits with those who work for him and does not provide them with health care or retirement savings plans.*

That wasn't unusual, was it? She knew the tourism industry in upstate New York and other places often relied on high school and college students for summer labor, but they had the advantage of still living in their parents' homes. Migrant workers did not. Many businesses didn't offer health benefits or retirement plans. But these businesses operated year-round. Students returned to the classroom. Immigrant workers kept the businesses running. Immigrants from Central and South America, for sure, but also from other countries. Europe. China. Ukraine. All you had to do was listen for the accents to know visitors and workers came to Lake George from all over the world.

Rose returned to the article, and another paragraph jumped out at her.

A recent investigation by the New York Attorney General's office zeroed in on the rights of immigrant workers and the accusations that some of them were victims of human trafficking. No evidence was found, but a spokesperson for the AG's office would not comment whether the investigation was ongoing.

Rose hadn't seen any references to human trafficking in the articles and notes in her father's folder. She knew that human traffickers often helped immigrants enter the country with the promise of work, but paying off the debt of their passage to the US often meant they were tied to their employers forever. She wondered how much her father was looking into the issue. It was one more question she wanted to ask Kelsey if Rose ever found her.

Mt. Marcy, the highest mountain peak in New York, grew larger in her window the closer she drove to Lake Placid. Now there were mountaintops in every direction. Towering Pines Inn competed with dozens of hotel chains and individually owned properties catering to visitors who wanted to see the former Olympic site. The familiar drums and cymbals theme from the Olympics played in her head as she pulled into the parking lot at Towering Pines.

Rose picked up her camera and looked over the manicured lawn. Of course, it was better maintained than the Queensbury Motel—people paid good money to stay here. She wandered to the pool where one man was swimming laps and a woman was reading a book on a lawn chair. Was there an outdoor spot for meals, or was the only restaurant inside? Rose took a couple of wide shots of the pool and stepped into the lobby. A breakfast buffet was set up on the far side of the room, with booths and tables scattered throughout.

"Can I help you?"

Rose turned toward the voice of a young woman with a warm smile. "I'm passing through on my way to Saranac Lake," Rose said, "and wanted to check out some inns in Lake Placid for a future visit. Is it okay if I look around?"

The woman reached over and picked up a brochure from the stand on the counter. "Here," she said, handing it to Rose. "This has photos of our guest rooms, the pool area, the restaurant. Do you have a date in mind for your future visit?"

Rose took the brochure. "Not yet, but thanks for the brochure. I'll just take a quick look around."

The woman's smile was a little less warm. "The brochure is fairly complete. You can see the restaurant area behind you. The fenced-in pool is close to the parking lot. I can get someone to show you the exercise room if you're interested, but we don't allow people to walk around the area if they aren't guests."

"Oh, sure, I understand," Rose said, looking around. She'd hoped to talk with some staff, a cleaning person, someone who helped maintain the property. But she saw only guests getting their breakfast. The woman stared at her, her smile dimming with each passing second.

"Thanks for your help. I'll be going then."

Rose took a few more photos of the property from the parking lot, then got in her car and headed toward Saranac Lake. Was she going to have to spring for a stay in these places to learn what information she couldn't get without a room key?

The town of Saranac Lake was a short drive from Lake Placid. It was twice the size of Lake Placid, at least when it came to year-round residents, but had fewer hotels and tourists without the history of the Olympic games. Rose easily located Browning's lakeside inn on the town's north side— again, just off the main road. She'd identified half a dozen Browning properties throughout the Adirondacks. Most of them were modest inns. One higher end property was in Lake George. And according to the magazine article, he made millions every year.

The staff of the Three Oaks Motel in Saranac Lake was equally nice and just as uncooperative as the woman at Towering Pines. Rose asked to use the restroom and eyes followed her as she walked down the hallway. She had the feeling that the woman at the front desk would send someone after her if she didn't return in a few minutes, so she didn't linger. When she left the restroom, she almost bumped into a guest.

"Sorry," Rose said, then added, "May I ask you a question about the Inn?"

The woman looked at Rose with wary eyes. "I don't work here."

"Oh, I figured you were a guest. I'm thinking of staying here next year. Do you like the rooms? Are they clean? Is the furniture comfortable? Is the staff friendly?"

"That's a lot of questions," the woman said. "The rooms are fine, clean, and comfortable. The staff is another matter. They're not really friendly. Most of them are Latino or Hispanic, you know—immigrants, which is fine. I don't have a problem with that. But it seems everyone is walking on eggshells. Like they're afraid of something. Or someone." She turned toward the restroom. "That's my opinion, anyway. I've got to go. Literally. Excuse me."

Rose hurried back down the hallway before the woman at the desk got suspicious. She waved goodbye and thanked her for the information, leaving Lake Saranac about fifteen minutes after she'd arrived. Her first two visits hadn't been very productive, except for the guest's comment about the staff. She steered her SUV south to the Western Inlet Inn on Lake George, where she hoped to learn something to make her trip worthwhile.

Chapter Twenty-Nine

Present Day

As soon as Rose drove through the busy area of shops, restaurants, hotels, and people on every corner at the lower end of Lake George, she sensed an immediate difference. Yes, the area was more developed, with dozens of outlet stores and an amusement park farther south on Route 9, but the lake drew most people. Lake George was not only one of the largest lakes in New York, it was also one of the cleanest, clearest lakes in the country. It was a prime destination for people wanting a summer by the water. To swim. To boat. And especially to fish.

And, Rose hoped, maybe immigrant workers more willing to answer her questions.

While not immaculate, the Western Inlet Inn was well maintained, with beautiful bushes and colorful flowers around the edges of the parking lot, the two buildings, and the walkways. Rose guessed every property in Lake George had to show off its grounds to appeal to guests. Other hotels and inns she'd passed looked freshly painted with blooming flowers at every turn: red and white geraniums, bright orange and yellow marigolds, pink and white impatiens, and tall ornamental grasses waving their feathery tops.

The patio restaurant at the inn was busy with people sitting down for a late lunch. Late in the working nine-to-five sense; not so late if you're on vacation and eat when you're hungry, not when you have to fit lunch into someone else's schedule. After ten minutes, Rose was seated at a table for two near the bar. She ordered salad with grilled salmon and a Saratoga Spring Water. She tried to engage her server in conversation, but she didn't say much. Rose's eyes kept roaming, looking for another server, groundskeepers, anyone she could prod with questions. But she found no one. She finished lunch and paid her bill. Slinging her camera strap over her right shoulder, she entered the inn through a side door.

The short hallway led to the reception area, with open doors to offices behind the counter. A woman studying the computer screen looked up when Rose approached. When the woman saw Rose, she froze. Then she shook her head. It was the woman from the Queensbury Motel who wouldn't talk with Rose when Rose had stopped by. She was even less likely to speak to her while she was working. Despite the woman's signal to stay away, Rose had to try.

"May I help you?" the woman asked with a tight smile.

Rose glanced at her nametag. "Hi, Ana. I'm considering staying here. I had lunch on the patio and really enjoyed the food and atmosphere, the way I could see Lake George. Is it okay if I look around the property?"

Ana reached down, picked up a brochure, and handed it to Rose. Handing an inquisitive nonpaying guest a brochure must be part of the training for people who worked the reception desks at Browning's properties. Rose thought of other places she'd visited where staff seemed more willing to let potential guests look around than the staff at Browning's inns. Maybe Browning had more to hide.

"You should find all the information you need in the brochure or online. Our website and phone number are right here," she pointed. "If you have any questions after reviewing our materials, please call."

Rose was about to try again to gain permission to roam the property when a man stepped out of the office.

"Do you need help?"

Was he asking Ana or Rose?

Rose suspected she wasn't going to get any further with this guy than she did with Ana. "I was just chatting with Ana about the inn. It's a beautiful property and in a wonderful location. I'd hoped to look around a bit."

He looked at the brochure in her hand. "I'm in charge of security at the inn. You have our information. We don't encourage nonguests to roam our property. Is there anything else you need, Miss—?"

Rose hesitated, but couldn't think of a reason not to give him her name. "Webster. Rose Webster."

Did he just flinch? What was it that just passed through his dark and brooding eyes? A flicker of recognition? Did her name mean something to him? She glanced at his name tag. Juan. "Um, no, Juan. I'm good," she said, but didn't move.

Ana smiled and glanced behind Rose as another guest approached the registration desk. Juan scowled.

"I guess I'll be on my way then."

Rose couldn't wait to get home and take a shower. The security guy creeped her out. The way he reacted to her name was unnerving. The way he looked at her with—what was the word she was looking for? Contempt. That was it. He'd looked at her with contempt. She fought the traffic and her nerves on the way back to Lake Amelia.

Chapter Thirty
July 2010

"I can't stay here much longer," Kelsey said. She pushed the hair off her face and rubbed her cheek. "They might trace me." Her eyes darted out the window to where her car sat in the driveway, over to the front door, then down the hallway to the back of Millie's condo.

"You haven't been out of the house since you got here," Millie said calmly. "You haven't used a credit card. How could they trace you?"

Kelsey finally looked Millie in the eyes. "I don't know what they can do, but Randall was suspicious of someone in the office. Not Mary. He trusted her completely, but he kept the investigation into the Western Inlet Inn between him and me. He even said I shouldn't print any documents unless I used the printer in his office. That I should never email him because he didn't want any communications that could be seen by someone else."

"That's certainly odd," Millie said. "And you had no idea who he didn't trust?"

"No," Kelsey said, urgency in her voice. "I don't know, but

I'm scared. Things were getting crazy before I left. And now Randall is dead. How do I know they didn't get to him? What if they killed him? What if they're coming after me next?" Panic rose in Kelsey's throat. "I have to get out of here."

"Kelsey, please slow down. Stay here for a while longer, a couple more days, or just one more day if you're that spooked. You and I can brainstorm about where you could go, someplace you'd feel safe. I'd be happy to help you, but right now, I have to get to work."

"Okay. Maybe somewhere south. Not Florida. California could work. Someplace far away where they won't come looking for me. Maybe in the middle of Iowa. I don't know." Kelsey had barely heard Millie.

"Sometimes it's easier to get lost in a busy place. Like New York. Or Boston," Millie said.

"No, they're too close. I have to get out of New York. Boston may be big, but I'm not going there." Kelsey closed the laptop and got out of her chair. "I need you to gas up my car. Can you do that?"

Millie walked over to Kelsey and took her by the shoulders. "Listen to me. I will help you any way I can. I just can't do it right this minute. I have to go into the city. Matter of fact, if I don't get going soon, I'll miss my train. Promise me you will stay put until I get home. I can probably take off work a little early, and I have a light schedule tomorrow so I can help you then. We'll figure out what to do next, okay?"

"I can't make any promises, Millie."

"Yes, you can. Promise me, Kelsey. Please. You're upset. You need help figuring out next steps. I will help you. This evening."

Kelsey nodded, her face grim. "Okay. Go. I don't want to make you late. I have five thousand dollars. For now. I have no idea how long it will last since I don't know where I'm going.

While you're at work, I'll come up with a plan. We can talk about it when you get home. I'll wait one more day, but I'm leaving here tomorrow morning."

Chapter Thirty-One
Present Day

Dr. Levinson held Rose's right forearm and removed the cast. Rose didn't want to look. And she couldn't wait to look. Wow, was that her arm? It looked paler than it did in the middle of winter. It was also dry. Very dry. Wait. Were those little flakes of skin? Did her arm have dandruff? She looked at Dr. Levinson.

"Is it normal for my arm to look like this?"

He smiled to reassure her. "It's fine. I'm pleased with what I see on the X-ray. I know it's not getting better as quickly as you want, but it's healing well. We can put some lotion on your skin before we put on another cast on, but it might only make it itch more."

Yeah, she'd wanted to scratch her arm the moment Dr. Levinson took off the cast. She'd wanted to scratch her arm plenty of times over the past several weeks, ever since it had been broken, when she'd been shoved to the ground. A surgeon in Philly repaired the broken bones. Two days later, Aunt Tess had called Rose and asked her to get to Lake Amelia as soon as she could because Rose's mother had fallen and was in the hospital. Dr. Levinson had been doing all of Rose's follow-up care in Saratoga Springs.

"At our last visit, you mentioned you might be able to put on a lighter cast, like one made of foam. It wouldn't be as heavy as the plaster of paris cast would it?"

"A cast of foam or plastic would feel lighter, but"—Rose hated sentences with a but in the middle—"I think a fiberglass cast would protect your arm more. The report by your occupational therapist said you want to get back to work."

Rose nodded, not telling the doctor she'd already been back to work.

"I'm willing to clear you for light work, but if I do, I'd prefer to have the fiberglass cast to protect your arm. It's more durable. I'd hate for you to have a setback."

"I'm not going to be covering breaking news or anything taxing," Rose said. "I've been asked to take photos at the library so they can update their website and promotional materials." Then she decided it would be okay to confess. "I did an assignment for the *Dispatch* at the last minute because someone called in sick. It was a ukulele picking party. Someone else carried my tripod. Events aren't much more low stress than that."

"Still, let's go with the fiberglass cast and not take any chances. I prefer you to be prepared for the unexpected."

Rose was hoping she'd be able to go without a cast soon, but it wasn't her decision. She understood the doctor's reasoning. She didn't want to impair her arm's healing, either.

"Speaking of being prepared for the unexpected, I'd like to ask you about a cardiac calcium scale test."

"What makes you ask about that?"

"Someone told me about it. My father died suddenly of a heart attack. He seemed in good health. I understand the test determines calcium levels in the arteries, whether the buildup of plaque has narrowed the arteries and increased the risk of heart disease. I wonder if my dad's heart attack could have been avoided if he'd had the test. And I want to know if I'm at risk for a heart attack like my father."

"You're healthy, Rose. I don't think you need to be concerned."

"By all indications, my dad was as well."

"How old was he when he passed?"

"Sixty-five."

"A man's heart attack risk increases beginning at the age of forty," he told her, "And a heart attack at sixty-five is not abnormal."

"But he'd had no indications . . ."

"How did your father's parents die?"

Rose's eyes shifted back and forth as she searched her brain for information. "Both of them died of cancer," she said. "My grandmother had breast cancer. My grandfather died of lung cancer."

If her father and his parents didn't have heart disease, or at least none her mother knew of, what had caused such a sudden cardiac attack?

"Let me think about it while we put that cast on. I'll get the nurse." Dr. Levinson left the exam room. Rose rubbed her arm, and the little flakes fell onto her jeans. She'd soak her arm in oil if that's what it took to get healthy skin again. But apparently, that was going to have to wait a few more weeks. After the doctor and nurse put the fiberglass cast on her arm, Dr. Levinson returned to Rose's question about the cardiac scale test.

"We can schedule you for a CT scan and see if your arteries have narrowed with plaque buildup," he said. "There are other genetic tests for familial hypercholesterolemia, dilated cardiomyopathy, and others. But let's start with the CT scan. Would that satisfy your concerns?"

Rose nodded.

"And of course, you can reduce your risk of a heart attack with a healthy lifestyle," he said, scanning the charts on his laptop. "You're fit. Blood pressure is normal. Cholesterol is good. You had an EKG post-surgery when you were in the hospital. All normal. I wouldn't worry about having a heart attack."

She couldn't explain that she was actually worried about whether her father *didn't* have a heart attack. She always thought her father was too vibrant, too full of energy to have life stolen away from him. Kirk said it was the cynic in her and pressured her to let it go. So she did. Well, not completely. Or she wouldn't be asking to have a test that could prove whether she had a genetic disposition to heart disease.

Chapter Thirty-Two
Present Day

Rose was back to work at her laptop after a quick stop for lunch at Aunt Tess's diner on the way home from Saratoga Springs. She'd wanted to make notes about her visits to Browning's Adirondack properties when she'd returned yesterday, but she'd been exhausted and went straight to bed. She didn't even pick up Gladys until this morning after the doctor's visit. The two of them had snuggled on the couch, then Rose got on her laptop, but before she could log onto the internet, she got a text from Bill. He was short-staffed again. Could she cover a birthday party that afternoon? She'd texted back yes with several exclamation points. She was eager for something else to focus on and let her mind work in the background on the immigrant abuse investigation.

She'd thought about checking in with Ricky and asking him more questions about Browning but rejected that idea. The other day he said he'd told her what he knew. He'd suggested she investigate allegations that were raised about Browning's activities over the years. She'd found a few articles from several years ago, but Browning was never charged with any crimes or violations. Either there really wasn't anything going on, which Rose did not believe, or investigators never found enough evidence to file charges. That's where Rose would put her money.

Gladys stretched and sat down in front of Rose with a pleading look in her eyes. Letting Gladys into the backyard would be easier, but Rose opted for a walk. After a long day in the car yesterday, it would feel good to stretch and move her body, especially after what Dr. Levinson said about maintaining a healthy lifestyle. Besides, Rose did some of her best thinking while walking the dog and letting her mind wander. The two of them were out the door in no time.

A few blocks later, Rose was around the corner from the newspaper and stopped in to confirm the birthday party details with Bill.

"It's just a birthday party at the nursing home, but it'll be fun," Bill said when she walked into his office with Gladys. Bill came around from behind his desk and gave Gladys a few rubs behind her ears. "It's three o'clock this afternoon," he said. "I need a couple of photos of the birthday girl, the cake, some balloons."

"From a picking party to a birthday party. You promised me assignments that wouldn't be too taxing, and you're keeping your word. Thanks for reminding me that the reason I didn't settle down in a small town to pursue my journalism career is because I wanted to cover hard news on a regular basis."

"We get plenty of hard news," Bill said. "Like the bike thefts that you helped put an end to a couple of months ago." Rose had read about the high number of stolen bikes in the region and tipped off Maxi to some suspicious activities, which led to the arrest of a deputy sheriff for aiding the thefts. Unfortunately, the brother of Rose's high school boyfriend was also caught dealing in stolen bikes.

"By the way, as promised, I asked around about those incidents of a woman run off the road and her apartment break-in," Bill said. "My contact didn't recall them, but he mentioned someone found a body on the Western Inlet Inn property several years ago. Homicide detectives were called to investigate. They determined the teenaged male committed suicide."

"Suicide?" Rose stuck that in the back of her mind to follow up. She intended to look into anything unusual involving the Western Inlet Inn, and a suicide fit that category.

"I have an update for you," Rose said. "I learned the name of the woman who claimed those things happened to her. It's Kelsey Jacobs. She was a paralegal, only worked at Dad's firm for about a year, and may have disappeared because of threats that she mentioned in that note with the cash."

"How did you find that out?"

"Mary, who worked with my dad for more than two decades, was talking with me about the note and money when she remembered Kelsey's name."

"Where's Kelsey now?"

"I don't know," Rose said. "That's my current search. Brandt Statler won't confirm Kelsey worked there, and he claims he doesn't have any employee records going back fifteen years."

Rose could tell Bill was arranging the pieces of this puzzle in his mind, the same way he taught her to organize facts to pull together a story.

"I'd like to talk with your contact about the teenager who committed suicide," Rose said. "He may have more information. Do you think he'll talk with me?"

"Maybe the three of us can grab a cup of coffee at the diner," Bill said after thinking it over. "He'll feel more comfortable if I'm there."

"I can live with that," Rose said. She lifted Gladys off her lap and stood, then gave Bill a half smile. "I'll upload the photos of the birthday party to the photo lab folder as soon as I can."

"Go easy on those old folks. The birthday girl is one hundred and five years old. She'd probably like to make it to one hundred and six."

So would I. So would I. Rose left his office.

Chapter Thirty-Three
July 2010

The Regalia George Hotel was one of the finest hotels in Lake George and its formal restaurant one of the fanciest. From the softly dimmed chandeliers to the white satin tablecloths, abundant floral centerpieces on each table, and diners in their fresh-pressed suits and elegant dresses. People planning on visiting Lake George knew they needed to book their dinner reservations as soon as they booked their accommodations, or they didn't have a prayer to get in. Sure, the hotel always held a few tables for last-minute reservations, but those were never given to the average tourist. The restaurant capped the waiting list at ten and cancellations were few. It helped to be a client of the owner, Leonard Browning.

Chandler Prescott was one of those lucky clients, although his name wasn't in any of Browning's official records. Prescott lived and worked in the financial district in New York City, visited the Regalia George three or four times a year, and always had a table when he wanted one. He also had a companion, thanks to Browning, whenever he wanted one.

Prescott signed the check and smiled at Vicki. He dropped

his napkin on the table and stood, came around behind Vicki, and pulled out her chair. As she rose, he placed his hand on her lower back and guided her out of the restaurant. She turned toward the front entrance of the hotel, but his hand moved from her lower back to around her waist as he led her toward the elevators just past the registration desk. She hesitated.

"Come on, Vicki. I've enjoyed our dinner together, and the night is still young. Let's have one last drink."

Never mind that she was eighteen and shouldn't have had wine at dinner. She wore enough makeup to pass for twenty-one, and the dress clinging to her body would have been banned from most corporate holiday parties. But no one in the restaurant at the high-end hotel would challenge the stylish man and his date, even if he looked old enough to be her father. They wouldn't be the first May-December couple to dine at the restaurant or stay in the hotel's luxury suites.

"The wine went to my head," Vicki said. "I should go home." She'd had drinks with friends before, when Alvaro or Danny got hold of a bottle of vodka. They'd passed it around while hanging out in the apartment Alvaro shared with his parents. His parents worked nights, so the teenagers always had a place to meet up. She knew what it felt like to get a buzz from alcohol. This was different from any of those times. More intense. She felt woozy.

"Not yet," the man said firmly. "I was told you are with me for the evening, and the evening is far from over."

Prescott had called that afternoon, said he was making a last-minute visit to Lake George, and could Browning find him a dinner date? Of course Browning could.

Vicki had only gone on a few dates. The other men hadn't asked her to their rooms, hadn't pressured her to do anything she didn't feel comfortable doing. Those men also didn't order two bottles of wine during dinner. Browning had other, older women used to dining with Browning's clients. But Prescott's call was last-minute and Browning had booked all of his regular escorts. Vicki was young and beautiful, and Browning knew Prescott would enjoy her.

Vicki stumbled on her four-inch heels as Prescott led her into the elevator and pushed the button for the eighth floor. His arm almost pinned her to his side, and the evening that had begun with smiles and laughter was giving way to Vicki's fear of what was next.

Later, she'd be asked for his name and room number, but she remembered neither, only entering his room, being encouraged to have another drink. Sitting on the couch so close to him, she could see the gray hair in his eyebrows. When his hand slid under her dress and up her thigh, she tried to push it away, but she was young, inexperienced, too afraid of what would happen if she said no. She wasn't strong enough to fend off his grip around her waist and hand squeezing her thigh.

She closed her eyes as tears threatened to spill out. The man brought her to her feet and led her into the bedroom, where he pulled her dress over her head and pushed her onto the bed.

Chapter Thirty-Four

Present Day

Rose slept in later than usual, thanks to being busier than usual.

"Do you have news for me?" she asked Maxi when she answered her call.

"What, no hello first?"

Rose couldn't see Maxi's smile, but she could hear it, even feel it. She was getting better at understanding her sister's wry sense of humor, at letting down her defenses, and not being offended when she thought Maxi was criticizing.

"Sorry. I just got up. I haven't had coffee yet. I'll try again." She cleared her voice. "Why, hello, Maxi. It's nice to hear your voice on this fine morning."

"You don't have to go overboard." Maxi laughed, and Rose did as well. "I'm calling about the computer. I picked up your laptop and thumb drive late yesterday . . ."

"Finally. I was worried your guy couldn't get in."

"Rose, it's been two days and we're not his only client. He does a lot of work for law enforcement in the area." Maxi paused. "You didn't hear that from me. There's something big going down that took up all of his time the past couple of days. You didn't hear that from me either."

"Okay. I only heard that you picked up the laptop and thumb drive."

"Yes. The tech unlocked both of them."

"Yay! That's great. When can I get them?"

"I worked the late shift, so I need to take care of the boys first," she said, referring to her two dogs that spent their days roaming the large fenced-in yard at Maxi's rural home. "How about if I head over around lunchtime?"

"You're going to make me wait that long?" Rose looked at the clock over the kitchen counter. Wow, it was almost half past eight. She was more tired than she'd realized.

"Want me to pick up a couple of sandwiches on the way?"

"That'd be great. See you in a while."

Rose hustled over to let an impatient Gladys back inside, thinking about what she might find on the laptop. Did it hold any more clues about undocumented immigrants and Browning's possible illegal activities? Would it provide the information—and help build a case for the police—to stop him from harming innocent people? She poured the coffee grounds into the filter, watched the coffee drip until it filled her cup, and headed upstairs to shower.

* * *

Rose paced the living room and pulled Maxi into the house the moment she arrived. Rose reached for the laptop, but Maxi handed her the bag with sandwiches and walked into the kitchen.

"Kitchen table or dining room table?" Maxi asked, then looked at both and shook her head. "Which one is easier for you to make some space?"

"Definitely dining room. Come on." Rose strode past Maxi and set the bag of sandwiches down on the end of the table. She stacked the file folders on top of each other, closed her own laptop, and set the folders on top of it. She slid the whole pile down the table. Then she grabbed the books and newspapers on the other side and put them on the couch.

"Better?" She smiled.

"Much." Maxi took a seat and reached for the sandwiches. "Food first, then the laptop."

"You drive a hard bargain." Rose took the sandwich Maxi offered and dug in. After a few minutes, Rose couldn't stand it any longer.

"Did your guy tell you what's on the laptop?"

"Nope. His job wasn't to read what's on it, only to make sure you could. That's what he did. There were a couple of folders he couldn't open that were only saved to the laptop and not backed up to the cloud. He said if you want him to take another crack at those, he could."

"Sounds good," Rose said, eyeing the laptop bag.

"Go ahead." Maxi wiped her hands on her napkin. "Take out the laptop and give me the power cable."

Rose unzipped the bag and yanked the laptop out, then grabbed the cable and pushed it across the table. After Maxi plugged the cable in, she sat in a chair next to Rose and pulled the rest of her sandwich across the table.

Rose smiled as the laptop came to life, the screensaver's swirls of black, red, and gray dancing across the screen.

"What's the password?" Rose asked, her hands poised over the keyboard.

"Sisters2025."

Her left hand moved toward the "s" key, then paused.

"With a capital 'S,' the rest lowercase," Maxi instructed quietly.

Rose flexed her fingers and forced the swelling tears to stay put. "Nice." She typed in the password and hit the return key. The screen filled with small icons and folders named for issues her father had been tracking. There were dozens of folders with names of clients and businesses. Some folders were labeled with the same topics Rose had found in the box of documents in the attic. Others were new topics. Her cursor flew around the home screen until it hovered over one folder. *Personnel.* Rose looked at Maxi. Looked back at the laptop.

"Could it be this easy?" She took a deep breath, then double-clicked. A small box appeared in the center of the screen, requesting a password. Rose typed in *Sisters2025*, but the password was rejected. Of course, it wouldn't be that easy.

"That must be a folder my guy couldn't access," Maxi said. She reached for the other half of her sandwich and Rose clicked on folders.

"Whatever is in that personnel folder may be the only way we can find someone who knows what happened to Kelsey. Mary told me that businesses don't have to maintain personnel files for more than four years, and that's one reason Brandt may not have had any info on Kelsey. That and the fact that something's going on with him. I just don't know what yet. But this laptop hasn't been updated since 2010. There's an excellent chance we'll find Kelsey's information in here."

After a couple minutes of watching Rose try to access the folder, Maxi stood. She put a hand on Rose's shoulder. "You need to keep poking around the computer. I have some shopping to do. I'll check in with you later."

"Thanks for doing this. What do I owe you? What do I owe your guy?"

"I took care of it. Stay put. I'll let myself out. See you later." With that, Maxi was gone. Rose dropped back into her chair. She kept her eyes on the computer screen as she reached for the rest of her sandwich and took a bite. *What would Dad use for a private password?*

She chewed on the question as she finished her sandwich and washed it down with a glass of water. Then she texted Kirk.

Chapter Thirty-Five

Rose stared at the laptop screen while she waited. Would this be one of those times Kirk didn't get back to her until he got home in the evening? She tried to think of passwords her father might use but was afraid if she tried too many times she would get locked out. Then she'd have to take the laptop back to Maxi's guy, and who knew how long it would take?

After glancing between the laptop and her cell phone for a few minutes, Rose stood and collected the white sandwich paper, dirty napkins, and other leftover lunch items. She walked into the kitchen and dropped everything into the trash. When her cell phone trilled, she rushed back to the dining room table.

"Hey, there. I was hoping you'd get back to me soon." Recently, Kirk had been returning her calls or texts soon after she sent them, much faster than he used to, and for a moment she worried his law practice wasn't busy. Or perhaps he was finally interested in learning who gave their father the money she'd found in the den.

"Hi. I'm impressed you accessed the folders on Dad's laptop."

"Not me exactly. After I struck out with a computer repair guy, Maxi took it to someone she knew who got into most of the files."

"Most of them? Not all of them?"

"At least one folder is protected with another password."

"That's why you asked if I knew any of Dad's passwords?"

"Yep. The folder I can't access is named 'Personnel.' It seems Dad put another password on it out of an abundance of caution, but that's probably the folder I care about most. It could lead to Kelsey."

"What was the password to get into the laptop in the first place?"

"Uh, Maxi didn't say. She and the computer guy created a new one that I'm using. Then I found the personnel folder. I was hoping Dad might have shared his password information with you. I mean, he must have told Mom since she used his laptop after he passed, but I didn't find any notes in the laptop bag or the table beside her recliner."

"Mom created her own passwords, but I doubt she gave Dad's laptop another thought after she had the Lenovo."

"Given where I found Dad's old laptop in the upstairs bedroom closet, that sounds right. And if Dad kept any notes about passwords or things like that his papers, we never found them when we cleaned out the office."

"Give me a minute."

Rose tapped her fingers on the table waiting for Kirk. She was never good at creating passwords or remembering them. Time moved on, and Kirk remained silent. Rose was about to ask if he was still on the line when he spoke.

"I just remembered a conversation I had with Dad not long after José was born. I was in the delivery room with Maria. When I saw José's little body, when I held him in my arms wrapped in blankets and taking his first breaths"—Kirk's voice cracked and he swallowed hard enough for Rose to hear—"I couldn't speak. I couldn't answer when the nurse asked if I was okay. I was in tears when I spoke to Dad later that day and told him what I'd been feeling. He didn't say anything for a while, and I think, uncharacteristically for him, he was moved. And then he said in a raspy voice, 'Your boys are little miracles,' or something like that. I think we were closer in that moment than we'd ever been before." Kirk blew out a breath. "What if he used the boys' names in his password?"

"It's a better guess than what I've come up with. Do you think he'd use both their full names, or parts of their names?"

"I have no idea, but what if you try *CarlosJosé* as one word with the first letter of each name capitalized?"

Rose put her phone on speaker next to the laptop and looked at the keyboard. She hesitated, then typed in the password box as Kirk suggested. She hit the return key. An error message popped up.

"Nice try, but that doesn't work."

"Try playing with some iterations of their names. That's my best idea."

"Okay. Thanks. I'll let you get back to work. I'll text you if —I mean when—I have success." Rose hung up, then quickly called Kirk back.

"Did you get in already?"

"No, I forgot to tell you I had the cardiac calcium test a couple of days ago. It's a CT scan, so the results don't take long." She paused.

"Rose, you buried the lede. Don't make me wait any longer."

"It was negative. The test was negative, meaning I don't have a genetic disposition to cardiac disease."

"That doesn't mean you can't still have a heart attack."

"I know, but it does make me wonder whether Dad really

did die of a heart attack. You should have the test done too. It's not a big deal."

Kirk was quiet for a moment. She braced for some critical or snarky comment from him about her having such a suspicious nature, but he surprised her.

"Okay. I'll think about it. But not because I think Dad didn't have a heart attack. I'd do it for my own peace of mind." He hung up.

Well, that was kind of positive, wasn't it? At least he didn't tell her she was crazy.

Rose set her phone on the table and returned her focus to the laptop. If the computer shut her out for trying too many times, she'd ask Maxi to take it back to her computer guy. She typed, *KirkMariaCarlosJosé*. It was long, but easy to remember. She tapped the enter button with her little finger. And got the error message again.

Now she *glared* at the screen. "Work with me, will ya?" She reached to the stack of folders she'd set aside when she'd cleared the table for lunch and found a notepad. She picked up a pen and wrote down the first two passwords she tried. She thought about the years the boys were born and tried *Carlos08José10*. Error.

Carlos2008José2010. Error.

She tried shortening the boys' names. *CarJos*. Error.

Error. Error. Error. She had to take a different approach.

Rose leaned back in the dining room chair and thought about her conversation with Kirk. What had Dad said to Kirk after José was born? He'd told Kirk his boys were little miracles.

She typed *LittleMiracles*. Error.

littlemiracles. Error.

Password possibilities flew through her mind. Then she typed *MiracleBoys*. She watched the screen, tried to think what it was thinking, and was rewarded when the personnel folder opened to reveal several more folders and documents. There should be trumpets blaring or something.

"I'm in," she whispered. Then, "I'm in," she hollered to Gladys. The fine hairs over the dog's eyes raised as she looked at Rose. Gladys shook her head once and went back to sleep.

Rose went to work.

Chapter Thirty-Six

"Are you busy? Can you come over?" she asked Mary after a brief hello.

"What's up?"

"I got into Dad's laptop. There's a folder labeled 'Personnel.' I'm hoping you could help me go through it. You were probably privy to some of this info already. I feel like I'm snooping into personal information." Snooping. That would be the word for it, but it would still feel better if Mary was there while Rose did it.

"I'll be there in twenty."

Rose led Mary to the table and pointed to the chair in front of the laptop.

"Have a seat. I opened the folder with Kelsey's name. You'll see the list of Word Documents. Application. Cover letter. Résumé. I clicked on a couple of them, but I don't have a right to look at these. Since you worked for Dad, sometimes in a managerial position," she asked with a question in her voice, "maybe it would be more appropriate if you read them first."

Mary nodded. Rose took the seat that Maxi had vacated.

Mary clicked on Kelsey's résumé and they both read it. It began with a summary of her work as a paralegal and her goals to continue working with underserved people in the community, with organizations or a law firm focused on the same issues. Then came her skills, listed in bullet points, including legal research, legal writing, organization, analytical thinking, and adaptability. Next was experience, which covered the years since she'd graduated college. She'd worked for an organization helping recent immigrants, women and children, who'd arrived in the US without a husband or father. Kelsey had also freelanced with a law firm in Westchester County which handled green card and undocumented immigrant issues.

"Pretty straightforward, don't you think?"

Mary nodded. "Kelsey didn't have a lot of experience, but it was focused in the same area, which would be important."

"Do you remember reviewing her materials, or interviewing her for the position when Dad hired her?"

"I don't. As I recall, someone recommended Kelsey to him, and he brought her on as a part-time paralegal, then moved her into a full-time position when she'd been there for a couple of months. I recall he respected her work. And he trusted her."

"Okay. Let's check out her cover letter. Isn't that where people list references?"

"References might be listed in the cover letter and the application. We'll look at the cover letter first."

As they opened the document, Rose held her breath. Mary scrolled to Kelsey's references: the two organizations she'd worked for in Westchester County, one of them in Peekskill, and a law firm in Bedford.

"We should print this, don't you think?" Rose couldn't keep the excitement out of her voice. These were connections to Kelsey, and one of them might lead to the missing woman.

"I'll print two," Mary said.

"Be right back." Rose walked down the hallway to the den and picked up the pages just as the printer finished.

"Let's see if there's any other helpful information on Kelsey's application," Mary said, closing one document and opening the other. After a quick review, they closed that document as well. "Is there anything else we should look at?"

Rose scanned the folders on the screen. She saw the folder with Brandt's name on it and fought the urge to open it. There was something odd about the way he went from nice guy to unfriendly when Rose had stopped by the office. But looking at his personal information felt wrong, inappropriate, intrusive, and a few other words, so she closed the laptop.

Mary looked at the notepad beside the computer as Rose handed her the printout. "What are all these?"

"The passwords I tried to open the personnel folder."

"Is the last one, *MiracleBoys,* the one that worked?"

"Yes, it is."

Mary smiled. "Your father was smitten with his grandsons. He didn't show a lot of emotion, as you know, but he was so proud of those boys. He beamed whenever I asked about them." Her voice lowered. "I'm so sorry he didn't get to see them grow up."

"Yeah. He would have been proud of them, for sure."

Rose wiggled the paper in her hand. "Should we contact these references? Ask if they know of Kelsey's whereabouts?"

"That's the logical next step, isn't it?"

Rose tapped in the number for the first organization on Kelsey's reference list and put her phone on speaker. The woman who answered said there was no one there by that name.

"I know," Rose said. "She worked there more than a dozen years ago and listed your organization as a reference. I'm following up to see if you have any current information for her."

"Let me see if I can get someone to speak with you." She came back on the line a few minutes later. "Sorry to keep you waiting. The executive director says Kelsey Jacobs did work here fifteen years ago, and she was a good employee. She has no current work or contact information."

Rose thanked her, hung up, and tried the second organization. She got the same result.

"I'm not surprised," Mary said. "If someone asked me about a reference more than a dozen years ago, I'd probably say the same thing. Younger people bounce from one job to another early in their careers, which is fine if they're trying to find the best fit. But some people don't like to stay in one place for too long. I wonder which kind Kelsey is?"

"Or was," Rose said. She couldn't help thinking about the threats Kelsey had mentioned in the note. Did someone track her down and harm her? Rose wanted to learn the answer to that question, but was afraid to find out. She pushed those thoughts to the back of her mind. "Let's try the last reference at the law firm."

"Millie Snyder doesn't work here anymore," said the woman who answered the call. "I believe she has her own consulting firm. I can give you a number if you like."

"Yes, please," Rose said, picking up her pen. She jotted down the number, hung up, and looked at Mary. "Okay, one more call."

It went to voicemail. Rose frowned and hung up.

"Don't you want to leave a message?"

"Yes, I do, but I wanted to think about what to say. I don't know what's going on with Kelsey, why she never returned, and I don't want to scare off anyone who might have information."

After talking it over with Mary, Rose called Millie's number again. When the recording beeped, she was ready. "Hi. My name's Rose Webster. I'm looking for Kelsey Jacobs.

She worked for my father at his law firm in upstate New York fifteen years ago. When I was cleaning his home recently, I found something that belongs to her. Could you please give me her contact information so I can reach out to her? Thanks." Rose left her cell number and hung up.

"How long do you think it'll take her to call back?" she asked, looking over at Mary.

"*If* she calls back." With that, Mary said she had some errands to run before dinner and to let her know if Rose heard from Millie.

Rose walked Gladys for something to do while she waited. As soon as she got home, Rose dug under the stack of file folders and found her own laptop. She looked up the two organizations on Kelsey's reference list first to confirm what they did, what clients they served. Then she Googled *Millie Snyder Westchester County.* Information about Millie's consulting practice came up first, with the cell number Rose already had called. She kept searching and bingo! She found a connection with Millie and the organization in Peekskill called Women and Children First, which helped migrants who'd recently come to the US. Kelsey had worked for them and Millie currently consulted for them. Not only that, but the organization was having a welcoming ceremony for dozens of recent immigrants the following day. Millie Snyder was one of the contacts for information about the event.

Rose called Mary and left her a message. "Do you want to go to Peekskill tomorrow?"

Chapter Thirty-Seven

As soon as Rose pulled into the driveway, Mary sprinted out the door to Rose's SUV with a bag in one hand and a tumbler in the other.

After saying hello and settling in, Mary asked Rose if Millie had called back.

"Not a peep. Maybe she's too busy with this event. Or she has nothing to tell us." Rose backed out of the driveway and onto the road. "And she could be avoiding us."

"We'll find out today."

"I hope." Rose glanced out the window. "This looks like a nice development to live in, Mary, but why did you move out of that sweet little house in Schuylerville?"

"I met Sam."

Rose looked at Mary with the unspoken question in her eyes.

"Sam, my husband. He's a retired cop. I hadn't planned on getting married this late in life, but it happened a few years ago, and here I am. A suburbanite."

"Do you miss your old house?"

"You bet I do. It was my home for more than thirty

years. I loved the house. I loved my neighborhood. And I made some special connections there." Mary grew thoughtful, taking in the view out her window, and Rose let the silence linger. This was the route to her father's old law firm and Saratoga Springs. It was also the fastest way to the highway.

"I've only lived out here a few years," Mary said, "but I barely know anyone other than Sam and that's not for lack of trying. In town, I knew my neighbors. I knew their joys, and I heard about their sadness. Sometimes their stories broke my heart."

"Sounds like you're thinking of someone specific."

Mary nodded. "There was this one young man. He was harassing me, making calls from burner phones, so it was hard to track him down. Then he made a mistake and bragged to a friend about what he was doing. The friend told his mother, and she told me."

"Who was he and why was he harassing you?" Rose turned on her left blinker and took the ramp to the highway heading south.

"He was a teenaged boy who lived around the block and often rode his bike in the neighborhood. One day, I caught him tossing trash on the flowerbed in front of my house—an empty soda bottle, a candy bar wrapper—and I asked him to stop. Rather than stop, he made a point of leaving trash there every day. That, plus the phone calls."

"What did you do when his friend's mother told you?"

"I found out where the boy lived and went to his home," Mary said, taking a sip from her tumbler. "I spoke with his mother. She was a single mom working two jobs. He was fourteen and was struggling with his parents' divorce. She apologized and called him downstairs. The boy came into the living room with his head down, unwilling to meet his mother's eyes or mine. She asked if what I said was true, and he nodded.

Then she asked him to apologize. He did, and that was the end of it."

"And he never bothered you again?"

"No, he didn't. As a matter of fact, he came by once in a while and asked if I needed any help around the yard, mowing the lawn, shoveling the snow. He was a nice boy. He was acting out because he was struggling. I think about him often and hope he's doing okay."

"Life can be filled with challenges. You never know what's coming at you next, and you can't always be prepared," Rose said.

"That's why I can't get Kelsey out of my mind now," Mary said. "I want to know why she left in such a hurry. Why she gave your father ten thousand dollars. I need to know if she's okay. She sounded so scared in that note. Who threatened her, and why? You know, it's part of being a paralegal, being in the field of law, wanting to get to the bottom of something."

"I get it," Rose said. "It's part of being a journalist too. You can't quit asking questions until you're sure you have all the answers."

"And we are a long way from having all the answers about Kelsey Jacobs," Mary added.

"Fingers crossed we'll know more in a couple of hours."

* * *

"I didn't return your call because I have nothing to tell you." Millie Snyder held her smile when Rose and Mary introduced themselves, but it lacked the sincerity of the smile she had just given a guest at the celebration of Women and Children First. When Rose and Mary had walked into the nonprofit organization's offices in Peekskill about fifteen minutes earlier, they were given a packet of information about the group's work, including a donation form with a prepaid envelope. The two of them had made small talk and wandered the room until they'd found Millie.

"Is Kelsey alive?" Mary asked.

"What makes you think she wouldn't be?"

"The note she left my father indicated she had been threatened," Rose answered. "More than once. She said she was scared and needed to disappear."

Millie's perfect composure cracked a little. "She told your father? Wait, what's your name again?"

"Rose Webster. Kelsey worked for my father, Randall Webster."

"The lawyer who—" She stopped abruptly.

"The lawyer who what?" Rose asked. "It's clear you know a lot more than you're telling us. Have you been in touch with Kelsey? Do you know where she is?"

"Millie?" A voice called out from behind Rose and Mary. "There you are." A woman hurried to Millie and took her arm. "Come along. We're about to make the presentations."

"I'll be right there." Millie removed the woman's arm and stepped closer to Rose and Mary. "Obviously I can't talk now. But really, I can't help you."

"Can't or won't?" Rose pressed. "Look, you're here today to celebrate an organization that's helping migrant women and children who came to this country seeking a better future, a life free from abuse. Kelsey was investigating the treatment of immigrant workers upstate when she worked for my father. She must have discovered something, and that's why she was being threatened. I don't know why she walked away from working on an issue that was so important to her—yes, the threats, I know—but she could have told my father, could have worked with him." Rose's voice had gotten louder. She lowered her voice, but not the intensity of her words. "Kelsey learned things that may help us stop what seems to still be going on. Please. If someone told Kelsey that this abuse is continuing all these years after she left, I think she'd want to help us."

Millie pressed the bridge of her nose, then looked to the front of the room at the podium where people were gathering. "I have to do this now."

"We'll be right here when you're finished."

Chapter Thirty-Eight

Rose and Mary stayed through the presentations, the applause, and the congratulatory handshakes. Most of the guests left, and a few people asked the two of them if they enjoyed the presentation. Did they need anything? Finally, Millie came over.

"Follow me. There's a room we can use."

They took seats around a small round table. Millie looked at Rose.

"So you're the daughter of the lawyer Kelsey worked for." She turned to Mary. "And who are you?"

"I was a paralegal in Mr. Webster's law firm for twenty-plus years. I was aware Kelsey was investigating something involving immigrants shortly before she disappeared, shortly before Randall died."

"You knew Kelsey?" Millie asked.

"It was a small office. We all interacted with each other every day. I never understood why she disappeared until Rose found the note and the money in her father's den."

"What money?"

"The ten thousand dollars she gave my dad to continue

the investigation," Rose said. "Kelsey was invested enough in finding out what happened to give my father money to hire someone and help finish what she'd started."

Millie nodded. "I'd forgotten about the money. Kelsey had told me she'd taken cash out of her bank account, some for Mr. Webster and some for her to live on until she figured out what to do. Didn't anyone at the firm wonder why Kelsey didn't return?" Millie asked.

"Randall died a few days after Kelsey disappeared," Mary said. "We were all shocked by his sudden passing and dealing with his death, as well as handling the firm's business. I'm sure we wondered at the time, but I can't recall anything more specific. Like I said, we were all stunned by Randall's sudden death."

"How did he die?"

"Heart attack," Rose said. Rose kept her eyes on Millie even when Mary spoke. Millie seemed to take most of the information they were sharing in stride. But she was a lawyer, and Rose knew lawyers were skilled at poker faces.

"You knew Kelsey when she began working for my dad. You were one of her references. She may have contacted you after she left. How long had you known Kelsey?"

Rose suspected Millie was trying to decide how much to share. She was the best lead they had. If Millie didn't help them, Rose didn't know where they would turn next. She held Millie's gaze until the attorney looked down at the table and sighed.

"Kelsey called me the day she suspected her apartment was broken into. She was a mess. Scared to death. Panicking. Said she feared for her life. I told her she could come stay with me. By the time our call ended, she'd calmed down and seemed her usual self." Millie glanced at Rose and Mary. "Then a few days later, maybe only one day, something happened. She called from the highway. She had that same panicked voice she'd had in that first phone call and said she was on her way to Westchester County, taking me up on my offer to come stay with me for a couple of days."

"She listed you as a reference, but Kelsey wouldn't call and ask someone who was just a reference for a place to stay. How long had you known her?"

"Since we were kids," Millie said. "We grew up in Westchester County, went to the same schools, were close friends in high school."

"Is that where you lived when Kelsey came to stay with you?"

"That doesn't matter," Millie said after a pause. "We grew up in Westchester. I went away to college then law school. Kelsey stayed in the area, became a paralegal. We reconnected when I moved back to the area for work."

"Was Kelsey someone prone to exaggeration?" Mary rejoined the conversation. "Do you think she was in as much danger as she'd claimed?"

It took a moment for Millie to respond. "I think she genuinely felt her safety, if not her life, was threatened. Her fear was real. Was the danger real? I don't know. I didn't have any reason not to believe her."

"How long did she stay with you?" Mary asked.

"Do you know where she is?" Rose asked almost at the same time.

Millie's face, which had been lit up with joy earlier in the day, was now drawn. Sadness filled her eyes. She rubbed her forehead.

"We need to talk with her, Millie. Please. You're the only person who can help us reach her."

Mille stood. "Give me a minute." She left the room.

Mary turned to Rose. "What do you think?"

"I think we have her attention. I think she understands why we feel so strongly about talking with Kelsey." Rose pressed her lower lip between her teeth. "But your guess is as good as mine whether she'll persuade Kelsey to talk with us."

Rose got out of her chair and wandered the small room, looking at the posters on the wall—images of women and children with dirt-smudged clothes and pained faces. On the other wall were images of smiling children playing outdoors in a grassy area and women cooking in a kitchen. From despair to hope and joy. Women and Children First changed the lives of these women. Could Kelsey help Rose and Mary change the lives of immigrants upstate?

The conference door opened and Millie walked in, holding her cell phone. She returned to her seat and set the phone on the table. Rose hurried to her chair, staring at the phone.

"Kelsey, I'm in the room with Rose and Mary, and I have you on speaker. I've explained a bit of our history and how you stayed with me after you fled upstate. As I explained, they have some questions for you."

Mary spoke first. "Hi, Kelsey. It's Mary. I'm glad you're safe. Do you remember me? We were both paralegals in Randall Webster's law firm."

"Yes, I remember you." Kelsey's voice was soft and tentative.

"I want you to know you can trust us. You never met Rose, but she's a lot like her father. Dedicated to helping others. Making sure people are treated fairly, and with respect. Rose?"

Rose explained how she found the note and the ten thousand dollars in her father's home office.

"You mean it sat there for fifteen years?"

"Yes," Rose said. "And I discovered it in a hidden compartment in my dad's den only after bumping my hand on a part of the bookshelf I was cleaning. Why didn't you give him the money at the office?"

"I was afraid someone might follow me. I didn't dare go to the firm. I slid the envelope through the mail slot at your father's house and drove away."

"Why did you give him money?"

"I wanted to make sure he continued the investigation into the abuse of immigrant workers. I knew he'd be short-staffed when I left, even for a couple of weeks, and I wanted him to hire someone outside of the firm to continue investigating."

"Why not someone else who worked at the firm?" Rose asked.

"Your father didn't trust someone at the office. I didn't know who. He never told me. But he stressed that I wasn't to tell anyone else what I was working on. Except Mary when she gave me a list of clients the firm had helped. Recent immigrants."

"It hasn't stopped, Kelsey. Actually, I don't know if it's been going on all these years, but Browning and the people who work for him are preying on his workers, abusing them, forcing them into an escort system, even teenaged girls. You were onto something. You have information that could help us stop this. Please. We need your help."

The silence lasted so long that Millie and Rose glanced at the phone at the same time. Rose thought Kelsey had hung up.

"It's not safe. I don't want to be dragged into this."

Rose hesitated. She heard the fear in Kelsey's voice but didn't know how to calm her. She decided to switch topics. Sort of.

"Let's set that aside for now. I want to return your money. I don't know many people who couldn't use ten thousand dollars. You intended for my father to hire an investigator. That didn't happen. I'll deliver your money to you. Then we can talk in person about what else you know that caused you to be the focus of so many threats."

Kelsey grew silent again. This time Rose pushed the conversation along.

"It's been fifteen years, Kelsey. I'll bet no one is looking for you anymore. Please help me help the people Browning may be hurting."

"*Is* hurting," Kelsey said. "There's no question he was hurting them before, and if he's still in business, he's hurting them still."

"Then help us," Rose said.

Kelsey sighed. "It's so complicated." She paused again. "Have you been to Cape Cod?"

Chapter Thirty-Nine

Rose's car rounded the curve, and the Sagamore Bridge arched into the sky with Cape Cod up ahead and the canal below. About fifteen minutes after crossing the bridge, she took the Barnstable exit and pulled into the Burger King parking lot. Then she waited. Cars came and went, people going into the fast-food restaurant for lunch or gassing up their vehicles at the Mobile station. A new text hit her cell phone, the first one since early that morning.

Exit left out of the parking lot. Turn right into CC Community College, then right. Park in the first lot.

What was it with all this cloak-and-dagger stuff? Rose did as instructed and waited again. Five minutes later, a woman wearing denim shorts and a bright blue T-shirt approached. Rose got out of her car.

"Hi, I'm Kelsey." The woman extended her right hand.

"Rose Webster. Thanks for agreeing to see me, but is all of this necessary?"

"I've been careful this long," Kelsey said. "I'm not about

to stop now." She pointed. "That's my white sedan. Follow me to my house in West Dennis. It's about thirty minutes."

It was a beautiful drive, despite the traffic, crossing over brooks with small ponds and the occasional larger pond dotting the landscape. Rose admired the well-trimmed lawns of the single-story saltbox homes and their cedar clapboard siding. Now and then a larger home appeared behind the pines, their dormers making more bedroom space on the second floors.

They pulled into the driveway of a single-story cottage, a modest home in a mostly modest neighborhood. Kelsey parked in front of the garage, and Rose pulled up close behind her. It was not a large house and Rose doubted there'd be room for her to stay overnight unless Kelsey had a sofa bed. The drive had taken more than four hours, and Rose had no intention of going back today. Hopefully, there'd be a B&B nearby, although finding an empty room on Cape Cod in August was like a dog searching for an inch of grass after a major snowstorm. She followed Kelsey up the walkway to the front door and stepped inside.

The living room had a matching beige loveseat and two chairs, one of them a recliner, a small side table, and a small television. A square table with two chairs was to the right. The kitchen was just beyond that, and a door to a bedroom was to her left.

"Would you like a cup of coffee or tea?" Kelsey asked as she walked into the kitchen.

"Actually, I'd love a glass of water." When Rose stepped into the kitchen behind Kelsey, she stopped. Beyond the kitchen was a narrow room that spanned the back of the home, with a couple of cozy chairs and tall windows looking into the woods. "That's a lot of windows for someone concerned about their safety and privacy," Rose said.

"When I moved in nine years ago, I kept the curtains on

these windows closed most of the time, especially in the evening. Now I let the light come in all day, but I still close them at night. The longer I'm here, the more comfortable I am. But I'm still cautious around strangers," Kelsey said, glancing at Rose.

"I'm not a total stranger, really, since you worked for my dad."

"He was a good man."

"Yes, he was." Rose took the glass of water Kelsey offered and drank half of it down.

"My tap water is filtered. Help yourself to more."

"I will, thanks. I'm a little dehydrated."

"I get it," Kelsey said. "Do you need to use the bathroom?"

"I'm good, thanks."

The electric kettle on the counter beeped. Kelsey poured the steaming water over a tea bag in a large mug, then picked up the mug and pointed outside. "I'm sure not many people take a hot cup of tea out into a hot August afternoon, but it's not as weird as it seems. Come on, let's go out onto the deck."

Two Adirondack-type chairs were separated by a table. A fly swatter leaned against the side of the table. Rose set her glass of water down next to her chair.

"How did you wind up on Cape Cod?" Rose asked, making a sweeping motion toward the woods.

Kelsey explained about the increasing tension and threats the last few days she was in upstate New York, and how she'd spoken with Millie.

"Millie knew what I'd gone through with Hal, so she understood how my fears could take on a life of their own. At first, I told her I was fine, but I was scared to death. My hands were shaking. I kept searching the shadows for danger. I couldn't stand the fear. After I dropped off the envelope with the note and money at your father's house, I headed south.

"I stayed with her for a few days and explained that I wanted to disappear for a while, intending to be gone a couple of weeks. Millie's family owns a house in Dennis with a two-car garage. Several years ago, Millie and her sister had a studio apartment built over the garage because they didn't want to stay in the house when everyone in the family gathered together. Her one brother had four very active children, and another had two kids. Millie and her sister needed a separate space. The apartment was small, but cute, as are so many places on the cape."

Kelsey reached for her mug and blew on the hot water. "The garage was far enough away that I could be on my own. I drove all over, walked the beaches for hours, then stumbled onto a landscaping and garden center that needed help."

"You were only going to stay a couple of weeks, but you decided to take a job?" Rose shifted in her chair to look at Kelsey. "I mean, you sound like someone who'd left and decided she wasn't going back."

"It was complicated. The landscaping center belongs to Millie's brother. She put me in touch with him, and he paid me in cash. I needed some money, you know, without tapping my bank accounts. When he said he couldn't pay me out of pocket much longer, Millie reached out to a friend from law school in Boston. He created a new identity for me. I was reluctant at first, but I realized I couldn't stay here, use a credit card in my real name, without someone tracking me down. The attorney helped move my money to the new accounts. I didn't ask a lot of questions. I was just grateful to feel safe again."

"At some point, you must have decided you weren't going back. Why?"

"Have you spent any time on the cape?"

"Not much. My family tended to head more toward Cape Ann or Maine when we vacationed."

"People here are friendly, helpful, but not intrusive. Actually, that's the way it is throughout most of New England. I'll always be an outsider because I wasn't born here, but I'm a homeowner now and that gives me some credibility." Kelsey smiled, something she hadn't done much since Rose had arrived. The smile softened her face.

"I still intended to return to upstate New York at the end of the summer. But then . . ." Kelsey's voice drifted off on a hot summer breeze.

Chapter Forty

"But then," Rose prodded.

"I always thought I'd go back," Kelsey continued, "but life is so easy here. I realized how stressed I'd been working for your father, even though it was important work. I heard so many heartbreaking stories. It was too much. Too much pain to witness after I'd lived through my relationship with Hal." She sipped her tea. "Believe it or not, I was very critical of myself for bailing on the women at the Western Inlet Inn, but I'd hoped your father would hire an investigator with the money I left, figure out what Browning was doing, and put an end to it."

"And now you know none of that happened."

Kelsey jerked her head. "Don't put that on me. I did what I could at the time. I was so scared, I felt myself slipping away. I couldn't distance myself enough. Have you ever had that kind of experience, that intense a feeling that almost shuts down everything you did or wanted to do?"

Rose had had some heart-stopping moments, for sure, sometimes while covering news and sometimes in her personal life, including when she found out about her father's affair and Maxi. But Rose had never experienced the kind of fear that makes a person want to run away from their life, the kind of fear that prompted Kelsey to leave upstate New York.

Rose couldn't reconcile the woman who'd investigated the Western Inlet Inn and pushed people for answers with the woman who'd fled. The woman sitting beside her now was independent, seemingly of sound mind, but still alone. Still hiding in a small house on the edge of the woods and so afraid of being located that she made Rose use burner phones when she'd given directions to Cape Cod.

"The other reason I stayed on the cape is my Uncle Henry and Aunt Jess. They own a house on the Atlantic Ocean side, in Harwich. They saved my life and raised me since I was fourteen."

"What happened when you were fourteen?"

"That's a story for another time, if ever," Kelsey said. "Bottom line, I lost my father, and Uncle Henry, my mom's brother, took me in."

"What happened to your mother?"

"That's not relevant," Kelsey said. "Because I lost my father when I was young, I looked up to other men as father figures. My uncle Henry was one. Your father was another. He reminded me of my dad, the good memories I had of him." Kelsey looked at Rose. "Your father once told me I reminded him of you. Strong. Determined. Capable. He was very proud of you, you know?"

Rose glanced down at her lap as tears threatened to spill onto her cheeks. She did know how much her father had loved her, knew he had respected her work, her awards, but he wasn't often expressive to or about his children. Losing her mother so recently touched on the ache that lingered after losing her father.

"Millie said that when you heard about my father's death,

you suggested Browning could have harmed my father," Rose said. "What makes you say that? Do you have proof?"

"I have suspicions, but no proof. Browning's security people were suspected of using force to intimidate people, and twice, from what I understand, they used a poison that was difficult to trace to stop someone investigating their activities. Randall was surprised when Brandt brought Browning in as a client, and Brandt had been pushing your father to meet with him. When I read in the newspaper that Randall died of a heart attack—a sudden heart attack—I thought Browning's people could have gotten to him, could have poisoned him. There were rumors that Browning had poisoned someone who was investigating him. They were after me. Why not your father?"

It was a stretch to think someone had poisoned her father, wasn't it? But why did Browning want to use her father's firm when he had other attorneys who handled his business? Browning could hire any attorney he wanted. Why did he ask Brandt and her father's firm to handle some of his legal matters?

"I had a cardiac calcium scan done recently, and it came back negative," Rose said. "So it seems there's no history of heart disease in my family. Other than that, I don't know how I could prove it wasn't a heart attack. I guess I could contact the medical examiner's office and ask to see the autopsy report."

Kelsey's tea had cooled enough for her to take a sip, which she did slowly, thoughtfully. "Look, Rose, I understand your skepticism. I see it in your eyes. I know you don't know whether to believe me, but it's not an outrageous suggestion, given Browning's reputation of stopping at nothing to protect his businesses."

Rose could only nod.

"I have to say that someone threatening you and possibly

murdering my father to hide their abuse of immigrant workers is a stretch," she said softly.

"Not if their actions also involved sex trafficking."

Rose turned back to Kelsey. "It's time you tell me more about what you know."

Kelsey set the mug back on the deck.

"You know the woman I told you about that Millie and I overheard at the Western Inlet Inn, the one who feared her daughter could be abused by the doctor who treated her husband?"

Rose nodded.

"I found out where many of the immigrants did their grocery shopping, and I visited the store. Once, I saw that woman with two girls I thought were in their late teens. I followed them, and when I had a chance, I pulled the two girls aside. I told them I was investigating the abuse of workers at the inn. Neither girl would say a word at first. One of them turned away, unable to meet my eyes. But the other girl, Ana, finally said she'd been asked to clean the doctor's office to pay off her father's bills. I can't remember the name of the doctor." Kelsey looked off into the woods. When she began speaking again, her voice was softer.

"Ana said the doctor made inappropriate comments and found a way to get physically close to her. Then one time, Ana told me, she was asked to dress up and meet a friend of the doctor's for the evening. He pressured her to go out with the man until she said yes. Ana was near tears when she told me she met the man in a restaurant in a nice hotel near the inn. After dinner, he pushed her to go to his room. She ran away from him, but Ana said not all the girls were as fortunate."

Chapter Forty-One

"Ana told me that she wanted to stop escorting men after her first time, but Browning threatened her family if she didn't continue. Her friend Vicki was also pressured. I asked Vicki to talk to me, but she wouldn't. I saw a hollowness in Vicki's eyes when she looked at me before walking away. Then Ana's mother walked over and pulled Ana away from me. I got in my car thinking I had proof that Browning was forcing these girls to do things they didn't want to, to have sex when they didn't want to, and basically, he held them hostage with threats."

"That's a more serious situation than you had mentioned to my dad and Mary," Rose said. "Why didn't you share this with them?"

"I planned to. Then the threats against me intensified. I couldn't tell Mary everything because I was afraid that would make her vulnerable. They knew where I worked. They'd followed me. I had to keep this to myself until I had enough evidence to report to your father because I knew he needed proof. I was determined to get it for him until I realized my life might be in danger."

Rose pushed a deep breath out of her lungs. Then she stood. "I need to use the bathroom. I'll be right back."

"You won't have trouble finding it," Kelsey said. "It's the only other door in the house, and it's next to the bedroom."

A few minutes later, Rose returned with her oversized handbag. She pulled out an envelope and gave it to Kelsey, then sat.

Kelsey looked at the envelope she'd pushed through Randall's mail slot all those years ago. "You brought the letter and the money."

"I told you I wanted to give back the ten thousand dollars. It's all there."

"I'm sure it is," Kelsey said, pushing the money aside and pulling out the note. She read it. "This was hidden in a secret compartment in a bookcase?"

"Yep, and it could have been lost forever if I hadn't been determined to clean and polish every inch of the bookcases in my dad's den."

"For the longest time, I thought I would move back," Kelsey said, tucking the envelope under her thigh. "Then when my lease at the Ft. Edward apartment came up five months after I'd left, I had Millie hire a mover and put all my stuff into storage. I waited until I bought this house to have it moved here, figuring my trail would have grown cold by then, hoping Browning's guys weren't still looking for me."

"I doubt they're looking for you anymore," Rose assured Kelsey. "I'm not done investigating Browning and Mary's helping me. If we need to, we'll hire someone, maybe even Mary's husband, who's a private investigator."

"Then you need to keep this money," Kelsey said, pulling the envelope out and thrusting it at Rose.

"No. We're not going to use your money."

"But I want to help," Kelsey said.

"Prove it. Come back to New York and help me find the

evidence to shut down Browning's operation, to send him and the doctor and whoever else is involved to prison for exploiting those poor girls and destroying their lives." Rose knew she was pushing, but she couldn't keep her frustration in check any longer.

Kelsey shook her head. "I can't, Rose. I'm sorry. I just can't."

They sat in silence for a while until Rose decided to find some common ground.

"I'd forgotten how beautiful Cape Cod is, but I don't know how you deal with all the traffic in the summer. That's actually one thing I remember most about visiting."

"Yes, shoulder seasons are the best time on the cape. My favorite months here are June—early, before the schools let out—and October when the leaves are changing." Then they talked about nothing important and sipped their drinks until late afternoon."

"Looking around my humble home, you can tell I don't have a guest room," Kelsey said. "I called a friend who owns a B&B in Yarmouth. She has a room available for you for tonight. Come inside, and I'll give you her address. It's ten minutes away." She smiled for one of the few times that after-noon. "Depending on traffic."

Rose stretched, rolling her shoulders and twisting side to side at the waist a few times before picking up her empty glass and following Kelsey into the house.

Kelsey wrote a note on a small pad and handed it to Rose.

"Here's the address. It's not far. I told Peggy you're a friend who's passing through. She knows not to ask any ques-tions." They stood side by side for a few awkward moments. "Thanks for coming and returning the money. I'm sorry I can't help you," Kelsey reiterated.

"I am too," Rose said, taking the paper. "You have my

number. Here's my email address so you can reach me anytime you want. I'll let you know what's going on."

Rose wanted to tell Kelsey how disappointed she was that Kelsey wouldn't help put an end to Browning's atrocious and illegal activities, especially when Kelsey once cared about it enough to give her father a chunk of money to continue the investigation. But there was nothing more to say.

Rose stopped at a fish shack for a lobster roll and French fries and joined other hungry diners at the picnic tables beyond the parking lot. After she finished eating, she drove to the B&B and pulled into the driveway of a beautiful creamy beige, three-story home with dark gray shutters. The enclosed porch at one end of the house looked perfect for snuggling into a comfortable chair with a book.

Rose introduced herself to the woman who greeted her in the foyer.

"I'm Peggy. Kelsey told me you'd be coming."

"How much do I owe you for the room?" Rose asked.

"Kelsey took care of it," Peggy said. "Breakfast is served buffet style at seven, but the coffee is ready earlier for those who may get up before the sun rises."

Rose told her seven was fine, took the key, and carried her bag up the staircase to her room on the second floor. The place was bigger than it looked from the outside, with the first and second floors extending out back around a patio with a firepit and chairs. Rose looked out the window and thought about joining the others outside, but the drive and conversation with Kelsey weighed her down.

She collapsed on the bed and fell asleep.

Chapter Forty-Two

Rose was tired from her trip but couldn't wait to get back to the contents of her father's laptop, especially to check out the folder with Brandt's name on it. She'd been reluctant to open it at first. Not anymore. Not after what Kelsey told her. She wanted to see what comments her father might have about Brandt, whether he was suspicious of him, and if so, why. Maxi had made it clear she had to remain on the sidelines. Rose promised to tell Mary all about her visit with Kelsey, and this was a good time.

"I just put a pie in the oven," Mary said. "Can you come my way this time?"

"Sure. Is now okay?"

Mary said yes, so Rose grabbed the laptop and headed out.

"Have a seat," Mary said. "How about a glass of lemonade? I make it myself and don't add a lot of sugar, so it's a little on the tart side."

"Sounds good."

Rose glanced around the room and spotted a few framed photos on the fireplace mantle. She walked over and studied them. One showed Mary snuggling a cat. Another photo was of Mary and a man with his arm around her waist.

Mary returned to the living room, set the glasses on coasters on the coffee table, and walked to Rose's side. "That's Sam. We married five years ago, not long after he retired from the sheriff's office."

"Which one?" Rose asked, turning to Mary.

"Warren County. He was the senior deputy at the time he left. He likes working as a private investigator now. He doesn't take a lot of cases, but he likes to keep busy. He's out of town on an assignment. Sam likes to travel, and, even though I miss him, I like a little alone time." Mary's eyes lingered on the photo before she turned to Rose. "Let's sit and you can fill me in on your time with Kelsey."

Rose perched on one end of the couch and Mary sat in the chair next to it. Rose took a drink of lemonade, proclaimed it the best she'd ever tasted, and launched into telling Mary all about her visit with Kelsey.

"She was concerned about the young women at the Western Inlet Inn and had suspicions about immigrant workers at other Browning properties. As I mentioned, I visited the inns in Lake Placid and Saranac Lake in addition to the Lake George property after doing research into Browning. The biggest thing I learned is that the front desk workers are trained to deter people who aren't registered guests. I need to stay there to investigate more. But I may have compromised myself. Someone might recognize me. You said Sam takes on private investigation cases?"

Mary nodded. "He should be back tomorrow, unless something detains him. I'll text him and see whether his schedule has changed." She took a moment to write a message, then set her phone on the table.

A moment later, Mary's cell phone pinged. She replied to

the text, then looked up at Rose. "He'll be home about midday tomorrow."

"Have you mentioned our trip to Peekskill to Sam?"

"Sure. I've filled him in on everything we've been doing."

"Could he help us with visits to Browning's properties?"

"I've been nudging Sam to take me on a weekend trip to the Adirondacks. Maybe we'll head to Lake Placid or Lake George." Mary smiled. "He could use a little downtime, and I would enjoy sitting by a lake or taking a boat ride."

"Talk it over with him and see what he says. At the very least, we can bounce ideas off of him, get his guidance on possible next steps."

"Sounds good."

"There's something else. I've left it for last, even though it might be the biggest news from my visit with Kelsey." Rose picked up her lemonade and looked at Mary. "Kelsey thinks Browning could have had a hand in Dad's death."

"What?"

"She suspects Browning could have poisoned Dad. Although I questioned whether Dad had a heart attack, I dismissed Kelsey's idea of his being poisoned as an overreaction. She admitted that she feared for her safety when she disappeared. She saw danger everywhere. But the more I think about it, I wonder if it's true."

"How would you even find that out fifteen years later?" Mary asked, leaning toward Rose, her eyes wide open with the shock of what Rose had just said.

"I haven't thought that through. Maybe Sam has some ideas."

"Yes, he might. There's no need to wait until he comes home. I'll run this by him the next time we speak."

"Thanks. That would be helpful. In the meantime, I was planning to check Dad's laptop and that personnel folder to see if he had any notes on Brandt, given what Kelsey said and because he's been acting so odd toward me. I brought the laptop with me."

Rose picked up the computer bag from the floor, zipped it open, and pulled out the laptop.

"Shoot." She had the wrong one.

"I don't believe it. I thought I grabbed Dad's laptop off the dining room table, but I left the house in a hurry and picked up mine instead." She closed it and put it back in the carrying case.

"It's fine. Go home. Look at anything you want to on your father's laptop. Given what Kelsey said about your father having reservations about someone in his firm, you shouldn't worry about accessing those folders on your own. Look at them when you get home, then call me and tell me what you've found. We need to get to the truth."

Chapter Forty-Three

Rose fought the urge to drive well over the speed limit on her way home. She raced into the house, found her father's laptop and turned it on, tapping her fingers on the keys as it booted up. She entered the first password, clicked on *Personnel*, and entered the next password. Taking a deep breath, she double-clicked the folder with Brandt's name. She scanned the list of documents, typical ones with his résumé and such, then spotted a document labeled *Concerns*.

The document was created on July 2, 2010, about three weeks before her father's death. She leaned into the screen and read.

I have become suspicious of Brandt's relationship with Leonard Browning, who I knew before Brandt brought him on as a client a few months ago. I recall that the State Labor Department and perhaps OSHA investigated Browning for conditions at one or more of his inns. I read about one case where the Department of Housing Preservation and Development looked into the places some of his immigrant workers lived —former motels that Browning provided to his workers at a low rate because he didn't pay them enough to find better housing.

I'm sure Browning has some high-powered lawyers who protect him from legal action, so why does he need a small firm like mine to represent him? When Brandt informed me that Browning had approached him about handling a minor case about one of his properties, I asked, "Why us?" He said he'd been working on establishing a relationship with Browning for some time. That was news to me. I had reservations about working with Browning, still do, although I appreciated Brandt's efforts to bring in new clients.

But my concerns about Brandt have led me to leave him out of the loop in some work we are doing, in the early stages of investigation, especially with Kelsey exploring how Browning may be mistreating, even abusing workers at the Western Inlet Inn. I don't have proof yet, but Brandt's relationship with Browning is causing me concern. If Kelsey's' investigation shows Browning has acted improperly, illegally, we need to cut ties with Browning immediately.

Rose continued to scroll through the document, seeing more entries with dates as her father updated his suspicions about Brandt. He mentioned nothing more specific than he had earlier, but seemed to be making short notes as he captured his thoughts. An entry dated July 23 prompted her to grip the arms of her chair.

I've finally agreed to Brandt's request that I have lunch with Browning to talk about our relationship. I told Brandt I wasn't interested in handling a lot of work for Browning, given some of the negative publicity and ethical questions about his operations, but Brandt pointed out the nonprofits that Browning has supported, the work Browning has done for the Chamber of Commerce and the regional business community, so I agreed.

Rose's body sagged in her chair. That was the last entry. How could she brush off Kelsey's comment that Browning had something to do with her father's death? This last entry was two days before her father died. Two days. Did Dad meet with Browning on the day he died? She kept staring at the document, words fading in and out of focus as she absorbed the implications of her father's notes.

She closed the document, then the folder. Ran her eyes back and forth across the home screen, then icons on the bottom. If Dad had a meeting with Browning, it would be on his digital calendar, wouldn't it? She looked at the calendar icon. Slowly reached out and touched the keypad. Clicked on it. If her father had met with Browning just before his death—the so-called sudden heart attack—it could take her investigation to a completely different place.

Rose tried to breathe. The calendar opened to July 2010, the last time her father must have opened it.

Reality stared Rose in the face. On July 25, 2010, the day her father died, he had lunch with Leonard Browning at the Western Inlet Inn.

Chapter Forty-Four

"What if Dad didn't die of a heart attack?" Rose asked. "What if he was poisoned and it was made to look like a heart attack? What if someone killed my father? He could still be alive today if it wasn't for Browning and his thugs. We have to go after them."

Rose had promised to call Maxi and tell her about the trip to Cape Cod, but as soon as Rose heard Maxi's voice, she exploded with the news of what she'd found on her father's calendar.

"Lunch with the man suspected of abusing his employees, of getting rid of prying eyes when they investigated his businesses. The more I learn about this guy, the more I realize what a hornet's nest Kelsey and Dad stepped into. I mean, we could be talking about murder. Murder, Maxi!"

"Easy now, Rose. It's only Kelsey's opinion. And it's all circumstantial."

"Okay, it's circumstantial, but there's a lot here. I'll find the proof. I swear I will find out if someone killed my father. Don't you care if our father was killed?"

"Rose, take a deep breath—"

"I swear I'll track them down—"

"Rose! Deep breath. Now!" Maxi yelled over the phone.

That startled Rose enough to stop screaming. She sucked in some air and pushed it back out. After she pushed out the second breath, Maxi spoke.

"I don't know what's true and neither do you. If Browning poisoned Randall—our father—I will help you find the proof. But I don't have any more time to chat now, so let's try to sort it out tomorrow. Aren't you taking photos at the library today?"

"How the hell am I going to focus on that when this is hanging over me?"

"Because you're a professional, and you'll focus on the task at the moment."

"You have more faith in me than I do."

"Hah! I doubt that. You have plenty of faith in your abilities. It's just that your logical brain is among the missing."

That got a laugh out of Rose. It felt good. Kelsey's comment about poison had stressed her ever since the visit to Cape Cod, which only intensified when Rose saw the lunch date with Browning on her dad's calendar.

"Thanks, sis."

"You're welcome. If you feel your stress level rising, remember to take deep breaths. I'll call you later."

Rose wasn't due at the library for more than an hour, and she'd already checked her equipment three times that morning. That didn't mean she wouldn't check it again before she left the house. She tried to compartmentalize, but she couldn't stop thinking about her father's death in light of the new information. What kind of poison would mimic or trigger a heart attack without being detected in an autopsy? She did a quick search on the internet, but she needed to talk with a person. She found a number and scheduled a call with the local medical examiner for the next day. Then she checked her gear once more and drove to the library.

Carter carried her tripod and light stands into the front rooms of the library, then helped set them up. Rose thanked him and said she'd let him know when she needed his help again.

When Rose took photos, whether in a chaotic news environment or a calmer setting—like a picking party, a birthday party, or still photos of a library—she became lost in her zone. Outside noises, even those of people talking, were white noise, pushed into the background. She concentrated on adjusting the lights, sliding chairs to put them in better spots, and dropping to her knees when she wanted a lower angle. That last part was hard because she still couldn't put her full weight on her right side and push up with her arm. Looking around to make sure no one was watching, Rose set her camera on the floor, slid from her knees to her bottom, and pushed up with her left arm. It wasn't pretty, but it was effective. Still, she decided not to take many more low-angle photos of the rest of the library.

When she was done on the first floor, Carter carried her gear upstairs and Rose completed the children's and young adult rooms in no time. Carter and Brianna, the assistant librarian, had already staged those rooms. All Rose had to do was adjust the lights and point her camera. The last images were the exteriors. The sun filtered through the clouds, just enough to bathe the building and surrounding gardens in soft light. One time, the sun popped through the clouds and struck the building like a spotlight hitting a set on stage. Rose couldn't press the shutter button fast enough. She was smiling when she walked up the front steps and into the library.

"You look happy—and exhausted," Carter said. "You've been almost nonstop the past few hours." He carried her gear to her SUV and set it in the cargo area. "And it's time for dinner. Would you like to join me and Ellie for Chinese takeout?"

That was unexpected. Rose slid her camera strap off her shoulder, ignoring the quick stab of pain, and smiled at him. "That would be nice, thanks. I have to go home and walk Gladys, spend a little time with her because she's been alone for a while now."

"Why not walk her over to our house? We're a couple of blocks from you, on Falls near Church. Ellie would enjoy spending time with Gladys. We both would."

Rose hesitated, but only for a second. She was tired. She needed to eat. Gladys needed attention. It sounded like a win-win.

Chapter Forty-Five

It was as if Gladys knew they were going somewhere new. When Rose placed the dish on the floor, Gladys inhaled her food like she hadn't eaten in days. Then she pranced around Rose's feet, waiting for her to put on her harness. They usually turned right when they left the house, but this time they went in the other direction. Gladys found new and interesting smells, slowing their walk. Rose didn't mind. She needed time to decompress from the hours focused on composition, lighting, and angles. Usually, after Rose had completed an assignment that didn't involve breaking news, she'd get home, transfer all the images onto her laptop, and scan them for the best ones. She preferred reviewing her work while it was fresh in her mind. That could wait until tomorrow, and while it interrupted her routine, it was a welcome one, and distracted her from dwelling on her father's death.

Ellie was waiting on the front porch. She skipped down the walkway while Gladys scampered toward the eight-year-old. They met in the middle with a squeal and a lot of little barks. Rose had never seen Ellie so animated, and she appreciated that Carter had thought to include her dog.

"I forgot to ask what you like," Carter said, opening the door and welcoming her and Gladys inside. "I got shrimp in lobster sauce, chicken with broccoli, vegetable fried rice in case you don't like either of those, and Ellie's favorite cashew chicken. Plus wonton soup and shrimp rolls."

"Thank goodness," Rose said. "I was afraid I'd starve." The two of them laughed as they walked into the kitchen, Ellie holding Gladys's leash and trailing behind.

"The food was just delivered. We like to put all the containers on the lazy Susan in the center of the table. You can help yourself to whatever you'd like."

"Sounds good," Rose said. "Could we give Gladys a little water first?"

"Oh, yes, of course." Carter pulled a bowl out of the cabinet, filled it with water, and set it on the floor. Gladys's little tongue lapped at the water as Ellie watched with delight. In the dining room, Rose waited for Carter and Ellie to take their usual seats, then sat with Gladys curled up at her feet.

"Guests first," Carter said.

Rose opened a carton of rice, put some on her plate, and added chicken with broccoli on top of the rice. Then she took another box and scooped out some vegetable fried rice. Ellie looked relieved that Rose hadn't touched the cashew chicken.

No one said anything for a moment while they dished out food and ate. Rose was famished. It had been a long time since lunch, and she'd worked hard all afternoon. Rose turned to Ellie.

"I saw you with a boy about your age in the library when I was taking photos today. Is he a classmate? A friend?"

Ellie nodded and put another forkful of cashew chicken in her mouth. After she chewed and swallowed, she said, "His mom dropped him off at the library while she went to the grocery store. Diego doesn't like to go with her because the other boys pick on him."

"Why do they pick on him, honey?" Carter asked. He'd been reaching for a container, but stopped to look at his daughter.

"His parents came here from Mexico. They're staying with family until they find jobs. The boys call him a beaner and tell him to go home." She looked from her father to Rose. "There was a swear word before beaner that I'm not supposed to say. I don't know what beaner means, but it upsets Diego when they call him that."

"When did this happen?"

"It was during recess on one of the last days of school, Daddy. It wasn't the first time they said mean things to him, but it got to Diego more than the other times. Especially when they said Diego's family should be put on a plane and sent back to where they belong."

"Did Diego tell the teacher?"

Ellie shook her head. "They were on the other side of the playground. I told him to tell the teachers what the other boys said, but I think he was too ashamed." She got another forkful of food.

Rose listened and watched Ellie's face. Diego was probably not just ashamed but maybe worried about what could happen to his family. With the latest push to send immigrants back to their home countries, many feared going to work or school because authorities might detain them. When school resumed in a few weeks, fewer children would return to the classroom.

"I'm glad you're Diego's friend. If other kids tease him again like that, it's okay to tell the teachers what they're saying."

"But wouldn't that make me a tattletale?"

Carter glanced at Rose. She shrugged. Parenting was not in her wheelhouse.

"If someone is hurting someone else, whether it's physical

or with their words, Ellie, it is okay to tell a teacher. Then maybe it will stop."

"Okay, Daddy. But why are they mean to him? Why do they tell him to go back to Mexico? And why do those boys think it's bad to be an immigrant?"

Carter put his fork on his plate. "Some people think too many people are moving here from other countries and taking jobs away from Americans. Some people also think immigrants are adding to the drug problem in this country and committing crimes against Americans."

"Are those things true?"

"There's almost always a little truth in everything you hear," he told her. "But immigrants often take jobs Americans don't want. And yes, some of them are drug dealers and adding to the drug epidemic. Plenty of Americans are drug dealers as well. But remember your history, Ellie. Your grandparents immigrated to America from Europe after World War II. America is a nation of immigrants."

As Carter and Ellie finished their dinner, Rose yawned so wide it was impossible to ignore. Carter sent her home with a mix of leftovers. She and Gladys trudged home, pausing long enough for Gladys to do her business. One final quick trip to the patio garden to make sure Gladys had last outs, and they headed for bed.

The conversation about Diego echoed in Rose's mind. She was glad Carter had advised Ellie to tell teachers what was going on with the boys. Diego might be too afraid to say anything, but Ellie had the power to tell on the boys and perhaps stop their taunting.

It was up to everyone to stop others from being used, abused, and hurt by others. The strong had to help protect others. Rose wasn't big on the Bible or the hierarchy of organized religion, but she believed people needed to lift each other up, not take them down.

Except when it came to Leonard Browning and his cronies. Rose would love to take him down.

Chapter Forty-Six

"When can you come over?" Mary asked. "Sam wants to tell you what he discovered during his visit to Browning's inn in Lake Placid."

"I have to finalize the photos I took yesterday at the library, but I'll be there in a couple of hours."

Rose reviewed the images and then put them in batches to adjust the lighting in Photoshop. She cropped another batch of the exteriors—smiling with pride at how she captured the sun and clouds—and selected fifty images to show Carter. That was a lot, but she wanted him to have choices. He could use the photos for years to come on the website, in the monthly newsletter, and in other promotional materials. Rose leaned back in her chair, satisfied. She'd look the photos over again later, then upload them to a site where Carter could download them when he had time.

She thought about last night's dinner. Even though she was exhausted from the photo shoot, eating with Carter and Ellie had been relaxing and a pleasant break from eating alone. Carter was a nice man, easy to look at, funny at times. She wasn't interested in romance, and he'd lost his wife less than a year ago, but she enjoyed his friendship. Ellie would approve. Rose could tell by how the girl looked at Rose and her father when she'd left after dinner.

Their conversation took an unexpected turn when Ellie told them about Diego. Rose felt for the young boy. Cases of bullying migrants—whether legal or undocumented, whether in a schoolyard, at a local bar, or on a Little League field—were increasing. Armed agents showed up on doorsteps. Families disappeared. No one knew who could be next, so people hid. Rose thought about Browning's employees. She was pretty sure most were here legally and had the papers to prove it. Maybe deportations didn't threaten them, but they lived under a different threat. She showered, stopped at the apple farm for a pie, and headed to Mary's.

Sam's handshake was firm, his eyes inquisitive yet gentle. He looked at Mary with such tenderness that Rose envied the older woman for finding someone to share her life with, especially since it hadn't happened until she was almost sixty. There was hope for Rose yet.

"I hope you don't want to make small talk," Rose said with a smile. "I'm eager to know what you learned."

"Darn. I'd planned a talk on the history of the Olympics in Lake Placid, including the historic men's ice hockey win in 1980. The play-by-play announcing of that game was riveting, and we listened to it on the drive. I could also repeat it word for word by now." Sam smiled and reached for a sandwich on the platter in the center of the table. "I guess it can wait."

"You guess right," Rose said, eyeing the sandwiches and taking one that appeared to be egg salad. She took a bite and set it on her plate.

"I know some people can see a cop in plain clothes coming a mile away," Sam began, "even one who's retired. The security folks at the Towering Pines Inn were no exception."

Sam explained how he'd walked around and chatted with

employees, sometimes with Mary, usually alone. "I'd leave her at the pool with a book and wander. One time I went back to our room right after we'd had lunch while Mary sat in the patio area. I spotted the security guard at the end of the hallway on our floor. I swear that guy is part cat, the way he got around without making a sound. The staff uses two-ways to communicate, so I heard when he was close. When he was called to the front desk, I approached a cleaning woman on the next floor and asked to speak to her."

Sam took a healthy bite of his sandwich and followed it up with a drink.

"She was reluctant, but I persuaded her that I was trying to stop the abuse of young women and Browning's mistreatment of workers. Then she told me about Dr. Collins."

"Is that the doctor the workers had to see because they had no health insurance?" Rose asked.

"That's him. The woman told me Dr. Collins travels to Lake Placid once a week to treat workers for illnesses or injuries. She said sometimes people have to drive to Dr. Collins's office outside of Lake George if they need treatment sooner. Sometimes, they have to go in the evening. When she mentioned the evening visits, she suddenly said she had to get back to work."

Sam took a drink. "I know she wanted me to leave, but I pushed her about Dr. Collins and Browning, asked her what she else she heard. The worry grew on her face and her eyes widened. She told me Browning manipulated—my word—the staff, including the mothers of teenaged daughters. The woman shook her head and said one teenager had disappeared after going to dinner with one of Browning's friends.

"She said, 'Please stop this. Stop him from hurting my people.' I told her I would do what I could. Then she walked into a guest room and closed the door almost all the way. The vacuum started right up."

Sam told Rose about a few more conversations he had. "But that was the most important one, implying that Browning and his doctor friend are involved in shady and illegal activities."

"Now what?" Rose asked.

"Now I keep looking around. I promise to keep you updated."

Rose had just returned home when her cell rang.

"It's Bob Night with the ME's office," he said.

"Thanks for agreeing to speak with me." Rose explained who she was, who her father was, and asked about the signature on his death certificate. "Is that the person who did the autopsy?" she asked.

"What's the name of the deceased?" he asked.

"Randall Wallace Webster. Date of death is July 25, 2010."

"Did you say 2010? Why are you inquiring now?"

Rose paused. How much should she tell him? Was he in cahoots with Browning and Collins? But she couldn't ask for information without giving some.

"I am following up because of medical issues that have come up in my family," she said. "We need to make sure he died from a heart attack and not any other complications."

"Did you ask his doctor? His records would indicate any medical issues your father was dealing with at the time of his death."

"That's just it. My father didn't have a history of heart issues, and yet the medical examiner cited that as the cause of death."

The clicks on a keyboard suggested the ME was looking for documents.

"According to this, yes, your father died of a heart attack. That's all I can tell you."

"Did you do the autopsy?"

"There was no autopsy."

"Excuse me? Why not?"

"I don't know. I didn't handle your father's case."

"Who did?" Rose blurted.

Her frustration grew as she listened to more keyboard clicks and waited.

"I know we went through a period of reorganization around that time. Doctors in the area sometimes performed autopsies or signed off on death certificates when we were shorthanded, usually after consulting with the family doctor."

"Who signed off on my father's death certificate?" she asked again. "His writing is atrocious. I can't make out his name on my copy." Typical handwriting for a physician. Why was a doctor's handwriting always so difficult to read?

The pause was a little longer.

"I believe that's Dr. Collins's signature."

Dr. Collins. Him again. Rose thanked the ME for his help and disconnected the call. She stared at the phone, then out the window. Dr. Collins signed her father's death certificate. And there was no autopsy. Add that information to the growing list, building the case that her father may not have died of a heart attack.

Chapter Forty-Seven

How long had Rose been staring into space with questions surrounding her father's death swirling in her head? Dr. Collins. No autopsy. Did Collins and Browning conspire to poison her father? Did they then cover it up by having Dr. Collins state the cause of death as a heart attack and indicate an autopsy wasn't necessary? Could one person have that much control?

The ringing doorbell brought her back to the present. She didn't want to answer it, didn't care who was there, too stunned to talk with anyone. But Gladys barked like it was FedEx with a delivery of her special food. It was easier to see who was at the door and quiet the dog. Besides, it might be Maxi. Rose could use her advice right now. She shuffled over and picked up Gladys. She opened the front door. And found Kelsey on the other side.

The two women stared at each other.

"Are you going to invite me in?"

"Sure. Sorry." Rose stood back and Kelsey walked into the living room.

"You could have given me a head's up," Rose said, closing

the door and setting Gladys on the floor. The dog ran to Kelsey and pawed her leg.

"Hello, there." Kelsey bent over and let Gladys lick her hand. "What's her name?"

"Gladys."

Kelsey smiled. "I like it. Hello, Gladys."

"When did you . . .? Why did you change . . .?"

"Let's sit down and I'll tell you."

They walked through the kitchen where Rose paused to pour a couple glasses of water, then they settled on the couch in front of the fireplace.

"Nice home," Kelsey said, looking around. "I've never been inside."

Rose needed to do something other than nod, but she was hard-pressed to form complete sentences.

"Sooooo," Kelsey said, dragging out the word. "I know you're surprised to see me because I was so adamant about not coming back here." Kelsey looked down, rubbed her hands together as if they were cold, then looked Rose in the eyes. "I explained about my history of abuse with Hal. But there was other abuse. For me. Against me. Why I was determined to stop Browning when I first discovered he and the doctor might be assaulting young women."

"Dr. Collins," Rose said.

"Right, Dr. Collins. That's the guy. I've been trying to remember his name. Dr. Collins. There's a man I'd like to see hauled off to jail." Kelsey took a deep breath.

"So, back to when my father died," Kelsey continued. "I was fourteen. I struggled with his passing, but my mother struggled more. Later in life, when I was in my early twenties, I realized how much my father had been an anchor for my mom. Without him, she was adrift. She started going to bars after work. Sometimes guys would come home with her and spend the night, both of them drunk. Sometimes Mom's date came looking for me. The first time one of her boyfriends climbed into my bed and fondled me, I woke up and screamed. He ran out of my room. I got up and locked the door."

Kelsey reached for her water and took a drink. Her eyes scanned the room, the photos on the fireplace mantle, the books on the small bookcase on the left, then came back to Rose.

"One night, my mother's friend wasn't as drunk as she was. He looked me over from head to toe before they went upstairs. He was creepy and I was afraid of him, so I locked my bedroom door. I'd gotten into the habit of doing that when Mom brought someone home. Sure enough, later that night, he tried to get into my room. The same man started coming home with Mom more often. One night, I went up to my room before Mom came home. I closed my bedroom door and went to lock it, but the lock was broken. I didn't know what to do. Mom and the man came home and went into her room. When I was sure they were occupied with each other, I ran downstairs. It was late, but I didn't know what else to do. I went into the garage and called my uncle, my mother's brother. He and my aunt came and got me."

Kelsey took a deep breath and fought back tears.

"My mom died a few days later after falling over drunk and hitting her head on the kitchen floor. I inherited some money from both of my parents, more than enough for my low-key lifestyle, and my aunt and uncle have been my adoptive parents ever since.

"After you left, I kept having flashbacks to those nights when I was so afraid that Mom's visitor would assault me, and then I couldn't stop thinking about what Browning and Dr. Collins were doing to those women. Girls. It hit me so hard, like a punch in the gut. I realized I couldn't live with myself if I didn't come back and help them the way my aunt and uncle helped me." She looked at Rose through teary eyes. "So here I am."

"I'm so sorry, Kelsey. What a horrible time it was for you. Thanks for sharing it with me. You know you can trust me with that information."

"I do or I wouldn't have told you."

Rose's phone rang. She glanced at the screen and hesitated. "It's Mary. Do you want her to know you're here?"

Kelsey nodded.

"She's either intuitive or it's lucky timing." Rose connected the call. "Hi, Mary. I've got you on speaker. Kelsey just walked in the door. She's sitting on the couch next to me."

"Kelsey's there?" Mary's high-pitched voice burst over the phone line. "We're coming over."

Rose looked at the phone in her hand. She hadn't expected visitors today, hadn't wanted to speak to anyone after learning about Dr. Collins signing her father's death certificate. Now events were taking over, and she had no choice but to go with whatever came next. She was going to tell Kelsey about Collins's role after her father died when the doorbell rang again.

"Seriously?" Rose said. "Is there a sign out front that says I'm giving away coffee and donuts?" She glanced at Kelsey and Gladys on the couch. Gladys didn't even bark this time. Rose hurried to the front door and opened it.

"Hi. Is this a good time?" Maxi asked, holding a six-pack of Thom's ale in one hand and a bag of tortilla chips in the other.

Chapter Forty-Eight

Rose hesitated a little too long.

"Oops. Do you have a date or something? I should have texted."

"No, it's fine. It's fine," Rose said. Maxi might not help officially, but she needed to know the latest developments. "Come on in."

Gladys ran into the living room. Maxi knelt down, put the beer and chips on the floor, and rubbed the dog's back. She glanced up when Kelsey strolled into the living room.

"Oh, you do have company. I'm sorry, Rose."

"Stop apologizing, Maxi. It's fine. This is Kelsey."

Maxi's head jerked up. She stopped petting Gladys and stood, the beer and chips forgotten, except by Gladys, who was trying to get into the bag most humans couldn't open without scissors.

"*The* Kelsey?"

Kelsey looked at Rose. "She knows about me?"

"She does, but don't worry. Kelsey, meet Maxi, my half sister and a deputy with the Washington County Sheriff's Office."

Maxi extended her hand. Kelsey looked at the woman with the short afro and shook her hand. "Half sister? How are you two half sisters?"

"Let's hold that story until later," Rose said. She turned to Maxi. "I'm glad you stopped by. Mary and Sam are on their way. Kelsey's decided she wants to help bring Browning and Collins to justice. We all need to put our heads together and figure out how we're going to do that." She looked at Maxi. "Unofficially, but we need you. Are you in?"

"Yeah, I'm in. Let's go into the other room."

Kelsey and Rose brought Maxi up to date on what they knew. When Rose mentioned her visits to Browning's inns, Maxi leaned forward on the couch.

"I thought you said you were going to be careful and not go off investigating on your own." Maxi looked from Rose to Kelsey. "Are you sure you two aren't related because, from what I've heard, you're both a little reckless."

Rose shrugged. Kelsey stroked Gladys. Neither of them met Maxi's gaze.

The doorbell rang. Again. Rose welcomed the break in tension. She let Mary and Sam in.

"We stopped for pizza and beer," Mary said, putting a six-pack on the kitchen counter as Sam set the pizza boxes alongside the two six-packs and the tortilla chips. Rose pulled plates out of the cupboard, then everyone grabbed some food and a beer, except for Maxi.

"I'm on call," Maxi explained. "I might have to leave early. Detectives in Warren and Washington counties are working on a sting, and it could go down tonight." She glanced at Rose. "Off the record."

Rose nodded. Then she and Kelsey pushed a couple of dining room chairs over to the couch. They all gathered around, pizza in hand and chips in a big bowl on the coffee table. After a few minutes of eating, Rose asked, "Where do we start?"

"At the beginning," Sam said. "Let's start at the beginning and we can hear everyone's stories in their own words. If you have an important piece of information to what someone is saying, jump in. Otherwise, we'll try to go chronologically." He looked at Kelsey. "You're first."

For the next couple of hours, with breaks for more food and drinks, and with Rose taking notes on her laptop, they reconstructed the events surrounding Browning, the people who worked for him, and Dr. Collins. When Rose revealed what the ME had told her about Dr. Collins signing her father's death certificate, Sam raised his eyebrows and asked Rose to repeat what the ME had said.

"I don't like that at all," Sam said when she finished. "I know local doctors fill in when the ME is out of town or over-loaded with cases, but this smells like a cover-up to me. It makes it more dangerous for us because of the broad reach of Browning's operation and how many people it may impli-cate." Sam looked at everyone. "I recognize I'm dealing with a few headstrong women—hell, I'm surrounded by them—but I don't want to say this twice. Nobody goes to any of Brown-ing's properties alone. Got it?" They nodded. "And Kelsey, you need to keep a low profile. I know it's been fifteen years now, but if Browning's security people are any good, they'll recognize you. That's a chance we can't take."

"Sam, you and Mary are probably the only people Browning or his staff might not recognize," Rose said. "And I'm not sure about Mary. How many of Browning's people were aware of Mary working in my father's office? It might just be you, Sam, unless you spooked anyone on your weekend trip to Lake Placid."

"I was careful, but it's true, you never know. I was in law

enforcement in the area for a long time and people remember cops. So, I would say all of us may be known to Browning and his people."

They discussed plans for another half hour. By the time everyone was ready to go home, they agreed to meet again the next day at Rose's. Except for Maxi, who said she would step back for now.

Maxi was the last one to leave. As the door closed behind her, Kelsey sighed. "I didn't think to make a reservation for tonight."

"Don't be silly," Rose said. "You'll stay here. Besides, and I know it's a long shot, but what if Browning's security guys put you on a watch list or something like that with area hotels and inns? What if he wanted to know if you came back?"

"I have credit cards with my other identity," Kelsey said. "And you think I'd be on their radar after all these years?" Kelsey smiled. "When you were in Cape Cod, you were the one saying it had been so long that Browning's people probably weren't looking for me anymore."

"I remember. I have no idea what Browning and his people are capable of, but like Sam said, let's be careful. I don't have any chocolates to put on your pillow, but there's a decent bed in the room across from the bathroom downstairs. I just need to put some sheets on it."

"Okay, I'll get my stuff out of the car."

Rose went to work and was fluffing up the pillows at the head of the bed when Kelsey walked into the room.

"This is a nice space," Kelsey said. "Was this your room growing up?"

"No, it was my brother's." Rose stopped, then tapped her forehead a few times. "We need to let Kirk know what's going on, especially what I learned about Dr. Collins signing Dad's death certificate without an autopsy." She looked at Kelsey.

"Kirk dismissed the idea that Dad could have been poisoned when I told him about your suspicions. Wait until he hears about this. Let's see if he still thinks Dad had a heart attack."

Chapter Forty-Nine

Rose texted Kirk the next morning to see if he had time to chat. She wanted to review all the information they'd covered with Maxi, Mary, and Sam the night before and get his input. Kirk responded that he was in a meeting but would call her in an hour.

Kelsey laughed. "I've never seen anyone type as fast as you did yesterday, trying to get all the information down as we talked about it."

"I haven't gone back to correct the mistakes yet." Rose laughed with her. "And some of it may not make sense if my fingers hit the wrong keys. Should I print out a copy for you?"

Kelsey nodded. They both sat at the dining room table, with Gladys tucked in her bed in front of the sliding glass door overlooking the patio. Now and then, one would ask a question to clarify something, and Rose would correct the digital copy.

Rose's phone chirped.

"Sorry I couldn't call sooner," Kirk said. "One thing led to another after my meeting. What's going on?"

"No worries. First off, Kelsey showed up yesterday, and I'm putting you on speaker so the three of us can talk."

"Kelsey?"

"Uh, yeah, a lot has happened since we last spoke." Rose gave Kirk the short version since he was at work. She planned to give him the whole story when they had more time.

"Tell me again about Dad's death certificate being signed by Browning's friend and not the regular medical examiner."

She repeated the info about Dr. Collins. "I'm going to make some calls and find out what I can," he said. "I agree this is suspicious, and I want to confirm it for myself."

"What? Don't you believe me?"

"It's not that I don't believe you, but I'd like to get some information firsthand."

"You don't need to get involved. I'm handling this with Sam. He has the contacts and credentials around here to make those inquiries. While his actions may also get back to Browning and Dr. Collins, it would be worse if the Webster name kept popping up. I'll keep you posted."

"Okay," he said. "I won't fight you, but I'm wondering if you're correct that something other than a heart attack caused Dad's death. What are you going to do next?"

"Mary and Sam are coming by again." Rose glanced at the clock on the side table. "Sam has another client that may delay him checking out Browning's inns in Saranac Lake and Lake George, but I'll know more soon. Yesterday, we kicked around some ideas and today we're going to narrow them down."

"And you said Maxi is going to help?"

"Yes, but not officially. Maxi won't be involved in day-to-day activities, but she'll be around to follow up if any information leads somewhere in Washington County."

"Okay. Let's talk tonight and you can give me more details. I've got some questions."

That was probably an understatement.

"I'm not sure I have the answers, but call me later."

As Rose disconnected the call, she looked up at Kelsey staring at her.

"So, about Maxi," she nudged. "Your half sister. Kirk's half sister. How?"

Time for Rose to share some family history.

"I can't imagine what it was like to come upon that information," Kelsey said when Rose finished speaking.

"We're taking it day by day. I'd already met Maxi, and I liked her a lot, but it was a shock to find out we're related. To find out my dad had an affair."

"Have you met Maxi's mother? Is she still alive?"

"Yes, she's still alive. No, I haven't met her. I'm not sure I want to meet her, but there's something inside me that needs to meet the woman who convinced my father to break his marriage vows."

"Your father was so proper and dedicated to his family. I only worked for him for a year, but the man I knew didn't seem like the type to have an affair."

"He and my mom had mended their marriage, and he rededicated himself to his family when you knew him. I always saw him as a family man too, which is one reason I'm curious about Maxi's mom."

Gladys yipped.

"Do you want to go on a walk with Gladys and me?" Rose asked, getting the dog's leash and harness. "Not a long one. It's getting hot already, but I think we can find enough shade for us and her little feet on the Falls Road side."

"Sounds good. I'd love to stretch my legs."

The three of them headed out, strolling to Felton Falls. When they got to the park, they sat at a picnic table enjoying the view, then returned to the house and resumed looking over the information they'd collected.

"Mary and Sam will be here soon. I'm going to review

these one more time and make sure I've gotten down all the questions I want to ask them."

"Makes sense," Kelsey said. "I've got a few questions of my own." She dropped her head and studied the document.

Rose looked at Kelsey, absorbed in the information and wondered what it must be like to live off the grid, keeping only a few close connections. She couldn't imagine how Kelsey lived such a private life in that little house in Dennis. Rose loved her two-bedroom condo in Philadelphia. She was growing more attached to her childhood home and the little town of Lake Amelia. Well, little until the tourists invaded every summer. Lake Amelia was more appealing now than when Rose was younger, but she couldn't imagine giving up Philadelphia—the restaurants, the museums, the challenge and fulfillment of her work. She grew more conflicted every day trying to decide between the two.

Rose was no longer the idealistic young woman out to make a name for herself, and Lake Amelia was no longer the sleepy town holding her back. She looked at the papers in her hand, the information building a case that could send Browning, Collins, that security guy Juan, and anyone else associated with their abuse of migrants and sexual trafficking to prison. First, she'd help get those guys off the street, then she'd figure out the next steps. She picked up her yellow highlighter and began flipping through the pages.

Chapter Fifty

Rose and Kelsey were fighting an uphill battle with Sam, but they refused to concede.

"I told you, I don't think anyone else should investigate in the field. It's too dangerous." Sam looked at them across the dining room table. Mary was at his side.

"We're not talking about visiting any inns," Rose said.

Kelsey jumped in to plead their case. "We want to stake out the grocery store where many members of the Hispanic and Latino communities shop," Kelsey said. "That's where I saw Ana and her mother that one time. And Ana's friend. That location should be safe enough."

"Don't you think Browning's guys might shop there also? All of his workers appear to be in the same tight knit community. And most of them live in the area where the grocery store is, correct?"

Kelsey gave one quick nod.

"Browning's security guy knows you," he said, pointing at Rose. "And he might remember you," he said Kelsey.

"We could disguise ourselves," Rose said.

Sam laughed. "You two light-haired gringos are going to stand out if you go anywhere near a Mexican grocery store."

Even Mary smiled at that.

"We won't get out of the SUV," Rose said.

Sam just kept shaking his head. "I don't like it."

"Come on, Sam. We'll be careful," Rose said. "You can't be everywhere. And we want to help."

"We need to help," Kelsey echoed. "We can't sit here and do nothing."

Sam glanced at Mary. He was losing the argument.

"It's settled then," Rose said. "You two head north to Saranac Lake and we'll check out the grocery store this afternoon after I have coffee with Bill and his police contact."

* * *

Rose slid out of the booth in the back of the diner and stood. Bill did the same and reached out to shake the hand of a man with a couple of day's growth on his face and almost shoulder-length hair.

"Shawn, it's good to see you. This is my friend Rose Webster."

"Rose, as in my *Wild Irish Rose*. It's nice to meet you."

Rose and Shawn shook hands and the three of them spent an awkward moment figuring out who would sit where. Bill finally nudged Rose to slide back in where she had been sitting, facing toward the rest of the diner. He joined her while Shawn took the seat across from them.

"I hear an accent, perhaps a bit of Irish brogue?" Rose said with a smile, "especially with your *Wild Irish Rose* reference."

"Yes, I'm Irish, by way of Galway. My parents immigrated to this country when I was a mere lad. My father's brother moved to the area first, thinking he was moving from Galway, Ireland, to Galway, New York." Shawn laughed. "Then he learned that Galway, New York, was first named New Galloway after Galloway in Scotland." He laughed again, rubbing his chin. "That's what happens when you've had a few too many pints. But the rural area of Galway suits them. I needed someplace a little more active. That's why I'm in Glens Falls." Shawn took a gulp of coffee and got down to business.

"Bill tells me you want to know more about the young man's body that was found at the Western Inlet Inn several years ago because you're investigating a human trafficking or sex escort business, right?"

Rose gave him a brief history of the chain of events that led her and Kelsey to the properties owned by Leonard Browning.

"Yeah, no matter how he tries to polish his image, he's no poster child for the Chamber of Commerce. As you may know, the Warren County Sheriff's Office is the primary law enforcement agency for Lake George. Other departments in the region provide backup, including the Glens Falls Police Department. I've been with Glens Falls PD going on twenty years now and have worked Lake George events many times, like the Winter Carnival. Then we get called in for serious matters like a multi-car accident at two in the morning, or a suspicious death, such as the one you asked about.

"I wasn't at the scene," Shawn continued, "and I wasn't involved in the investigation of that young man's death, but I pulled up the report the other day." Shawn nodded in appreciation as the server filled his coffee cup.

Shawn pulled his notepad from his back pocket. "The county sheriff asked the Glens Falls PD to provide assistance at the Western Inlet Inn the morning of July 22, 2018, with the suspected homicide of a young man whose body was found." Shawn flipped over the page. "Name of the deceased is Alejandro Lopez. Nineteen years old. No parents or other relatives listed. He was a resident of the Queensbury Motel

Complex and worked at the inn as a barman and waiter. Had been working there since he was sixteen. After investigating the scene and speaking with other staff at the inn, it was determined the young man committed suicide."

"Why? Did other staff at the inn say he was depressed? On drugs?" Rose knew suicide was the last option for some severely depressed people and for people who struggled to kick painkillers. Truth was, far too many people decided life was too painful to continue. Rose's heart always ached when she read or heard about people taking their own lives.

"Blood and tissue tests showed no legal or illegal drugs in his system. He seemed to be in excellent health and used the inn's exercise room in off hours. Investigators couldn't find any evidence of foul play. They suspected Alejandro could have died during a sexual liaison with another man. There was semen on his clothing, but again, no blood anywhere. With no other evidence to contradict it, they ruled it a suicide." He closed his notebook.

"Off the record?" He squinted at Rose.

"Off the record," Rose confirmed.

"It was July. The Saratoga racing season was in full swing. Communities all over the Adirondacks and beyond were holding blueberry festivals, book festivals, crafts festivals, flower festivals, you name it. And then three young men home from college crashed their car into another vehicle on Route 9 in the early morning hours the day after Alejandro was found. It was a head-on collision." Shawn shook his head. "Seven people died, including two of the college students and five members from one family in the other car. The family members were active in the community and their deaths reverberated throughout the region. The death of an immigrant worker was not a top priority compared to the loss of those seven lives. No one came forward to claim his body or dispute the possibility of suicide. With no additional info, the ME closed the case."

"Wow," Rose said. "Who was the ME who signed off on Alejandro's death, do you know? Could it have been Dr. Collins?"

"Bob Night, the county ME, should have signed it but let me check." He flipped through his notes. "Hmm, it was Dr. Collins."

"Leonard Browning doesn't provide health care to his workers," Rose said. "He sends them to Dr. Collins and many of them struggle to pay their medical bills. Some of them are pressured to work for Dr. Collins, or do other work, in return for their health care. The ME told me Dr. Collins also helps when his office is short-staffed."

Or it could be they called in other doctors when they wanted to cover up a poisoning. Maybe Alejandro's suicide was also a cover-up. Add those to the list of questions on the list.

"I've heard Dr. Collins's name, but nothing comes to mind," Shawn said. "If I remember anything, I'll let Bill know." He tipped his coffee cup and swallowed the rest, grimacing. "Is there anything else I can help you with?" he asked, setting his cup down on the saucer.

Rose shook her head. "You've been very helpful, thanks."

Bill put a ten on the table and all three of them got to their feet.

"Wait," Rose said. "There is one more thing. Most employees, when they begin working at a new place, have to fill out paperwork, including providing an emergency contact. I know you said Alejandro didn't have any relatives, but he must have had some friends, even a fellow staffer who he hung around with."

Shawn considered the question. "I can't recall any other

names. I'll double-check the report and let Bill know if I come up with anything."

"I appreciate that. It might be someone I could chat with," Rose said. "I'm grabbing possible leads wherever I can find them."

Chapter Fifty-One
Summer 2018

"I have a bad feeling about tonight," Vicki Gomez told the handsome young man fussing with his curly black hair. He ran his hand down the front of his shirt as he admired himself in the full-length mirror in her bedroom. Vicki curled up on the bed. Her children's laughter drifted in from the living room where they were watching TV. She was alone in the evenings five or six days a week. Her husband worked the night shift at another inn in Lake George, one not owned by Leonard Browning. Visits from Alejandro helped pass the time.

Alejandro laughed. "Do you know how often you say that?"

She shook her head.

"Almost every time. And what happens?"

She soaked in his beautiful face and shook her head.

"Nothing. Nothing has ever happened. And nothing terrible will happen tonight." He tilted his head and checked himself out in the mirror one more time.

"I'm worried that one of these times you won't come home. You're my bestie, you know."

He preened as he danced over and flopped on the bed next to her. "And you are mine." He threw his arm over her shoulders and pulled her close.

"Have you met this one before?"

"Vicks, honey, you know the deal. Browning or his guy calls and I have to show up. I don't know who I'm seeing until I get there. No one ever says please or thank you. It is what it is."

Vicki admired his attitude. He always had a smile on his face, whether playing with her kids, tending bar, or getting ready for a night out. Despite everything, he still had a positive outlook, even though life had thrown him a few curves.

"You'll text me when you get home?"

"Don't I always?" He turned his head and kissed her cheek. "Love you, Vicks." With that, he hopped off the bed and hurried out the door. He said goodbye to the children and the front door closed behind him.

He was right. She always worried about him. Worrying had been in her bones since she was about twelve. She had Browning and Collins to thank for that. She had them to thank for getting Alejandro into this escort business as well. So many of life's decisions were made for her by others. The same was true for Alejandro. But he managed to rise above it. She'd resented Browning and Collins for years. Alejandro helped her recognize that she was only feeding the anger and resentment, and in doing so, denying herself the joy in life with her children and husband. He had helped her enjoy life again.

She slid off the bed and walked over to the dresser next to the mirror, picked up the tin of Alejandro's hair gel, and held it in her hands. Then she wrapped her arms around herself and asked God to keep Alejandro safe one more night.

Chapter Fifty-Two

Present Day

"If we park any farther back, we can't see anyone going in and out of the store," Kelsey said, her hair tucked into a baseball cap, big, black-rimmed glasses resting on the bridge of her nose. "Move closer."

Rose glanced in the rearview mirror and caught a look at her tan floppy hat and oversized sunglasses. She also wore bright red lipstick. A first. She put the SUV in gear, drove closer, and backed into a spot that gave them a clear view of the grocery store's front entrance.

It was midafternoon and the cloudless summer sky left them sitting in a hot SUV, even though they'd found a spot partially under the trees. Rose turned the engine on now and then, but they couldn't sit there with the engine running for too long. People would notice. Yesterday's conditions weren't much better and after two days of sitting in a hot vehicle, they'd both questioned the wisdom of their stakeout. Sam and Mary had the better assignment.

"I'm getting hungry," Rose said.

"Me too. And I'm going to need a bathroom soon."

"Me too."

Rose noticed an older sedan pull into the lot. A woman got out of the driver's side, but Rose heard two doors close. Then she saw the girl come around the front of the car.

"Look at those two." Rose pointed. "That's Ana, the woman I spoke with at the Queensbury Motel. She freaked out when I saw her at the Western Inlet Inn."

"Are you serious? Ana was a teenager when I spoke with her fifteen years ago," Kelsey burst out. "And it looks like she has a daughter."

"We need to talk with Ana when she comes out."

"Only one of us should go at first," Kelsey said. "She might feel overwhelmed if we both approach her, especially since her daughter is with her. You go. You saw her most recently."

Rose was glad she was the one to talk to Ana, but she was also anxious. So much was at stake. She didn't want to scare her off, and Ana had made it clear that Browning didn't like his workers talking with other people. Rose drummed her fingers on the steering wheel while Kelsey bounced her legs on heels, tapping the same beat as Rose's fingers. Then the front door of the grocery store opened. Ana and her daughter came out, each holding a large grocery bag. Rose hurried to Ana's sedan.

"Hi, Ana. My name is Rose. I saw you at the Queensbury Motel."

"What are you doing here?" Ana's eyes swept the parking lot.

"I need to talk with you. It's important. Please."

"Isabella, put that grocery bag on the floor behind your seat," Ana instructed. "Get in, but don't close the door. It's too hot."

Ana motioned Rose to step away from her car so she could put the other bag of groceries on the floor behind the driver's seat.

"I can't be seen talking with you."

"Then meet me somewhere." Rose handed her a piece of paper with her phone number.

Ana shook her head. "Please leave us alone. I can't help you."

"Ana."

Ana whipped her head around at the sound of a second voice.

"It's Kelsey. Remember me? We spoke here more than a dozen years ago. Before you became a mom."

"What are you doing here?" Ana looked back and forth between them. "Do you two know each other? And why are you wearing those hats and big glasses?"

Rose felt the burning heat of the pavement through her sneakers. Kelsey explained why she and Rose had tracked down Ana.

"Rose and I know what Browning and Collins are doing," Kelsey said. "We're trying to stop them from hurting more women and girls. We can't do it without your help."

Tears filled Ana's eyes. "He will hurt me and my daughter if I talk with you."

"He will continue to hurt others if you *don't* talk with us and help us stop him," Kelsey said. "You know how much power he has over everyone. Please help us."

The three women stared at each other.

"Not here." Ana looked at the paper Rose had given her. "I'll call."

Kelsey shook her head. "We don't have time to wait. We need to stop this now."

"Do you know where Lake Moreau State Park is?" Rose asked Ana. "About fifteen minutes south of here? Meet us there now in the main parking lot near the beach."

Ana clutched the piece of paper as she looked around

again. Her fear was so palpable. Rose didn't want to put her in this position, but they had no choice.

"Talk to us and then we'll let you be," Rose promised.

"Okay," Ana whispered. "But I'm not following you. I have to take these groceries home and put them in the refrigerator. And I promised Isabella ice cream."

* * *

Rose and Kelsey looked out over Lake Moreau. Children and parents ran on the beach and splashed in the water. It was a small lake and shallow, perfect for young children. Hiking paths led into the woods and around the lake. Rose had parked under the trees, not much of a challenge given they were in the middle of an Adirondack park. She and Kelsey both had their windows open. They kept watch for Ana's sedan.

"How long do you think it will take Ana to drive home and put the groceries away, then get ice cream?" Kelsey asked.

"I don't know. Half an hour, forty minutes. Then fifteen minutes to get here. I hope she hasn't changed her mind."

"That makes two of us."

Rose let out a sigh of relief when Ana's sedan cruised into the lot to a spot near them. She and Kelsey hopped out of the SUV and hurried over.

"Come on. Let's take that path so we can talk," Rose said.

Ana looked at her daughter.

"How about if Isabella and I wander down by the water?" Kelsey said, pulling her baseball cap down over her eyes and almost knocking the black-framed glasses off her nose.

Ana hesitated. "We'll be fine," Kelsey insisted. "Talk with Rose. You can trust her."

Kelsey and Isabella wandered to the beach while Rose and Ana took to the path.

"Have you been here before?" Rose asked.

Ana looked at her. "We have little time for beaches and walks in the woods. And I don't want to spend a lot of time right now. What do you want to ask me?"

"We suspect Browning forced you and other teenaged girls, young women, to act as escorts for people who paid Browning. Is that true?" Rose didn't want to be so blunt, but she needed to get Ana talking. This was not the time for a slow, gentle approach.

Ana nodded, then shared the truth. "We would go to dinner with them at a fancy hotel restaurant, and if the man asked us to go to his hotel room, we were supposed to do whatever he wanted."

"So you were forced to have sex with the men?"

Ana stroked her upper arms with her hands. "Yes."

"How many girls did he force to do this?"

"I have no idea," Ana asked. "I only know about Vicki and me for sure. We were best friends back then. There was maybe one other girl I didn't know well, but we sometimes saw her with a man too."

"Do you know her name?"

"No, and I haven't seen her in years."

"What about Vicki? Is she still an escort, or is she working at one of Browning's properties?"

Ana blinked back tears. "I haven't seen Vicki in some time. She got married and had a couple of children. I don't think she worked for Browning again. Lucky Vicki."

Chapter Fifty-Three

ose felt the hurt in Ana's eyes when she spoke of Vicki. Her heart went out to both women for the suffering Browning had put them through. She hated to make Ana relive such a painful time in her life, but she needed Ana to tell her what happened with the two men to help build the case against them.

"Tell me how it started with Dr. Collins. You were a teenager, right? Was cleaning for him the first time Browning made you do something?"

Ana dropped her eyes. "I began cleaning Dr. Collins's office to pay for Dad's treatment. He got hurt working at the inn. Mr. Browning sent him to Dr. Collins because, like most of us, we had no medical insurance."

As gently as she could, Rose asked, "Is that all you did, clean Dr. Collins's office? Did he try to take advantage of you?"

"He didn't do anything in the beginning. It was several weeks before he . . ." Ana paused and both women exhaled. Rose suspected what Ana was getting ready to say and waited for her to find the courage to say it. "Then he forced me into sex. I cleaned his office twice a week, and almost every time I was there, he raped me."

"Did you tell anyone?"

Ana shook her head. "I was afraid. I didn't know what would happen. My parents talked about how much money they owed Dr. Collins. Dad needed many appointments when he hurt his back and knee." Ana stopped walking and turned to Rose. "I did what I had to, what was expected." She paused. "I tried to quit once. I never told my mother why I wanted to quit, but I know she suspected something because of what another woman told her about her daughter and Dr. Collins. Mom didn't want me to keep working for Dr. Collins either. But then Mr. Browning came to our apartment. He threatened us. My father got angry. He stood and faced Mr. Browning and told him to leave me alone. Then Mr. Browning said I was already 'damaged goods.' I thought my father was going to hit him. But Mr. Browning laughed and said, 'You'll keep doing what's needed if you know what's good for you.' And he looked at me with such evil in his eyes."

"Is Dr. Collins your daughter's father?"

Ana looked so sad. Rose was sorry she'd asked the question. But she needed to.

"I don't know. Mr. Browning came to the office some evenings." Ana wiped a tear from her eye and looked away. "The first time I got pregnant, I told my parents. They told Mr. Browning. One evening, after all the clients had left, Dr. Collins said he needed to examine me because I was pregnant. I didn't know what to say. Didn't know what to do. But I got on the table and he moved his hands between my legs. I felt a lot of pressure down there and then a sharp pain. That night I bled a lot, and I knew I was no longer pregnant. I stayed home in bed for a few days." Ana had been keeping pace on the path with Rose, but she slowed down as she relived the horrible memory. "I didn't tell anyone when I got pregnant the second time. I didn't want to have a child yet, but I was sure they would stop what they were doing to me if I was pregnant."

"How far along were you when they found out?"

"I hid my growing belly well. Even my parents didn't know. I was almost five months pregnant when I told them. Too late for anyone to do anything about it."

"I'm so sorry, Ana. I'm sorry they hurt you and that there was no way out." Rose wanted to comfort Ana, but she didn't know her well enough to give her a hug, and any touch now would be inappropriate. "How did you deal with what was happening?"

"This might sound funny," Ana said. They had resumed walking, but Ana stopped on the path again. "I've always escaped into books. My mother started taking me to garage sales when I was young, just a little older than Isabella. She bought most of my clothes there, and she'd let me buy some books, the kind with soft covers. They were mostly books about girls my age having adventures, sometimes in far-off places. When it was happening at Dr. Collins's office, I'd mentally disappear into the happy places and shut out everything else. Sometimes I still do."

Ana turned around. "We should go back. There's not much else I can tell you."

As they resumed walking, Rose asked if Ana knew of anyone else who would be willing to talk with them.

"No, they would be just as afraid to get involved."

"Do they still force you to be an escort or to have sex with either Dr. Collins or Mr. Browning?"

"No, they never did again after Isabella was born. I wasn't ready to be a mother, but I saw what happened to other girls who got pregnant and knew it was almost a way of life in the immigrant community. Girls, women, are not treated with respect. I wouldn't say they treated me with respect after Isabella was born, but they left me alone. The job I have now is better than most, and my daughter is a good girl. I tell her how to protect herself and make sure she learns how to treat other people with respect."

Ana's voice caught. "The only reason I'm talking with you is because I'm afraid of what they'll try to do with Isabella." Tears filled her eyes. "She's getting older. I can't let what happened to me, to Vicki, happen to my little girl."

Their walk back to the beach was quicker, quieter.

Kelsey and Isabella were sitting on a bench chatting when Rose and Ana emerged from the woods. They met them at Ana's car. Ana pulled the paper with Rose's phone number out of her pocket and handed it to Rose. But Rose wouldn't take it.

"That has my cell phone number and Kelsey's cell number. Please keep it in case you need it."

"I have nothing else to tell you, and I don't want someone else to find this. I don't want anyone to know we've met."

"I understand," Rose said. "Hide it. But keep it in case you ever need to reach out to us."

Rose and Kelsey watched Ana drive away. "It's everything we suspected," Rose said, "but we have to find more people to talk to us, people willing to expose Browning and Collins for what they're doing, for what they've done. Ana is just one piece of this puzzle. We need more women to come forward, or we won't be able to put an end to it."

"What do we do next?"

"We find Vicki."

Chapter Fifty-Four

Kelsey used Rose's phone to text Maxi on the drive back to Lake Amelia. When they got out of the car at Thom's BrewPub, Rose tossed her floppy hat and large sunglasses onto the back seat. Her need for a disguise was over, but they agreed Kelsey should continue wearing the baseball cap and glasses. They settled into a table with four chairs and ordered drinks.

"This is a nice place," Kelsey said. "And just a few blocks from home. Do you come here often?"

"At least once a week," Rose said. "Sometimes I stop in for lunch, sometimes for dinner. If it's not too crowded with tourists, it's a comfortable place to eat alone."

"Just not beer and burgers for breakfast, huh?"

"No, I go to Aunt Tess's diner for breakfast."

"Is she your Aunt Tess or is that the name of the diner?"

"The Main Street Diner is on Main Street at the northern end of town. And she is my aunt, my mother's sister." Aunt Tess, the woman who taught Rose to appreciate good cooking, but never convinced her to do much cooking for herself.

"I'd say you have your meals taken care of." Kelsey smiled.

"That I do," Rose said as Maxi walked in and headed for their table. When Maxi came closer, she looked at Rose and stopped.

"That's a new look for you, isn't it?" Maxi asked.

Rose didn't understand, until Maxi ran her finger around her lips and pointed at Rose. "Ruby Woo isn't your best color."

"Ruby Woo? Oh, I forgot I was wearing lipstick," Rose said, wiping her lips with her napkin. "And how is it you know the name of my lipstick?"

Maxi just smiled. "Besides a new lipstick color, what's up with the two of you?" Maxi waved to Thom at the bar, motioning that she wanted a draft. The server dropped it off a couple of minutes later and took their food orders.

Kelsey told Maxi about their stakeout at the grocery store, and Rose filled her in about her conversation with Ana at Lake Moreau.

"Browning and Collins are a couple of bad actors," Maxi said.

"How do you figure they've been getting away with this for so long?" Kelsey asked.

"I learned Browning was under investigation for human trafficking several years ago, but he was never charged. I suspect he cleaned up his act for a while until the pressure eased. If he's at it again, he and his cronies are probably keeping people in line with threats," Maxi said. "They target the most vulnerable. Immigrant workers, even fully documented ones, often feel they can't challenge anyone's authority, or it could mean losing their green cards and a trip back to an awful life in Mexico, or Colombia, or pick your country in Central and South America, or Eastern Europe. These days almost anyone who looks different or speaks different is in danger of being deported. It's a scary time."

"How do we persuade Ana or any of the others to file a complaint?" Rose asked.

"I don't know that you can. Threats against their way of life are one thing. Threats against their families are another. The Latino communities are tight. They'll go to great lengths to protect each other. Guys like Browning and Collins use it against them." Maxi sipped her beer as Thom approached with their food.

"What you'd do, fire the help?" Maxi smiled.

"I wanted to say hi." He put their plates in front of them, Kelsey's last, and waited for an introduction. When none was coming, he asked.

"Does your friend have a name?"

"Olivia," Rose said.

"Evelyn," Maxi said at the same time.

Thom looked at Rose, then Maxi, then Kelsey. "Okay, then. Welcome, Olivia Evelyn." He walked away.

"Thom?" Rose called out. He turned and looked at her.

"Boxes in the attic," Rose said.

Thom dropped his chin, pursed his lips, then nodded.

Maxi and Kelsey watched with amusement.

"Was that a secret language?" Kelsey asked.

"Sort of." Rose laughed. "Thom knows I found Maxi through the photos in the box of books in the attic. It's a key phrase now among the three of us whenever Maxi and I want to say something without going into details."

Kelsey looked at Maxi, who smiled even though her mouth was full of cheeseburger.

"That's how you learned you are half sisters? I imagine it was quite a surprise."

"That's the understatement of the year," Maxi said, swallowing. "Maybe the understatement of my life."

"And you're Black."

"Apparently." She smiled. "So's my mom."

The three of them ate their lunch in silence for a while.

"Rose said the two of you were friends before she found out about her father's affair and you. I'm guessing it's been a big adjustment," Kelsey pursued.

"I always wanted a sister," Rose said, "and now I have one. But I'm still wrapping my head around the fact that Maxi is also my father's daughter."

"Yeah, when you put it like that . . ." Maxi's her eyes drifted to the tabletop.

Rose knew Maxi was having a harder time understanding that Mr. Randall, as Maxi had known him, was not a family friend, but her father. Maxi had gone through life as an only child, and she once told Rose that had suited her just fine. She liked Rose as a friend. The sister thing was coming a little slower.

"So back to this investigation," Maxi said. "What's next?"

"We want to update Mary and Sam on what we've learned but haven't been able to reach them," Rose said.

"They could still be in Saranac Lake," Maxi said. "You know how sketchy cell service is around here and in the mountains. It's a crapshoot whether your call goes through."

"We'll reach them eventually," Kelsey said.

"There's nothing urgent, right?" Maxi looked at Kelsey and Rose.

"No, nothing urgent," Rose said.

Chapter Fifty-Five

"I just got off the phone with Shawn," Bill said when Rose answered. She and Kelsey had been comparing notes from Rose's conversation with Ana and the report about Alejandro's death. Rose considered putting Bill on speakerphone, but he didn't know about Kelsey.

"Isn't it early for you to be at work?"

"Shawn called me at home because he has a court appearance this morning and isn't sure when he'll be free."

"And?"

"It was smart thinking about the emergency contact, Rose. It turns out that young man, Alejandro, did have an emergency contact. A Vicki Gomez."

"Vicki!" Rose exclaimed as Kelsey listened and studied her face.

"It sounds like that name means something to you."

"She's a friend of Ana, the woman we've been in touch with from the Queensbury Motel."

"*We*?" Bill asked.

Not much escaped his attention. She should fill him in.

He was helping with the investigation, after all. "How about I swing by this morning?"

"I'm going in soon," Bill said. "Come by at ten."

"I'll have someone with me," Rose said.

"I always love seeing Gladys."

"This female walks on two legs. See you soon." She disconnected the call and looked at Kelsey. "I'm not sure what to make of this yet, but Vicki was the emergency contact for the young immigrant whose body was found at the Western Inlet Inn several years ago, the one ruled a 'suicide' by the ME." Rose nodded as she thought. "Browning and Collins may have been involved in his death as well." She and Kelsey talked more about where their investigation was going, then left for the newspaper.

Bill had cleared Rose's guest with the receptionist, so the two women walked down the hallway and into the newsroom. Bill waved them to his office and came around his desk as they walked in.

"Bill, this is Kelsey. Kelsey Jacobs. Kelsey, meet Bill Poole, my friend and first mentor."

The two shook hands, then Bill pointed. "Let's sit at the table."

For the next half hour, Rose, with help from Kelsey, brought Bill up to date on what they'd learned.

"You've been busy."

Rose nodded. "We were at a dead end, though, until Shawn discovered Alejandro's emergency contact was Vicki."

Bill retrieved his notepad from his desk. "In addition to Vicki's name, Shawn also gave me an address. He has no idea whether that information is still good, but here it is." He wrote Vicki Gomez's address on a separate sheet, tore it off, and handed it to Rose.

"Wow, that's great. We might have to buy Shawn lunch instead of just a cup of coffee next time."

"There you go again with the 'we' thing," Bill laughed. "As I recall, I paid for coffee."

They all laughed. Then a serious look crossed Bill's face.

"Shawn also reviewed the witness list in the police report on Alejandro's death. Cops never spoke with Vicki."

"Isn't that odd? Not to interview the emergency contact of someone whose death is suspicious? And especially since no one claimed the body. Wouldn't they ask the emergency contact if they wanted to claim the body and handle the burial?"

"There's a lot about this thing that strikes me as odd," Bill said. "Shawn too. It's one more thing that doesn't quite add up with Alejandro's death. Where do you go from here?"

The three of them shared ideas, then Rose and Kelsey returned to the house. As they sat down at the dining room table, Rose suggested they call Sam with an update.

"That's good work, getting Ana to talk and tracking down contact information for Vicki," Sam said as soon as they connected. "Why don't you give me Vicki's address? I'll stop by on our way back tomorrow."

Rose and Kelsey looked at each other.

"We were going to drive there next," Rose said. "We don't have any other leads to follow. Where are you anyway?"

"Saranac Lake. We stayed two nights at the Three Oaks Motel. Didn't make much headway here, but I want to check out a few more things and we may swing by Lake Placid tonight and stay somewhere other than Browning's property. It depends on what else we learn today. I promised Mary a boat cruise on this trip, and we haven't done it yet."

"We already looked up Vicki's address. It's not any of the motels we've connected to Browning. It's a small apartment complex near Amsterdam."

"Are you sure it's not close to Browning's motel in Amsterdam?"

"No, it's not," Rose reassured him. "And that's why I think it's safe enough for us to head over there. I promise we'll be careful."

Sam finally conceded. "But if there's any sign of trouble, or anyone looks at you twice, leave immediately, okay?"

A little later, Rose and Kelsey were driving west. They found the apartment complex, which looked better than Browning's motels, but no one answered the door. They waited a few minutes but saw no activity. It was probably the wrong time of day. More people would be home after work. Rose and Kelsey decided to come back in the evening.

They returned to Lake Amelia and had just walked back into the house and were giving Gladys some lovies when Rose's phone chirped. She didn't recognize the number and hesitated for a moment, wondering if any of Browning's people would have tracked her down. She shook her head, thinking that wasn't likely, and answered the call.

"Rose?" Ana's panicked voice said. "Isabella didn't come home from day camp."

Chapter Fifty-Six

"What do you mean Isabella didn't come home from day camp?" Rose repeated Ana's question for Kelsey's benefit as she put the phone on speaker.

"They let out early because of a staff meeting," Ana said. "Officials from the county health department inspect the camp once every summer. When I called the camp office, they said the staff is getting ready for that visit. I didn't know Isabella was getting out early or I would have been watching for her. I'm not working today."

"And she hasn't called or texted you?"

"Isabella doesn't have a phone. I called her friend's house to see if she was there. The girl said Isabella never got on the bus home. It's been over an hour." Her voice broke. "Where could she be?"

"Stay calm," Rose said. "Don't go imagining the worst." Rose tried to think of a spot where they could meet, but she didn't know the Queensbury area. She opened her laptop and searched Google's map.

"Meet us at the McDonald's just before the Northway. Do you know it?"

"Yes."

"We'll be there as soon as possible." Rose stood and walked over to the sliding glass door. She opened it and Gladys scurried out. "How about if I pack some drinks and a couple of protein bars?"

"Yes, please." Kelsey hurried down the hallway to get her handbag from the bedroom.

Rose grabbed the insulated soft pack from a drawer, dropped in protein bars and a couple of drinks. She zipped it shut and filled two bottles with water. Rose filled the dog's water as well and gave her some treats. Then the two women sped out the door and hopped into Rose's SUV.

"What if Browning's security guys saw us with Ana?" Kelsey said as Rose stepped on the gas. "What if they're threatening Ana by taking her daughter?"

"It's as good a guess as any," Rose said. "Try calling Sam and Mary. We need to tell them what's going on."

But Sam and Mary weren't picking up. Rose drove as fast as she safely could, pulled off the highway at the Glens Falls exit, and spotted Ana's car when she turned into the McDonald's. She hesitated. Should she drive up next to Ana? What if someone was watching her? If they had Isabella, would it make any difference now if Browning's guys knew Ana was talking with Rose and Kelsey?

"The damage may already have been done, Rose," Kelsey said, as if she could read Rose's thoughts. "Pull up next to Ana."

Rose took the spot and motioned Ana to get into the back seat.

"I called the camp office again. This time I got the camp director," Ana said as soon as she closed the door. Her voice shook and her words came out so fast Rose had to concentrate to follow her. "When I told the director that Isabella was missing, he pulled the staff from the meeting to search the grounds. So far there's no sign of Isabella."

Ana looked at Rose and Kelsey. "What do we do now? How do we find my daughter?"

Rose tried calling Sam and Mary. Still no answer. She called Maxi.

"Hello. What's new with you?"

"We think Browning's guys may have taken Ana's daughter."

Maxi's voice went from light to serious in a heartbeat. "Where are you?"

"At the McDonald's in Queensbury. Just off the Northway."

"Stay put. I'm on my way."

Twenty minutes later, Maxi's dark blue Jeep pulled in. She hopped out of her vehicle and into Rose's, joining Ana in the back seat.

"Okay, tell me everything," Maxi said to Ana.

When Ana finished, Maxi pointed out that they were in Warren County, out of her jurisdiction. "There are all kinds of summer camp activities for kids throughout the Adirondacks and surrounding counties. Day camps. Sleepover camps. Does Isabella go to the day camp at Lake Moreau?"

"No, not there. It's the Woods Edge Day Camp north of here."

"Okay," Maxi said. "Let's canvass the neighborhood and check your apartment while the camp director and the staff continue their search. If we need to, we'll go there."

They drove around the neighborhood, even stopped in at Isabella's friend's house, but she couldn't add anything more than what she'd told Ana on the phone. The girl's mother gave

Ana a hug and promised to let her know if she heard from Isabella.

"Let's check your apartment." Maxi said.

As Rose pulled into the parking lot, Ana spotted her daughter sitting on a chair next to their apartment's door.

"Isabella!" Ana shouted as she opened the door and jumped out. She ran to her daughter and pulled her into a hug, running her hand over her daughter's head again and again. "Where have you been?"

"Two men told me you had been injured in an accident and wanted to drive me home right away," Isabella said, looking up at her mother with wide eyes. "One said you were at the hospital. So we drove around for a while, and they took me to an apartment where we had drinks and some crackers. Then they brought me home. Did I do something wrong?"

"Did you know the men?" Maxi asked.

"When they walked up to me at camp, one of them looked familiar, so I thought it was okay to go with him. But then I realized I didn't know him after all. Lo siento, Mamá."

"It's okay, baby. I'm just glad you're safe." Ana hugged her daughter, then picked up the knapsack sitting on the ground next to the chair.

"Can you describe the men?" Maxi asked.

Isabella looked from her mom to Maxi and shrugged. "Not really. They had dark hair. One had a moustache. They were dressed like people around here dress. Jeans. Shirts. That's why I thought I knew them."

"Okay. Hang tight. I'm going to call the camp, then the sheriff's office to let them know Isabella has come home. It's up to the sheriff what to do next." Maxi was already on her cell phone as she turned and walked away from them.

"Are you sure you're okay?" Ana said, her arm around her daughter.

"Sí, Mamá." Isabella snuggled into her mother's side.

Ana looked at Rose and Kelsey. "I'm going to take Isabella inside. We're sorry for the trouble."

Ana turned toward the door. A slip of paper fell out of Isabella's knapsack. Ana picked it up, glanced at it, and a frown crossed her face. She spun away from Rose and Kelsey, unlocked the door to their unit, and led Isabella inside.

Chapter Fifty-Seven

"Did you see that?" Rose asked Kelsey under her breath.

Kelsey looked from Rose to the closed door, then shook her head.

"Something fell out of Isabella's knapsack. A piece of paper. Ana looked at it and frowned. We should ask her what it was."

"Because?" Kelsey asked.

"Because of how Ana frowned when she read the note. Her eyes darted between Isabella and us. I think she was trying to figure out if we saw the note. I'm going to ask her about it." Rose took a couple of steps toward Ana's door.

Kelsey reached out and grabbed her arm. Rose turned toward Kelsey. "What?"

"Let's wait and ask Maxi to check it out."

"We're right here. I saw the piece of paper. Maxi didn't." Rose turned to look at Maxi. "She had her back to us when I saw Ana pick up the note and she still does while she's on the phone. Why don't I ask Ana?"

"I don't know what's going on, but because the sheriff's office is involved, they should take the lead."

Maxi ended her call and returned to where they stood. "You both have funny looks on your faces? What's going on?"

Rose told Maxi about the piece of paper.

Maxi nodded. "The Warren County Sheriff's Office sent one deputy to the camp and the other one is coming here. Let's wait for them before we do anything else."

The deputy pulled into the lot several minutes later and parked next to Rose's vehicle. She stepped out of her cruiser and walked over to them.

"Deputy Patterson," she said, after Maxi introduced herself.

"I thought I'd met everyone in the Warren County Sheriff's Office," Maxi said.

"I transferred in from downstate a few weeks ago," Deputy Patterson said.

"Welcome to the area." Maxi introduced Rose and Kelsey and explained the situation.

"Do you know the woman whose daughter went missing?" Deputy Patterson asked Maxi.

"A little, but these two people know her better." Maxi explained why Rose and Kelsey were involved.

"I'll speak with the woman and her daughter," Deputy Patterson said. She stepped up to the door and knocked. Ana opened the door and walked out of the apartment. When Deputy Patterson asked to speak with Isabella, Ana balked.

"Is that necessary? She's had a scare and been through enough already."

"Yes, ma'am. I understand. But we need to investigate what happened today, whether there was a threat to your daughter's safety. I need to ask her about the men who picked her up at the camp. Camp officials are also upset that someone came onto their property and left with one of their campers. If there's a predator targeting children, especially around these summer camps, we need to know."

Ana told the deputy what Isabella had told her.

"Yes, ma'am. Could I speak with her now?"

Ana flinched but seemed to realize she had no choice. She led the deputy inside. Rose followed, but a quick look from Deputy Patterson stopped her from taking another step.

"May I join you?" Maxi asked. "In an unofficial but interested capacity."

Patterson nodded and the three of them went inside.

Rose suggested to Kelsey that they could get into her SUV and turn on the AC, but Kelsey was content to stand outside and wait for them to finish their questioning. They found a little shade under a pine tree near the building. As soon as the door opened and the two deputies walked out, Rose and Kelsey hurried over.

"What did you learn?" Rose asked.

"The daughter confirmed her story that the men claimed her mother was injured and were taking Isabella to her," Deputy Patterson said. "When they brought her home here, the men told her they thought she was someone else, another girl, that's why they picked her up. It doesn't make sense, but Isabella can't identify them. Still, we'll send a notice out to all the summer camps to be on the alert for two men in an older light blue sedan. We'll relay the information to the state campgrounds as well. That's about all we can do, unless the camp director has more information."

"What about the piece of paper from Isabella's knapsack?" Rose asked.

"She said it was nothing important," Patterson responded. "I asked to see the paper, and she put me off, so I looked to Deputy Stover."

"I told Ana that you'd seen her frown when she saw the

paper," Maxi explained, "but she brushed it off. Said it was nothing."

"I pushed her to show us the paper," Maxi said. "She went into her daughter's room where the knapsack was and came out with a piece of paper. It was a note from a classmate about a playdate in a couple of weeks."

"Why would Ana frown at that?" Rose asked.

"Not a clue," Maxi said. "Maybe Isabella didn't know the girl well or it was a family that Ana didn't want Isabella to get involved with."

"Or maybe it wasn't the piece of paper I saw Ana pick up," Rose said.

"We don't know, and Ana isn't telling us. I think we're at a dead end," Deputy Patterson said.

Was it? Rose was the only one to see it, but that didn't mean she imagined it. She played the scene over in her mind. Ana with her hand on Isabella's shoulder as the two of them turned to go into their apartment. A piece of paper falling out of the backpack. Ana picking it up. Then frowning. That's what Rose saw, and Ana's frown hinted of something serious.

Deputy Patterson said there was nothing more for her to do. She thanked them for their help and tipped her hat.

"I'll walk you to your car," Maxi said. Rose smiled as the two deputies walked away.

"What?" Kelsey asked.

"Nothing important." She looked at Kelsey and grew serious again. "Why do you think Ana won't tell us what was in the note?"

"I think we should ask her," Kelsey said, "but not before Deputy Patterson leaves."

When Maxi returned, Rose smiled at her. "Did you get her number?"

Maxi started to protest, then stopped. Grinned.

"Okay, you two. Can we please get back to this note and whether there's any significance to it?" Kelsey asked.

"I'm going to wait in the car, or next to it since I don't want to become a casualty of a heat stroke. You two do what you need to," Maxi said.

Rose walked up to the door and was about to knock when Ana opened the door.

"I'm glad you're still here. My car is at McDonald's. I need a ride."

"First, will you tell us what the note is that fell out of Isabella's backpack?"

Ana shook her head. "It's nothing. Please drop it. I'm going to get Isabella. I don't want to leave her here alone. Will you please take us to my car?"

"Of course," Rose said.

Rose and Maxi climbed into the bucket seats in front. Isabella nestled between her mother and Kelsey on the back seat. No one spoke on the short ride to the fast-food restaurant. Ana thanked them for their help and got into her car with Isabella.

"Did Ana say anything else when you knocked on her door and asked again about the piece of paper?" Maxi asked as she and Rose watched Ana drive away.

"No," Rose said. "She was more concerned about getting her car. But her face says enough. She's scared. I think whoever picked up Isabella did it to send Ana a message." Rose turned to look at Maxi. "And I would say the message has been received."

Chapter Fifty-Eight

Maxi stepped into her Jeep and left for the sheriff's office in Ft. Edward. They were going to meet up again at Rose's house after Maxi's shift, which was already halfway over. Even though she'd been off duty when she'd joined Rose and Kelsey to search for Isabella, her boss put her on the clock when she told him what was going on. Maxi said she expected the rest of her shift would be making sure no one was targeting girls or any kids at day camps, overnight camps, even state campgrounds in the region.

"Are you hungry?" Rose asked.

"Starving," Kelsey said. "I need a big salad with lots of stuff on it like carrots and olives and some kind of nut. Maybe walnuts or sunflower seeds, with tomatoes and even an avocado. And, oh yeah, cheese. How about goat cheese? You got any place like that?"

"Eat-in or take-out?"

"Take-out. I'd love to eat someplace comfortable, with a little doggy in a nice, cozy family room."

"It didn't take long for Gladys to win you over, did it?"

Kelsey smiled.

"Okay. Let's get some salads from Rock Hill Bakehouse in Glens Falls."

"Bakehouse? Does that mean they have baked goods as well?"

"I am not the kind of gal who shies away from cakes or pies or muffins. They have all that, plus excellent salads."

They continued to discuss Isabella's story, Ana's reaction, and what was going on with Leonard Browning at his properties. It was late afternoon, and the sun beat down. Even the oak and maple trees seemed to wither from the blistering summer sun.

After a bit of a wait and using some restraint—ordering only a couple of pastries—they made it back to Lake Amelia and let Gladys out onto the patio before they settled in to eat.

"Let's suppose the two men who picked up Isabella knew what they were doing. That Isabella was their target. If it was a warning to Ana, what happens next? If she doesn't talk with us, maybe they leave her alone, but that leaves us with no more leads," Kelsey said.

"Unless Sam and Mary come up with something at the inns, I agree."

Kelsey glanced at the clock on the fireplace mantle. "We still have Vicki."

Rose smiled. "Do you want to finish our salads and then take a quick trip back to Amsterdam and see whether she's home?"

"Sounds like a plan."

They were developing a steady routine. Eat. Feed Gladys. Let Gladys out. Search for information against Browning. Eat. Feed Gladys. Let Gladys out. Search for information against Browning. The only part of the process not working well was the search for information. Rose knew that many leads could end up at a dead end until you hit pay dirt, the one lead that sent you further along into your investigation. Rose wasn't giving up, but she had to think of how to approach this from a different direction. She couldn't wait to brainstorm with Sam and Mary again and see what ideas they had. And just as important, to find out what they had learned.

Traffic was heavier this time when they drove to Vicki's apartment, and there were more cars in the parking lot of the modest complex. Rose and Kelsey walked up the sidewalk and rang the bell. Rose thought she heard a child's voice, but as she listened closer, she couldn't hear anyone. She rang the bell again and knocked. No one came to the door. She and Kelsey turned to walk back to the car when something caught Rose's eye. There. In the curtains in the front window. It was as if someone had pulled them back a little and then let the curtain fall back into place when Rose turned that way. The curtain continued to sway. Rose touched Kelsey's arm and tilted her head toward the windows. She spun around and knocked on the door again. All the time, she watched the curtain. She waited, then took a card out of her wallet and wrote on the back.

Please call. We need to ask you about Alejandro. And we're trying to protect children like yours. Rose stuck the card in the crack between the door and the molding.

"Did you see the curtains move?" Rose asked as she rejoined Kelsey as they continued down the walkway.

Kelsey shook her head. "Is that why you went back and knocked again?"

"Yep. I think someone's here but doesn't want to talk with us."

"What else is new?"

"If they don't want to talk, they probably have a reason. We're not done with Vicki yet."

Chapter Fifty-Nine

"I'm sorry you can't go with me," Rose told Kelsey as she tidied up the kitchen. "I know Bill is comfortable with you, but Shawn doesn't know you. He trusted Bill about me, but I'm not sure he'll open up with a new person there."

"No worries. I get it. I'll hang here with Gladys. And I'll try again to get Sam on the phone."

Rose was seriously annoyed at how difficult the cell signals could be in this part of upstate New York. Some calls dropped in the middle of a conversation or didn't connect because of the mountains. Other cell issues were attributed to solar flares. There had been a lot of flares lately. It was frustrating in an age of technology where more people had cell phones than land lines in their homes. You never knew when a call might connect. When it wouldn't.

Rose was first to arrive at the diner and found a booth near the back. She slid in and the server came right over.

"Coffee?"

"I'll take an iced tea. You can bring three waters as well. Thanks."

Bill and Shawn came in the door together. Shawn had bags under his eyes and a crease in his forehead. He shuffled over to the table and sat down, asked for coffee, and ordered a sandwich.

"I believe we've poked the hornet's nest," Shawn said as he added a dash of cream to his coffee. "The chief called me into his office yesterday. He doesn't like to be left out of the loop on any investigation, so he got right to it and asked me why I'd pulled the report on the suicide of the young male at the Western Inlet Inn." Shawn took a quick sip of his drink and looked at Rose.

"The chief's a good guy. He's been on the job for more than a decade and I trust him, so I told him everything. About a possible sex trafficking ring involving immigrants, how Alejandro's death may be connected to it, and how Leonard Browning could be behind it all. The chief nodded several times, then tapped his desk with his pen. I waited. Then he told me he got a call from someone in the ME's office. He didn't say who and I didn't push him on that—yet—and that person asked what was going on."

"How would someone know you'd pulled the file?" Rose asked, picking at her tuna sandwich.

"We still have evidence lockers, of course," Shawn said, "because we have to have a place to lock up physical evidence, but everything else is digital. Investigating officers sometimes save their written notes and forget to put them in the digital file. That's where they are supposed to go. Whenever someone accesses a digital file, an alert is sent to the officer in charge. A red flag, if you will. Someone flagged my access and asked the chief about it."

"Do you know who flagged it?" Bill asked.

"Because it was a suspected homicide at first, the Warren County Sheriff's Office led the investigation. It was one of their guys. A deputy named Larkin. I don't know him well, but I'm surprised he made it a point to contact the chief. The chief and I were both surprised that the ME's office got involved."

Rose glanced at Bill, then back to Shawn. "Sorry, I don't know how all these agencies work together in rural areas. I mean, you explained during our first meeting that while some municipalities or townships have police departments, they rely on the county sheriffs to assist, especially in cases like homicide." Rose hesitated. "So the authority of the county agency overrides the municipal police department's authority, so to speak."

Shawn nodded. "Yep. And while everyone knows that's the system, not everyone is happy about it. If someone from the sheriff's office fails to follow up on a lead or interview, for example, they're inclined to point the blame at the municipal agency. Like the Glens Falls Police Department." Shawn shrugged. "The chief and I can handle the heat."

"What else did the chief say about Alejandro's case?" Bill asked.

"He remembered it, although he admitted the details were vague. He accessed the file and skimmed it while I was there. Then he noted that there were some loose ends, like no interview with the emergency contact and no comments from Browning's staff. Then the chief's office phone rang."

Rose leaned in. She imagined officers in the Glens Falls Police Department didn't like someone looking over their shoulder. She didn't like that either. One of the things she liked most about freelancing was being her own boss.

"The call was from the officer in charge of the evidence locker and case files. He noted that it was the second time our department had accessed the file and asked what was going on. The chief asked him why it was flagged. The deputy didn't mince words. 'Can't say. Don't know.' The chief was vague with the deputy on the phone, said we were reviewing the case for a possible link to something else we were working on. That earned another grunt on the other end of the line." Shawn smiled. "After he hung up, the chief asked me again to explain the possible connection to Browning."

"Did he ask if you were talking to anyone else? Like the media? Like us?" Rose asked.

"He asked why I was interested in the case, and I told him I'd gotten a tip from someone who'd been looking into unexpected deaths in the area, including suicides, and that person believed Alejandro's death wasn't a suicide. It was a weak explanation, I'll admit, but the chief didn't press me about where I'd gotten my information, and I didn't offer it."

"Thanks for that," Bill said. "I don't know what we're into either, but someone isn't happy with us poking around. How did the chief leave it? And where does that leave us?"

"He said if I suspected a sex trafficking ring, I needed to contact the Albany FBI office, and if I thought there was something illicit going on with the county sheriff's office, I needed to tell him stat." Shawn finished his coffee and glanced at the clock above the counter. "I've got a contact in the ME's office—a staffer, not a doc—who I trust. I tried calling him this morning, but he doesn't come in until two. I'm going to find out why the ME's office has also taken an interest in my digging into the case. Someone is worried about the renewed attention."

"That's for sure," Rose said. "Thanks for checking this out. Let us know what else you learn."

Shawn nodded and eased out of the booth. Bill stood and shook Shawn's hand, then returned to his seat. Rose and Bill stared at each other until Rose pointed out the obvious.

"Got any ideas who we spooked?"

"After everything Shawn told us, I think it goes back to the investigating officers, the county homicide detectives. But it's interesting that the ME's office was alerted. Maybe it's both."

"Can we track down those guys?"

Bill smiled. "Shawn let me keep a copy of the report as long as I promised to file it in a secure place and destroy it once we had what we need."

"And you still have that report?"

"It's your turn to pay," he said, sliding the bill over to her with a smile that spread from ear to ear. "Then let's get to my office."

Chapter Sixty

"Remember, Dr. Collins signed off on Alejandro's death," Bill said as he, Rose, and Kelsey sat at his conference table looking over the police report. Rose had called Kelsey and told her to meet them at the newspaper and she'd rushed right over.

"Yes, but Collins is called to help with autopsies often enough that he must know the staff. If Alejandro's death is tied into Browning's sex escort or sex trafficking ring, then Collins may have asked someone to watch for any cases that are connected to Browning. After all, Collins is pretty deep in it himself." Rose looked at the other two. "Does that make sense?"

"We can't go looking into every death certificate that Collins signed," Kelsey said.

"Actually, we can." Bill tapped the page of the report. "Death certificates are digitized. We could check which ones Collins signed. See if any of them are connected to Browning's properties."

Kelsey looked at Rose. "You're still wondering if

Browning contributed to your father's death and that's why Collins signed his certificate, aren't you?"

"I'd be lying if I didn't admit it's crossed my mind." Rose paused. "At least ten times a day." She tried to smile.

"You don't need to convince me," Kelsey said. "I was suspicious early on. When you found out your father's heart attack was the same day he had lunch with Browning, that's more fuel for the fire. I haven't seen anything to change my mind."

"Yeah, but isn't it too much of a coincidence that the ME, Bob Night, wasn't available to handle my father's death certificate that, remember, was signed without an autopsy? And Night wasn't around for Alejandro's case either?"

"Shawn told us there was a lot going on around the time of Alejandro's death, with that accident involving so many fatalities. That's a time when extra help would definitely be called in," Bill said.

"I don't get how someone can step in and sign off on a person's death without more questions being raised," Kelsey pointed out.

Rose shrugged. "Small towns. Everyone helps everyone else in a time of need, and friends cover for friends without asking questions." Sometimes covered for friends, sometimes lied for them. Rose knew it could go either way.

"We don't know that the ME and Collins were friends," Kelsey said.

"No, but they were colleagues. Sometimes that passes for friends."

"Do you think it's the way many municipalities operate, with a bare-bones staff in the ME's office and other medical people on call to help out as needed? Is it about budgets, or is it about control over the medical examiner's office?" Kelsey asked.

"I've lived in the area long enough and covered enough

stories, talked to enough cops, that I think it's more that they don't need a large staff on a daily basis. That's why people like Collins are called in as needed. Look," Bill said, "I don't know if we'll connect Browning to your dad's death, but we can try to make the case that Collins and Browning were involved in covering up Alejandro's death. Even if it was arranging the escort that night. I mean, sometimes men having sex has resulted in accidental deaths."

"The question is how do we get to the bottom of that?" Rose said. "I keep coming back to Vicki."

"Vicki was the other teenaged girl I saw going into the grocery store with Ana and her mother that one time," Kelsey said. "Vicki was withdrawn. She looked scared. She had paused long enough to hear my question to Ana about Browning, then hurried away."

"Ana said Vicki doesn't work for Browning now, so how did she get out of the escort situation? Was she also moved out when she became pregnant? Or did she meet her husband and get out of Browning's grasp that way?"

Bill and Kelsey looked at Rose. They shuffled through the report again, trying to find links and leads and someplace to take their investigation next. Then Bill's cell rang.

"Hey, Shawn. What's up?"

Rose and Kelsey watched as Bill nodded several times. Then his eyebrows shot up—his telltale sign that he just received an important piece of information.

"Great work. Thanks." He disconnected the call.

"Shawn called his contact in the ME's office. He told Shawn that a woman who's been there for almost twenty years is most likely the leak."

"Is Shawn sure?" Kelsey asked.

"Pretty sure. The woman's name is Leigh Browning."

"Seriously? Talk about a direct connection. Is she Browning's daughter?" Rose asked.

"Daughter-in-law."

"Close enough," Rose said. "What do we do now?"

"Shawn asked us to give him time to talk with the woman. He can lean on her if she isn't cooperative. I think he wants to get her to admit she's been doctoring death certificates on her own or helping Collins. Either way, he needs time to follow up."

"So we sit and wait?" Kelsey asked.

Rose's phone rang.

"It's Sam." She put him on speaker. "Where are you? We've been trying to reach you."

"We're at Saratoga Hospital. Mary's been vomiting with severe stomach and other digestive pain. I think they might admit her."

"What happened?"

"I don't know. We checked into the Western Inlet Inn late yesterday so I could follow up a lead with one of their groundskeepers. After lunch today, Mary got sick, and when she couldn't stop vomiting, I brought her to the ER."

"We're on our way," Rose said. She disconnected the call as she stood. "You handle things from here," she said to Bill. "We're going to the hospital."

Chapter Sixty-One

Vicki Gomez sat on one of the few benches in the shade of the towering white pine trees and watched her children play on the swings and the slide in the park several blocks from where they lived. How did their bodies tolerate the heat and keep climbing the steps and coming down the slide? Wasn't the hard plastic hot on their bums from the sun beating down on it? She was so focused on her children she didn't hear the footsteps behind her until the man was at her side and easing himself onto the slatted wood bench.

"Hello, Vicki."

She didn't look at him. Didn't want to. Didn't need to. She could pick that voice out of a crowd of thousands. Her stomach churned at the smell of his cologne, and she swallowed hard. These were sounds and smells she'd always associate with some of the worst moments of her life.

"What do you want?"

"Is that any way to greet me?"

Her children laughed, and she tried to calm herself with the sound of their familiar voices. "I said, what do you want?"

"Careful now, Vicki."

She rested her arm on the bright yellow knapsack with light green straps that held her children's treats and drew in a breath. Tried to calm down. Provoking him never ended well. She'd had the bruises and scars to prove it.

"Your daughter's beautiful. How old is she now?"

Vicki flinched. "You know how old she is."

Browning dropped his hand onto her thigh. The tension in her leg spread to the rest of her body. His hand rested there and she feared what might come next. Of course, nothing physical could happen in this public place. That didn't mean he couldn't hurt her. Wouldn't hurt her.

"Some people have been poking into my business," he said, an easy tone contradicting his actions. "Talking to people they shouldn't. Have they contacted you?"

"I don't know what you're talking about."

He squeezed her thigh with so much pressure, she bit her tongue to stop from crying out.

"If anyone contacts you asking questions about me," he said, his voice hard like he was gritting his teeth, "you let me know. Do you understand?"

She nodded quickly and searched the playground for her children. There, coming down the slide. First, her six-year-old son, waving his arms in the air and laughing. Then her ten-year-old daughter, making sure her brother was clear of the bottom before she slid down.

He squeezed her thigh one more time. "And if you see your old friend, Ana, you tell her that I stopped by. Tell her to stop talking to the cops. Don't talk to anyone about me. Do you understand?"

"Yes," she whispered.

"Good. I'd hate to see anything happen to that beautiful daughter of yours."

He left as quickly as he'd come. Vicki stood but immediately fell back onto the bench, her legs too weak to hold her up. Browning had already done so much damage to her life. There was no telling what else he could do. Would do.

Vicki wrapped her arms around her body. What had Ana gotten into?

Chapter Sixty-Two

Rose and Kelsey speedwalked back to the house.

"We'll be home soon," Rose said, petting Gladys's head and setting a dish of food on the floor next to her water bowl.

Rose knew the route to Saratoga Hospital well, thanks to trips she'd made with her mom over the past couple of months, and to Rose's ongoing occupational therapy sessions. At least those were only once a week now, thanks to Rose's determination to heal her arm and shoulder.

She parked across the street from the ER and the two women rushed inside. They didn't see Sam anywhere. Rose waited behind another person at the receptionist's desk. Was Sam in the back with Mary in an ER bay, or had she been admitted? Kelsey took another pass around the waiting room and rejoined Rose.

"He's not out here."

"I could text him, but let's ask first."

Rose stepped up and gave the receptionist Mary's name.

"And you are?"

"Rose Webster."

"She's being admitted," the woman said. "Her husband told me it was okay to give you the information. He's in the cafeteria while they finish processing his wife and moving her to a room. Do you know where the cafeteria is?"

Rose smiled. "I sure do. Thanks."

After several hallways and twist and turns, they found Sam sitting at a table in front of the windows, his face drawn, his hands folded around a cup of coffee. They hurried over. He stood and hugged each of them.

"What happened?" Rose asked.

"I can't tell you much more than I did on the phone." He collapsed back into his chair. "We were on our way back from Saranac Lake and stopped at the Western Inlet Inn late yesterday. The woman at the receptionist's desk said the inn has a two-night minimum during summer months. We said that was fine." Sam ran his fingers through his hair and took a gulp of coffee. "We woke up late and had lunch at the patio restaurant. Mary started having stomach cramps soon after we returned to the room. The cramps got worse, and she began throwing up. Then other things happened." He waved his hand in the air. "You know, the things that go along with cramps and vomiting."

Rose and Kelsey nodded.

"How long did that go on?" Kelsey asked.

"A couple of hours. The cramps got worse. She couldn't even keep down a sip of water. Then she was too dizzy to stand up to go into the bathroom. That's when I brought her to the ER."

"What did the docs say?" Rose asked.

"They admitted her because she was so dehydrated and the stomach cramps wouldn't let up. They also put her on a saline IV. I asked them to do a tox screen. When they asked why, I showed them my PI license and said I'd been looking into a case and that it could be a poisoning." He spun his coffee cup around in his hands. "We won't get the tox screen for days, maybe a few weeks, but it's worth doing. The nurse who helped wheel her gurney up to the patient floor said they would text me when I could see her." Bill looked at them. "I'm hoping she'll feel better as soon as they get fluids in her. Sorry I had to pull you away from whatever you were doing."

They filled him in about what Shawn had told Rose and Bill about the ME's office and Browning's connection, a connection that might explain Collins's access to information and his occasional, but timely, work with the department.

"What's next?" Sam asked.

"You're going to stay here with Mary, right?" Rose said.

He nodded. "I need to make sure she's recovering from whatever this is. Here's the thing," Sam said. "I called the inn to ask if anyone else had told them they'd become ill after lunch. The receptionist said she didn't think so, but she put me through to the inn's manager. He expressed his apologies for Mary's illness and told me no one else had contacted the staff to report feeling unwell. I said Mary couldn't be the only person to have the tuna salad over greens, and he promised to check with the kitchen staff. But he didn't seem very concerned. Wished Mary a speedy recovery and hung up before I could ask any more questions."

Rose looked at Kelsey. "My floppy hat and sunglasses are still in the back of the SUV. You tossed your cap and eyeglasses into the back after we met Mary at the pub, didn't you?"

"I did."

Rose turned to Sam. "Why don't you give us the key to your room?"

"Not gonna happen," Sam said. "I don't know what happened to Mary, but the inn's staff has identified both of you. They know we're investigating, and they won't hesitate to hurt you."

Rose leaned across the table. "Kelsey and I are both smart,

careful, and resourceful. We've both done investigations and know how to keep our heads down. We can take care of ourselves."

"And we'll have each other's backs." Kelsey pleaded with him. "Sam, the trail is hot. Let us stay in the room tonight and we can look around. Find out if anyone else got sick, maybe whether someone was sending you and Mary a message."

Sam's phone pinged.

"Mary's in a room. I've got to go."

All three stood. Sam picked up his cup of coffee. Rose held out her hand.

"Promise me you'll call Maxi before you leave the hospital parking lot and tell her what's going on. Tell her where you're headed?" Sam said.

"Consider it done," Kelsey said.

"My gut is telling me not to give you the key, but I agree people know we're looking at them, and that's often the time someone makes a mistake. They'll get sloppy if they haven't already." He reached into his pocket. "Text me when you get into the room. Text me if you so much as take an evening stroll around the property. And text me in the morning."

He dropped the key into Rose's outstretched hand. "Lakeside Building One. Room 219."

"And you text us if there are any updates about Mary, okay?"

They walked to the closest elevator. Sam got in. As the doors closed between them, he reiterated: "Be careful."

They followed the hallways back to the ER. As soon as they stepped outside, Rose called Mrs. Shaw.

"Something's come up. I need to go to Lake George to help a friend. Could you get Gladys and keep her overnight?"

"Of course, dear. I hope it's nothing too serious with your friend," Mrs. Shaw said.

"It'll be fine, but I need to be with her tonight. Grab some food from the fridge or a bag of treats from the cabinet if you need them. Thanks for helping. I'll see you tomorrow."

They retrieved their disguises out of the back seat and climbed in front. Rose realized her red lipstick was at home. She thought about doing without, not sure whether bright red lipstick would draw attention to her or prompt someone to brush her off as a flashy woman who couldn't be Rose.

"I think it's best to change your appearance as much as you can," Kelsey said, studying Rose's face.

They stopped at the drug store on the way north. Great. Now she had two tubes of bright red lipstick she'd probably never use again.

The evening sun cast pink and purple stripes in the western sky. They pulled into the inn, checked to see whether any staff was around. Then they got out and strolled to the building where Sam said his and Mary's room was, like they had every right to be there.

Rose keyed them into the side door of the building. They took the stairs to the second floor. No one was around as they strolled down the hall until they found room 219. Rose swiped the key, and the green light on the electronic pad blinked. They stepped inside and closed the door behind them. Rose stopped a few steps into the room. Kelsey bumped into her from behind.

"Do you smell that?" Rose whispered.

Kelsey nodded. "Someone's either here or been here. I don't remember Sam wearing cologne."

Chapter Sixty-Three

Voices. They froze. People talking. How close were they? The door to the room next to them closed with a *thud* that shook the hallway wall. The voices moved away. Rose let out a sigh of relief.

"Whoever was here is gone," Kelsey whispered.

"I think you're right. I hope you're right." Rose flipped on the switch on the wall next to her and the recessed light overhead cast a welcome light. Three more steps and they were in the kitchen, which was separated from the living space by a counter. The bedroom was on the right. Sliding glass doors in the living room led to a small patio and a beautiful view of Lake George.

Rose sniffed the way Gladys did when she'd found a fresh scent of a squirrel or the dribble of another dog. The smell of sweat and cologne lingered. She glanced at Kelsey, then tilted her head toward the open bedroom door. Rose crept toward the door, peeked in, and found it empty. The bathroom door was still closed. She looked back at Kelsey.

"I think we're okay. Want me to get out my phone and get

ready to call 911?" Kelsey said so softly Rose had to lean back to hear her.

Rose nodded. She crossed the bedroom into a small area with the closet. Across from the closet door was a large shelf covered with cosmetics, deodorants, facial cream, and a shaving kit. She opened the folding door to the closet, then opened the door to the bathroom and stepped back, just in case.

Both women sighed. The suite was empty. Unless someone was hiding under the bed—and Rose threw a quick look at it just in case—no one was here who shouldn't be. But someone had been here. She hurried over to the door and flipped the security bolt into place. Someone might try to get in with a master key, but the bolt would stop them.

Kelsey closed the curtains to the sliding glass door and the window in the bedroom.

"We need to check in with Sam," Kelsey said, walking over to the couch and sitting. She tapped his number. He picked up right away.

"Where are you?"

"We're in your suite."

They told him how the room smelled of sweat and cologne.

"You need to get out of there," Sam said. "Right now."

"No, wait. Listen," Rose replied. "We don't know who did it, but someone checked out your room. They probably won't be back, so I think it's safe."

"Does it look like they went through our luggage?"

"No, it doesn't," Kelsey said. "I'd say you two keep a tidy space."

"I also don't leave anything around for someone to find."

"Then we should be fine. Kelsey and I will go for a stroll and see what we can learn."

Kelsey looked at Rose, who was still wearing her floppy

hat. At least she'd taken off the sunglasses and put them on the counter. "I'm so glad we stopped for red lipstick to enhance your disguise," Kelsey said with a smile, "but I think you'll attract attention if you walk around wearing a big floppy hat and sunglasses after dark. Which it is. Getting dark."

"You two need to stay put," Sam said.

Rose deflected his request. Order. Whatever. They didn't come here to sit in the room and do nothing.

"How's Mary?" she asked.

"She's sleeping. She hasn't vomited in a while, but she's still not able to drink any water. And food is out of the question. But she's sleeping, so that's good."

"You're still staying the night?"

"Yes, of course. If she's able to drink a little juice and eat a piece of toast, they'll release her in the morning."

"But they don't know what happened to her, do they?" Kelsey said.

"No, and they may not be able to. The symptoms of stomach bugs and food poisoning are about the same, so they can't say for sure. But it's one or the other. Probably. Maybe."

"Probably? Maybe?" Rose asked.

"I'm suspicious by nature and profession," Sam said. "There's a bit of me that wonders if someone slipped something into her food. Maybe they did it to get us out of our room so they could check it out, or it could have been a warning. If it was poison of some kind, it wasn't enough to kill her, just to make her very ill. The tox report should tell us one way or the other."

"Okay. We'll talk to you in the morning," Rose said.

"Call or text me if you need anything—especially if anyone tries to get into the room again. What did Maxi say when you told her where you are?"

Oops. "We are calling her next," Rose said, disconnecting the call before Sam could remind them they were supposed to call Maxi from the hospital parking lot. Kelsey switched her phone to vibrate.

"Give Maxi a call. I'm going to go look around," she told Rose as she headed toward the door.

"I'm coming with you."

"You can't."

"Yes, I can."

"Let me rephrase that. I don't think you should come with me."

"And why is that?"

"One person can sneak around more easily than two. I can wear my disguise because guys wear baseball caps whether it's day or night, so it won't look out of place like a sun hat would. I have the big glasses for additional cover. And," Kelsey said, "the strongest argument I can make is that no one has seen me in fifteen years."

Shoot. Kelsey was right. Rose hated to lose an argument, but she agreed to stay put.

"I'll text you, but don't text me unless it's urgent," Kelsey said. She slid back the security lock, stuck her head out the door to see if anyone was around, and slipped into the hallway.

Rose slid the lock back into place and settled on the couch. She picked up the remote and turned on the TV. "Let's hope urgent doesn't happen," Rose said out loud, as if trying to convince herself. "Because if it gets too urgent, we could be in trouble with no backup."

Chapter Sixty-Four

Rose fidgeted while she waited. Surfed channels on the TV but couldn't focus until she heard from Kelsey. Her phone rang, reminding Rose she was supposed to try getting through to Maxi. She'd do that as soon as she hung up from this call. Rose didn't recognize the number, but Kelsey carried a couple of disposable phones, so it could be one of those. Rose muted the TV and swiped to connect the call.

"Where are you? Is everything okay?" she asked.

"Rose?"

She didn't recognize the voice. The person spoke just above a whisper.

"Yes. Who is this?"

"It's Ana. I'm sorry to disturb you, but I tried calling Kelsey, and she didn't answer."

Rose sat up straighter. Where was Kelsey? Why didn't she pick up when Ana called? Was Kelsey in trouble? And what was up with Ana now?

"What's going on, Ana? Where are you?"

"I'm at the Western Inlet Inn," she said, "filling in on the night shift. A guest called the front desk a few minutes ago. She was crying, said she was assaulted. She begged for help. Juan, the head of security, overhead me talking to her. I said I needed to call 911. He said no."

"No? Why?" Rose got up from the couch and looked for her floppy hat.

"He said he would handle it, but it's not the first time something like this has happened and he wouldn't let me call the police. I'm afraid for the woman."

"Where is she? What's her room number?"

"Why do you need to know that?"

"Don't let on to your security guy, but Kelsey and I are here at the inn. We're in a friend's suite. Give me the woman's room number and name. We'll go help her."

"She's in building two, room 184. Her name is Rita. Should I call the police?"

"Let Kelsey and me find out what's going on first. The cops won't be happy if they're called here for a domestic dispute. We'll check it out."

Ana thanked her and hung up. Rose walked into the bedroom and found her hat where she'd left it on the bed. Then she spotted Sam's Buffalo Bills' cap on top of a small suitcase in the corner. That would look better than her floppy sun hat at this hour. She adjusted the band on the cap to fit her, reached for the tube of red lipstick but remembered how Maxi had reacted when she saw her at Thom's BrewPub. Yeah, just a dab of the lipstick this time. She used the bathroom, then picked up her phone and set it on vibrate. She texted Kelsey to meet her at room 184 in Lakeside Two, grabbed the room card off the small table, and scooted out the door.

Don't act like you shouldn't be here. Walk like you own the place.

She pushed her shoulders back and thought about how Maxi walked, especially when she was in full uniform. Confident. Cocky. Don't mess with me. Maxi had all of that in her cop's stride and Rose did her best to imitate her. A man coming down the hallway nodded at her.

"Go Bills," he said with a smile.

Rose didn't react at first, then remembered she was wearing Sam's cap. She gave a hearty fist pump. "Yay, go Bills." Her voice had a little too much energy and was much deeper than her own. The man's smile faded, and he tilted his head. *Maybe draw a little less attention to yourself,* she thought and kept walking. *Try using your normal voice and skip the fist pump next time.*

At the end of the hall, she opened the door and hurried down the stairs. No one was in the first-floor hallway, and she had to go all the way to the other end to get out of this building she was in to reach the other one. She strolled like her deputy sheriff half sister again and encountered no one else. As she stepped out of the building, a motion detector cast a soft glow but faded when she left its space. Rose crossed the manicured lawn on a slate path illuminated by small solar lights planted alongside it. White pine trees dotted the area. Smaller cedar and spruce trees joined the occasional maple or oak to create the Adirondack Mountain ambiance of the property.

Rose jerked her head when she spotted movement at the other end of Lakeside Two. A figure ran from the other end of the building toward the beach. Rose started after the person, but paused and took cover beside a cedar tree when someone ran after the first person. Was that Kelsey? Rose squinted to see better. Yes, it was. What was going on? Then, just as she was about to run after Kelsey, a third person, bigger than the other two, exited the far end of Lakeside Two.

Rose didn't hesitate any longer. She took off after all of them, staying on the grass to minimize the sound of her feet hitting the ground. As she ran, she tried to keep a low profile in the safety of the trees. The man, the last person to run from

Lakeside Two, suddenly turned in her direction. Rose scooted behind a small shed with window boxes overflowing with flowers. She held her breath and peeked around the corner of the building. She pulled back quickly, then looked again. A shovel leaned against the wall. A weapon.

Rose crept toward the shovel, picked it up, and raised it about shoulder high with both hands. It was heavier than it looked. She pressed her back against the shed wall and heard movement. Gripped the shovel tighter and prepared to swing. A person with a baseball cap rounded the corner and Rose almost hit them.

"Hey, it's me," Kelsey whispered.

"Jeez, I almost hit you. What's going on?"

"I should ask you that. You were supposed to stay in the room."

Rose explained about the call from Ana.

"She must be talking about the woman who ran out of the building ahead of me. I saw her at the end of the hallway coming out of the stairwell and told her I could help her, but she took off. I don't know if she couldn't hear me, couldn't understand me, or was too scared to trust me."

"Where'd she go?"

"I think she snuck into this shed. I ran from the security guy and just circled back to see if she's in here."

"We need to get her out of there to safety. How about if I act as a decoy and distract the guy who ran after you?"

"Rose, you can barely hold the shovel." Kelsey took it from her and set it on the ground. "I'll distract the guy. You get the woman and run back to our room."

Rose nodded.

"Okay. I'll meet you back there." Kelsey took off.

Chapter Sixty-Five

Rose waited half a beat, then crouched low and circled around the shed on the side away from the beach. She tapped on the door.

"My name's Rose. I'm here to help you. We need to hurry before the security guy comes back."

The door opened a crack. Rose extended her hand, and the door almost closed on her fingers.

"Hey, I'm serious. The security guy will be back in a minute. My friend is distracting him. Please trust me. We need to get out of here."

Rose extended her hand again. The door opened a little farther. "Come with me. Hurry."

The young woman stood behind the door, her dark hair a mess of curls, her eyes red and swollen, her shoulders hunched over.

"Come on. There's no time to waste," Rose said, looking toward the beach and grateful she couldn't see anyone charging in their direction.

Rose tried to be firm, but gentle, as she took the woman's hand and pulled her out of the shed. They raced across the lawn from tree to tree, not stopping until they reached Lakeside One. The motion detector came on as Rose keyed the door open. She and the woman ran down the hallway, up the stairs, and into the safety of room 219. Rose flipped the security bolt on the door and fell to her knees, all her strength sapped by the events in the last half hour.

Kelsey was right. Rose lacked stamina. Her lungs were sucking in air so fast her ribs complained. The doctor said her ribs had healed from the incident at the rally, but they sure didn't feel healed now. Rose had pulled the woman's hand with her right arm and now the shoulder was also screaming in pain. She focused on taking slower, more shallow breaths, hoping that helped. It did, and she glanced up to see the woman she'd taken from the shed huddled in the far corner of the couch, staring at her.

"¿Rita, sí?"

The woman hesitated, then nodded.

"¿Hablas inglés?"

"A little." The woman sniffed and wiped her nose with the back of her hand.

Rose took a few more breaths and stood. She found a box of tissues in the bathroom nook and brought it into the living room. She sat on the couch next to the woman and held out the box. The woman pulled out a couple of tissues and wiped her nose. Rose set the box on the couch between them and studied the woman's face. She couldn't be older than twenty. Her cotton dress was torn at the waist, blood spots splattered across the right side and one sleeve.

Rose tried to remember the Spanish word for water but had no idea what the word was for glass, so she hoped the woman would understand.

"¿Agua?" she asked with raised eyebrows.

Rita shook her head.

Rita might not need a glass of water, but Rose did. She

pulled a couple of glasses out of the kitchen cabinet, turned on the tap and filled them, and returned to the couch. She set one glass on the table in front of Rita and took a long drink from the other. Rita watched Rose as she picked up the other glass and sipped.

Now what? Rose hesitated to call Ana at the reception desk in case there might be another security guy who could see what room she was calling from. She could call from her cell phone. Even if they realized it was her, they wouldn't know where she was. And she needed to try Maxi again. Maybe Rose needed to call 911. She had just picked up her phone when someone banged on the door.

"Rose, it's me. Let me in."

Kelsey sounded as out of breath as Rose had been. She must have been running the entire time since Rose had seen her. Rose rushed to the door as Kelsey called out again.

"Rose, hurry, before he sees me."

As she flipped back the security bolt and turned the doorknob, Rose wondered how Kelsey entered the building without a key card. But that thought came too late.

The door pushed open and Kelsey stumbled into the room, falling into Rose who struggled to remain on her feet. The security man, whom Rose knew as Juan from her first visit to the inn, rushed in behind Kelsey, waving a gun in the air. He slammed the door shut and studied Rose and Kelsey's faces.

"Mujeres estúpidas," he said, shaking his head, then he reached out and shoved Kelsey. Kelsey reached for Rose's arm, but the move caught Rose off guard. The two of them fell to the floor in a heap. Rose cried out when Kelsey landed on top of her.

As Kelsey pushed herself up on her feet, Juan shoved her toward the couch, where Rita remained tucked in the corner as if trying to disappear.

"Sit down over there. And you"—he nudged Rose with the toe of his shoe—"you get up and join them."

But Rose didn't move. She stayed curled up in a ball moaning in pain. She should have trusted her instincts and not opened the door. Now she had to get all of them out of this.

Juan glared at Rose, then Kelsey.

"¡Idiotas! Han armado un desastre!"

"No, you're the idiot," Kelsey shouted. "You're brilliant to lock us in this room with you. People know we are here and they're on the way. It's a disaster, alright—for you."

Juan crossed the room in three strides and slapped Kelsey across the face so hard he almost lifted her off the couch.

Kelsey cried out. As Juan walked back toward the kitchen, Kelsey glanced at Rose. Her eyes opened wide when she noticed Rose was alert, her lips moving.

"Shhh," Rose said under her breath. She didn't want to lift her head and let Juan see that she wasn't as injured as she appeared. Kelsey looked at Juan to see if he'd noticed. Juan was somewhere behind Rose, and while Rose couldn't see him, she kept her eyes on Kelsey to get an idea where he was, what he was doing.

Rose heard the beeps of a cell phone. Kelsey started to get up from the couch, but Juan must have seen her.

"¡La parada!" he shouted. Kelsey dropped back down, her eyes shooting back and forth between Juan and Rose. Rose continued to moan as if in pain, sometimes pulling her legs tighter to her chest, then stretching them back out. In addition to letting Juan think she was too hurt to get up, Rose wanted to stay limber enough to jump up in a hurry should Kelsey come up with a way to take down Juan.

Juan launched into a tirade spoken so quickly Kelsey didn't seem able to understand, given the frown on her face. She looked at Kelsey, who closed her fingers into her palm, her pinkie and thumb raised in the universal sign of a phone call.

Got it. Juan was on the phone. But who did he call? Browning? The manager from the inn? Maybe they were also in on this human and sex trafficking ring Browning operated. Rose thought about how she could use her position on the floor to upend Juan, but he had a gun. She didn't. He also had a functioning body. And she definitely didn't.

Chapter Sixty-Six

Rose looked at Kelsey and raised her eyebrows, but Kelsey gave a quick nod at Juan, then shook her head. Maybe she was signaling that she didn't understand what Juan was saying. If they were going to get out of this mess, Rose needed to put herself in a better position despite the pain. She pushed up a little and leaned back against the coffee table leg, keeping her arms wrapped around her body. The tricky part now was to look at Juan and Kelsey without whipping her head back and forth. She kept her gaze on Kelsey as much as possible. They'd have to coordinate whatever they were going to do if they had any hope of getting out of here without getting shot.

Juan banged his phone down on the counter. Kelsey jumped. Rose tried not to. Another cell phone chirped. It was Rose's, sitting on the coffee table in front of the couch. Kelsey reached for it, but Juan must have started toward it too, because Kelsey pulled her hand back in a hurry. She put both of her hands up in a sign of surrender and leaned back on the couch. Rose shot a glance at Rita, still curled up on the couch, streams of tears flowing down her cheeks.

Rose's eyes drifted to her cell phone on the table. That call could be from Sam or Maxi checking up on them, although Rose wasn't sure if her message to Maxi had ever connected with the towers. Maybe Sam had called Maxi and let her know what was going on, where Kelsey and Rose had gone. Maybe Sam would alert Maxi or the cops if he didn't hear from them soon. Maybe the cops were on the way. Maybe someone was about to help them out of here. Maybe. Maybe. Rose had to come up with something better than maybe because there was no *maybe* about whether she and Kelsey were in trouble.

Everyone jumped when someone banged on the door and called out in Spanish. Then whoever was pounding on the door switched to English.

"Give it up, Juan, and open the door. We know you have hostages."

Rose gulped. Hostages. Yep, they were in a locked room with a man who had a gun, and she had to figure out how to end this. Rose looked at Kelsey, whose lips were pressed together so hard they were white. Kelsey was still holding her face where Juan had hit her, and the crease between her eyebrows grew larger. She looked like the word hostages had frightened her as well.

Kelsey, who'd disappeared fifteen years ago because she'd feared for her safety and had lived a low-key and safe life in Cape Cod until Rose had stumbled onto her note and ten thousand dollars. Kelsey, whom Rose had convinced was no longer in danger from Browning and his thugs. Kelsey, who'd come back to upstate New York to help Rose shut down Browning's human trafficking ring, to protect the immigrant women and men he'd been abusing.

Rose pictured the two of them chatting on Kelsey's back porch in Cape Cod, where the biggest danger they'd faced was the hungry mosquitos that came out by the hundreds as the sun dropped below the horizon.

"Sorry," Rose said softly.

Kelsey shook her head. "Not your fault. I came back to help. We'll get through this. I know we will."

A fist banged on the door again, harder this time. Rose flinched.

"¡Détente!" Juan's face was red with anger. He yelled at the door again and picked up his gun, waving it in the air.

Rita sobbed. Kelsey's eyes shot back and forth between Rose and Juan, who was pacing in the small space. He glared at Rose and Kelsey as he walked to the sliding glass door near the couch. He opened the curtains a crack, then jumped back. Juan raced across the room and shut off the overhead lights. The only remaining light in the room was on the table at the end of the couch where Rita huddled.

"Apaga la luz," he said, pointing the gun at her.

"Sí. Sí," she said, reaching over and flipping the switch on the base of the light.

Well, this wasn't good. Now the room was almost fully dark, except for a red glow from the smoke detector in the ceiling and a soft white glow from an outlet between the kitchen and the living room. Rose hoped her eyes adjusted soon because she couldn't see Kelsey's eyes and didn't know how they would communicate. Juan was pacing again, and Rose noticed that he came closer to her the last time he walked past. When he came by again, Rose thrust her leg out. Juan stumbled, and Rose was about to jump up when he swung around. Even in the low light, Rose saw the gun pointed at her. She held up her hands.

"Sorry. Sorry."

He took one step closer and kicked her thigh.

Rose screamed. Holy shit. Did he wear shoes with steel-reinforced toes? Rose leaned over to her side and rubbed her leg.

Juan swung his leg as if to kick her again, and she curled up as tightly as she could.

The pounding on the door resumed.

"Juan. Come on. Let those women go."

Rose didn't recognize the voice, but it was not the same one that called out in Spanish. Hopefully the cops were in the hallway.

A soft *click* indicated the lock was released. The door pushed open, casting a ray of light into the room. But the security bolt kept it from opening more than an inch. So did the sharp crack of Juan's gun and the thud of the bullet slamming into the door.

All three women screamed.

The door was pulled closed, leaving the room darker than it had been before.

Chapter Sixty-Seven

Rose's heart pounded. Juan wasn't afraid to use his gun to warn the police on the other side of the door. Would he use it on Rose and Kelsey? On Rita? Rose recalled a time she was covering a situation in Newark, New Jersey, where a man had taken his wife and three children hostage, along with a friend of his wife's, after shooting the woman's husband. The man barricaded himself in a first-floor apartment in the largest public housing complex in Newark. The SWAT team had been called in, and several armed officers in full protective gear huddled behind the armored vehicle. The media was kept a quarter mile back, out of danger, except for the three people who were selected to be the media pool—the journalists who would report back to the other reporters, the print photographer whose images would be shared with all other print media, and the TV videographer whose video would be copied for all other TV and media outlets to use.

It was Rose's turn to be the print photographer in the pool. She'd stood alongside the police negotiator, who was trying to calm down the man in the apartment. What she'd learned from the SWAT negotiator, as well as from TV shows and movies she'd watched, was that it helped to talk with the hostage taker, to calm him down, and to convince him to give up his weapon without hurting anyone. Of course, Rose didn't have help from a SWAT negotiator or an armored vehicle to hide behind, but she figured talking to Juan was worth a try.

"This can still end peacefully," Rose said, keeping her arms wrapped around herself to keep up the impression that she hurt too much to stand.

Juan wheeled around and pointed his gun at her. "Shut up!"

"I'm just saying—"

Even though it was so dark, she could see him take a step toward her and point the gun at her face.

Rose shut up.

Kelsey tried next.

"We know what Browning's been doing," Kelsey said. "He's abusing his workers and sexually assaulting women who worked for him. If you want to get out of this mess, you should tell the cops what you know about Leonard Browning. And Dr. Collins."

"You disappeared," he said, stepping closer. "I guess you got the message when I ran you off the road all those years ago. You were stupid to come back."

There wasn't much light in the room, but it was enough to see the hard edge to Juan's eyes that went along with his commanding voice. Evil voice.

Rose was about to speak again, but Kelsey quieted her with the motion of her hand. Juan hadn't told Kelsey to shut up. Was he intrigued to find her back in the area? Is that why he let Kelsey speak? Now was not the time to get into a debate about which one of them was in a better position to negotiate.

"I knew you were bad news the first time I met you,"

Kelsey said. "And while we're clearing the air here, was that you chasing me through the woods outside my apartment one evening? Or who left papers in my car?"

Juan's laughter sent shivers down Rose's spine.

"I don't handle the petty stuff."

"Only the big stuff, huh? Like poisoning Randall Webster?"

Rose took a sharp breath. Was Juan responsible for her father's death? Did Browning order him to poison her father, did he do it on his own, or did the men carry it out together? Rose stared at him, waiting for an answer, but he was done talking.

The voices grew louder on the other side of the door. Whoever was out there decided to open the door again. A shaft of light came into the room, and Rose scrunched back onto the floor, making herself as small as possible. Kelsey slid off the couch, pinned between the coffee table and Rose.

"I'm going to shoot one of these women if you don't close that door," Juan yelled.

The only one not on the floor was Rita. Juan pointed the gun in her direction and fired.

All three women screamed.

Juan was good at shooting doors. His shot had gone wide of the couch and hit the sliding glass door to the patio. It didn't shatter the glass, but the gunfire did shatter the nerves of the women in the room.

"Stop shooting," Kelsey said. "We get it. You have a gun. You can hurt us. But I don't think you want to go that far. I think you just want to get out of here."

He glared at her.

"All you have to do is give up Browning." She paused. "And Dr. Collins."

"What do you mean, 'give up'?"

"Tell us what they did. Tell the cops that the information

we've uncovered about them is accurate, and that Browning abused and assaulted people who worked for him. That he made some of them act as escorts, and to provide sex to men who paid Browning."

"I don't know what you're talking about." Juan turned toward the front of the unit where someone was opening and closing the door, trying to break the security bolt. Each time the door slammed, the ray of light seemed to grow a little wider. Then someone kicked the sliding glass door. The wall shuddered and voices on the patio grew louder. Rose looked at the sliders. Was that Maxi? Were the cops distracting Juan by trying to break into the unit from both sides?

Juan tensed and swung his gun from one side of the room to the other. When he turned to the main door, the light from the hallway showed the tense set of his jaw and a hint of fear in his eyes.

It was just the opportunity Rose and Kelsey needed.

Juan had been standing a few feet in front of them. He leaned toward the sliders, then glanced at the door to the unit. He turned toward the sliders again long enough for Rose to nod to Kelsey.

Juan took a step toward the sliders. In one swift motion, Kelsey lifted the coffee table up and onto Juan. The table didn't knock him over, but it threw him off balance and he stumbled. He tried to keep from falling and he still had the gun in his hand. Rose scrambled to her feet and launched her body at Juan, aiming for the back of his knees.

The gun went off.

Rita screamed and Rose feared the bullet had struck her. Rita jumped up and stomped on Juan's arm. Then she kicked him in the head. Then she kicked him again. Kelsey raced to help her and grabbed the gun that Juan had dropped, then she pointed the gun at Juan.

Rose smiled and slid back down on the floor, holding her right arm against her chest as she bent over in pain.

Chapter Sixty-Eight

"You were supposed to call me," Maxi said.

Rose and Kelsey sat across the table from Maxi in a small room at the inn, their faces drawn and tense. Rose held her bad arm with her good one, Kelsey rubbed the deep red spot on her cheek that was showing purple splotches around the edges.

"We tried several times. It wouldn't go through," Rose said. "I even left a message. Did you get that?"

Maxi shook her head.

"And you weren't supposed to leave the room," Sam said. "But other guests at the inn reported seeing both of you running around the property. You two. Another woman. And that security guy. Juan."

Maxi's eyes swept over Rose and Kelsey. "You've been through a lot. Rose, you look like you're in pain. Do either one of you want to see the paramedics with the ambulance out front?"

They both shook their heads. Rose hurt in a lot of places, but she wanted to go home and seeing the paramedics might delay that.

"Then tell us what happened," Maxi said. "Starting with when you left the hospital."

Rose reiterated how she had tried to call Maxi. Then she explained about the phone call from Ana and rushing off to find the woman.

"But you were already out of the room, right?" Sam turned to Kelsey.

"It was dark. It seemed like a waste of time to sit in the room. I took a walk to see if I could learn anything. The door to Lakeside Two was propped open with a rock, so I stepped inside. I was almost at the end of the hallway when a woman rushed out of a room, sobbing and clutching her dress. I ran after her, out the door at the other end and outside."

"That's when I spotted them," Rose said and explained how she almost hit Kelsey with a shovel. "Then Kelsey took off to distract Juan, and I grabbed the woman, Rita, and we ran to Sam's room."

Kelsey described how Juan had hidden behind a tree near the waterfront and grabbed her when she ran by. "I didn't see him double back," Kelsey added.

"Why did you let Juan into the room?" Maxi asked Rose.

"It's not like I opened the door and welcomed him with open arms," Rose said, an edge of annoyance in her voice. "Kelsey sounded urgent when she banged on the door. I realized a moment too late that she didn't have the room key to enter the building. Juan stormed in."

Maxi and Sam nodded. They all knew what happened next, more or less.

Maxi had kicked the slider where Juan had shot it. The bullet had cracked the glass enough to weaken it. She kicked it again, harder. Maxi and Deputy Patterson pushed aside the curtains and ran into the room. At the same time, the security lock on the room's hallway door broke, and the Warren

County deputy rushed into the room with two Glens Falls police officers, their guns drawn.

"And you know the rest," Rose said. She looked at Sam. "How's Mary? Is she feeling better? Do they know if it was food poisoning or other poisoning?"

"She's getting better and was eating some lemon Jell-O when I left. She'll be fine. I'll pick her up in the morning. Well, later this morning," he said, glancing at the clock on the wall. It was after midnight. Rose and Kelsey still had to give formal statements to the police. "We have no firm answer yet whether she'd been poisoned. That's a question investigators will ask Juan."

"Is Juan in custody?" Rose asked.

Maxi gave a curt nod. "Ana called 911 while you two were playing detective. Deputy Patterson asked Ana how her daughter was doing, and Ana broke down. She admitted that the real note she found in Isabella's backpack was apparently written by the two men who'd told her daughter that Ana was hurt. Ana got the message. Browning could hurt her daughter anytime he wanted to."

"The look on Ana's face told me something more was going on," Rose said. "I'm glad she told the detective the truth."

There was a knock on the door. Detective Patterson walked in with an officer from the Glens Falls Police Department. Patterson looked at Maxi.

"We need to take statements."

"Can it wait until tomorrow?" Rose asked.

Patterson shook her head. "Kelsey needs to go into another room with this officer. I'll take your statement, Rose."

"Can I stay?" Maxi asked.

Patterson smiled. "Of course."

Sam stood. "I'll go with Kelsey if that's okay."

Patterson nodded. "You'll both have to come to the sheriff's tomorrow to review and sign your statements," she said, looking from Kelsey to Rose. "But let's get it down while it's fresh in your mind."

"Oh, it's going to stay fresh in my mind for a while," Rose said. "I've covered hostage situations. I sure didn't like being on the other side."

Kelsey, Sam, and the other officer left as Patterson took the seat next to Maxi.

"Alright. Tell me what happened."

"Where do you want me to begin?" Rose asked.

"I think you should begin with the note and the ten thousand dollars," Maxi said.

Patterson whipped her head and stared at Maxi, then Rose, eyes wide, eyebrows raised, pen poised over her note pad.

"Here." Maxi pulled a notepad out of a side pocket in her pants and handed it to Patterson. "You're going to need a bigger notepad."

Chapter Sixty-Nine

Rose and Kelsey were exhausted when they'd returned to Lake Amelia, but they had too much adrenaline racing through their bodies to sleep. A bottle of wine helped them unwind as they relived the past few hours until they trudged off to bed.

Rose moaned and reached for her chirping cell phone. Her eyes longed to remain closed.

"Maxi, it's not even eight o'clock. I've barely slept. Can you call later?"

"At least you've slept," Maxi said. "Get up and answer the door."

Maxi was out front? Rose pushed herself up, pulled on a lightweight sweatshirt, and set Gladys on the floor. Did Maxi have an update for her and Kelsey? Rose trudged down the stairs and shuffled to the front door.

Maxi's eyelids drooped, and her face held no smile.

"You look exhausted," Rose said.

"Ah, the intrepid journalist nailed it," Maxi said with a hint of a smile. "I just came from headquarters and thought you'd like to know the latest. But it will cost you a cup of coffee and a blueberry muffin. I sure hope you have both because I'm not only tired, I'm hungry."

"I can do better than that. How about some eggs?"

"Can you make an omelet?" Maxi asked as the two of them entered the kitchen.

"Not as well as Aunt Tess."

"Okay. Scrambled eggs with a blueberry muffin will be fine."

"Let's keep our voices down so we don't wake Kelsey," Rose said.

"I'm up." Kelsey rubbed her eyes. "I heard a car drive up and then the front door open. Hi, Maxi."

"Hey, Kelsey. Join us. Rose is making breakfast." Maxi's smile was a little bigger.

"I'll take care of the coffee."

Maxi placed her hat on the dining room table as she walked over to the couch at the end of the room and sat. She leaned her head back and a minute later was snoring.

"Time to eat," Rose said a few minutes later, setting plates of eggs and a basket of muffins on the dining room table. "Come on, Maxi. Breakfast is ready."

"I guess I drifted off." Maxi shook her head, then joined them. When they'd finished eating eggs and were nibbling on muffins and sipping fresh cups of coffee, Maxi filled them in.

"Juan isn't as tough as he seems when faced with the possibility of a long prison sentence. He told us all about Browning's treatment of his immigrant workers, how Browning abused some men and sexually assaulted some women, how he forced younger women to act as escorts for men who stayed at his fancy hotel, the Regalia George. Juan confirmed what you two learned. He also implicated Dr. Collins, saying Collins also assaulted the young women. When we'd heard enough, two deputies from Warren County paid a visit to Browning at his estate on East Shore Drive.

They got him out of bed. He denied everything, of course, and is in custody."

"What about Dr. Collins?" Rose asked.

"When the police arrived at his condo, his car was gone. They searched the condo. It appeared someone packed a suitcase in a hurry. The dresser drawers in the bedroom had been rifled through. There was no suitcase in the bedroom closet or anywhere else in the house." She paused. "There's an APB out for Collins. We'll find him."

"Wow. I can't believe it's over," Kelsey said.

"Almost over." Maxi turned to Kelsey. "You're going to need to testify when these cases go to court." Then she looked at Rose. "You too. You also have firsthand knowledge that the police need to convict Browning and Collins. If the two of you hadn't been so persistent, there's no telling how long they would have gotten away with this."

Rose knew she should be smiling for bringing those men to justice, but there were still loose ends.

"What about my father? Our father? Did Juan admit to poisoning him, or helping Browning poison him?"

"Juan became less cooperative when the discussion turned to poison and murder. Juan blamed Browning and Collins for your . . . um, our father's death. Deputy Patterson says she suspects Juan had a role in that. Juan's in jail, and investigators will question him again. They'll ask Browning. They'll ask Collins when they bring him in. We're almost there, Rose. Almost there."

Maxi stood. "Thanks for breakfast. I'm going home to get some sleep, and you two need to get to the sheriff's office in Lake George to sign your statements."

"Will I see you later?" Rose asked.

"I don't know. If I can't come by, I'll call." Maxi picked up her hat, then looked at Kelsey.

"I know it took a lot for you to come back here, but Rose

couldn't have taken these guys down alone. You two should be proud of yourselves. Let's celebrate after the dust settles."

Kelsey sighed. "I'll have to take a rain check. As soon as I sign my statement I'm going home. I have a job and a life on Cape Cod. I can't wait to get back there. Who knows, maybe I'll even start using my real name again." Kelsey pushed back from the table and stood. She and Maxi shook hands.

"I'll see you next time you're in Lake Amelia." With that, Maxi walked through the kitchen and living room and out the front door.

"Do you mean that about leaving so soon?" Rose asked.

Kelsey smiled. "I've been here a while. Aren't you ready to get rid of me?"

"Not really. It's nice having you around."

"Well, like I said, it's time for me to go home."

"If you need anything before you go, just let me know."

"There is one thing I've been meaning to ask."

"What's that?"

"Could you show me the secret compartment where your father hid the money?"

Rose smiled. "Right this way."

Chapter Seventy

"Can you and Kelsey meet me at that Lake Moreau Park?"

"When?" Rose asked.

"Now?"

Ana's call caught Rose and Kelsey by surprise. The two of them were leaving the Warren County Sheriff's Office after reviewing and signing their statements. Kelsey was eager to get on the road, and Rose was looking forward to some quiet time. But it sounded important.

Rose looked at Kelsey, who nodded. "Okay. We'll see you in about twenty minutes."

They spotted Ana's car at the far end of the parking lot and pulled up. Ana and Isabella got out of the car, and another woman and two children walked up to them.

"Rose and Kelsey," Ana said, pointing at the other woman, "this is Vicki."

"*The* Vicki?" Rose stammered.

"Yes, *the* Vicki," the woman said, an arm wrapped around each child. "And these are my kids."

"Can we chat—you, me, and Vicki?" Ana said. "I don't mean to exclude you, Kelsey, but do you mind taking the kids to the beach?"

"Not at all," Kelsey said. "I'd love to catch up with Isabella and meet these two. What are your names?"

The children's soft voices drifted into the air as Kelsey led them away.

"Let's go over there." Ana pointed to a picnic table just past the parking. They brushed the pine needles off the bench and sat, Vicki next to Ana and Rose on the other side.

"Thank you again for helping last night. I don't know what I would have done if you and Kelsey hadn't been on the property."

"It worked out for everyone."

Ana nodded. "As you know, when the deputy sheriff showed up at the front desk and asked how Isabella and I were doing, I broke down and told her the truth about the two men who had picked up Isabella at the day camp. I told the deputy what I knew about the abuse that's been going on, by Mr. Browning and Dr. Collins." Ana's eyes filled with tears. "I told them everything because I have to stop them. I won't let them get near my daughter. Ever."

Vicki slid closer and put an arm around Ana, who dropped her head and wiped the tears from her eyes. Rose tried to swallow the lump in her throat. These two women had been through so much. Ana's fear for her daughter and Vicki's fear for her children must have weighed on them every single day. But Browning wielded so much power over them and their families, they were powerless. Rose wiped the tears from her face with the back of her hand.

Ana looked up at Rose and apologized for her reluctance to get involved.

"You don't owe me or anybody an apology for loving your

child so much and protecting her so fiercely. I'm just glad you told Deputy Patterson what really happened with Isabella. What happened with you."

Vicki cleared her throat and sniffed back tears. "A couple of days ago, I was at a park near our apartment," Vicki said. "Mr. Browning appeared out of nowhere and sat down next to me." She told them how Browning had threatened her and told her to keep her mouth shut.

"We're both pretty resilient," Ana said, "but Vicki's more of a fighter. When she realized I must have told someone about Mr. Browning, she reached out to me, despite Mr. Browning's threat. We agreed that if we didn't stop them, Mr. Browning and Dr. Collins could target our daughters next."

"That made my heart stop," Vicki said. "I had to do anything I could to protect my daughter from . . . her father."

"Ana told me she doesn't know for sure who Isabella's father is," Rose said. "But you're sure Mr. Browning is your daughter's father?"

Vicki nodded. "I had to protect my precious daughter from him. And yours." Vicki leaned back into Ana. A look passed between the two women. Rose understood intellectually that a mother's urge to protect her children was strong enough to accomplish incredible physical feats, and emotional ones. Browning had challenged them, and he was going to pay the price.

"I'm on my way to the sheriff's office to tell them how Browning threatened me, how he assaulted me, how he forced me to go out with men."

"You two," Rose said, taking a deep breath and pushing it out. "I'm honored to know you both. Your story, with Ana's and Rita's, will help police put those men away for a very long time." Rose didn't try to hide the tears that flowed down her cheeks. "You've survived some terrible times, but you've risen above them and helped others. Not just your children, but so many immigrant workers and their families. There's no telling how far Browning's reach extends and how many people he's hurt. But it ends now."

Chapter Seventy-One

Kelsey's bag sat by the front door. Rose tried to convince her to have one more cup of coffee, but Kelsey declined. She stretched her neck from side to side, then reached out and put her hands on Rose's shoulders. "I need to tell you something else." Kelsey's voice cracked. "Going after Browning and Juan helped me face the abuse in my past and accept it for what it was without criticizing myself, without wondering why I was too weak to stop it. It's taken a while, but I can move on and take back my life. That's been so healing. I can't thank you enough."

Rose nodded. "Promise you'll keep in touch."

Kelsey reached into her pocket for her cell phone, tapped it a few times, then a ping hit Rose's cell. "That's all of my contact info. My real cell phone. And come visit me."

"I will. Just not in August."

They both laughed.

"Millie must have been thrilled when you told her you were going to see her. Give her my best and thank her for trusting me."

Kelsey let out a deep breath. "Thanks for everything." The

two women wrapped their arms around each other in a tight hug, then said goodbye.

Rose stood in front of the living room's bay window and waved as Kelsey pulled away. Then she took Gladys for a walk that was so long, Rose had to carry the dog home. The fresh air cleared her head, and the walk tired them both out. Rose fed Gladys and watched until the dog had cleaned her dish so thoroughly it looked like it had just come out of the dishwasher. Gladys made a quick trip outside, then hopped onto the couch and fell asleep. Rose sat down beside her and drifted off.

She awoke to the ping of a text. Kelsey was in Westchester County. Already? Rose checked the time. Wow, she'd been napping for a couple of hours. She replied to the text with a thumbs-up, then wandered the house, feeling the emptiness. She had a bite to eat, poured a glass of wine, and headed out to the patio for a change of scenery. Rose opened the sliding glass door and followed Gladys out. She was closing the slider when her cell phone chirped. She rushed back into the kitchen and picked it up off the counter.

"Tell me you have news."

"I have news," Maxi said. Rose thought she could hear a smile in Maxi's voice.

"Do you want to come over?"

"I'm still wrapping things up, but I need to tell you something before it leaks out." Maxi's voice was all business. "I know your friend Bill has excellent sources, and I don't want you to hear this from him or anyone else."

Rose walked back outside and dropped into one of the Adirondack chairs. "Okay," Rose said, drawing the word out as her anxiety ramped up. "What is it?"

"Police in Reading, Pennsylvania, pulled over Dr. Collins for a broken taillight. The cop had seen the APB and took Collins into custody. Two deputies from Warren County drove to Reading. They questioned Collins while waiting for him to be released. Collins blamed Browning, said Browning was responsible for everything, including . . ." Maxi's voice caught in her throat. She took a deep breath. "Including poisoning our father."

Neither tried to fill the silence needed to absorb the awful news. The confirmation. The horrible reality.

"Tell me everything Collins said."

"Okay, but this stays between you and me. Collins claimed Browning forced him to get thallium, which they used to scare off people getting too close to their sex trafficking and abuse of immigrant workers, going back years. Collins said Juan put it in our father's coffee. Collins claimed Juan put in too much, but deputies think he's just trying to cover his ass."

Thallium. Murder. Rose gulped some wine. While she had believed Kelsey when she said her father may have been poisoned, finding out what happened was different. Her mind was numb, and her heart ached so much she could barely take in a breath.

"Rose?"

"Here."

"I wish I could be there with you."

"I wish you could too." Gladys must have sensed Rose's despair, because she ran over and pawed her leg. Rose picked her up and pressed her nose behind the dog's ear.

"I need to tell Kelsey she was right."

"Not yet, okay? We're still questioning people and don't want anyone else who may have been involved to be tipped off."

"Yeah, like all the police activity at the Western Inlet Inn didn't already tip people off. I wonder how Collins found out."

"We think Browning's daughter-in-law told him. She's the one who worked at the ME's office. We suspect that the day your father died, Browning may have ordered her to call Collins in to sign your father's death certificate. She's being questioned now, so we'll find out what she knows."

"Are you and the investigators questioning anyone else?"

"Brandt. He owed Browning close to a hundred grand. Browning covered Brandt's gambling debts. We don't think Brandt had a hand in our father's death, but he may be complicit in the abuse of the immigrant workers and the sex trafficking ring. At the very least, Brandt knew and looked the other way without telling Dad and Kelsey."

A phone rang.

"I gotta go."

"Call me when you get home?"

"Yep." And Maxi hung up, leaving Rose alone, her mind spinning.

Brandt. Collins. Browning's daughter-in-law. Rose couldn't wait to talk to Bill. She couldn't tell him anything yet, but when she could, he'd have one hell of a scoop.

Chapter Seventy-Two

"Rose? Are you back here?" Maxi came around the side of the garage as Rose lifted her chin and opened her eyes.

"What time is it? What are you doing here?"

"It's late. I needed to see you." Gladys ran over to greet Maxi and she knelt and picked up the dog. Then Maxi sat in the chair next to Rose. "How are you doing?"

"About how you might expect of someone who'd learned their father was murdered." Rose shuddered and sat up. Falling asleep in the chair did not help her aches. She studied Maxi's face. "You're beat. Do you want a glass of wine or a beer?"

"No thanks. It would put me right to sleep." Maxi stroked Gladys's back. "My cop brain is still organizing the pieces of this case. After my initial reaction of learning that Browning poisoned our father—not disbelief, not shock, but something that hit me in my core—I haven't processed it. Not as a cop, but as Mr. Randall's daughter." Maxi's face showed her exhaustion, but Rose saw a softness she'd never seen before. "These last few months have been a roller coaster."

Rose didn't disagree. "What does Browning have to say about Collins's claim that he bought thallium for him?"

"Browning lawyered up when the topic switched to murder. I don't think we're going to learn much more from him. But Juan and Collins are talking. So are Ana and Vicki. There's enough evidence to convict all three of them."

"Including for Dad's murder?"

"Including for Dad's murder." Maxi frowned. "We've requested the full report of our father's death, including bloodwork. They could have done bloodwork and a toxicology report. That might tell us if he died of poison. But I'm no longer skeptical."

"Me neither." Rose picked a bug out of her wine, flicked it into the air, and took a sip. "I have another question."

"Of course you do." Maxi almost smiled.

"Juan is Latino. Why would he hurt his own people, let Browning and Collins abuse, rape, assault those girls? I don't get it."

"Browning was a master at finding people's weaknesses and holding it over them," Maxi explained. "With Brandt, it was his gambling debts. For Juan, it was also about money. Browning gave him a luxury SUV, took him to fancy restaurants, and paid him a lot. Juan liked expensive things. When Browning told him to do something, Juan couldn't say no."

Rose sighed again and figured she'd be sighing a lot in the coming days, releasing the pain, thinking about the lies that had been exposed.

How many more years could her mother and father have had together, how many more years could her father have enjoyed watching his grandchildren grow up? How many more years and special times might Rose have had with her father if he had not been poisoned? Her eyes brimmed with tears.

She glanced at Maxi, who was looking into the night sky. Rose tilted her head back.

"Look at all of those stars," Rose said. "It's beautiful, almost magical, the way they fill up the sky, isn't it? I never saw this many stars in Philadelphia. The sky is so much clearer here." Rose bolted upright. "Oh, look, there's a shooting star." She pointed, but the flash of light was gone before she'd finished her sentence.

Rose looked at Maxi, whose eyes were almost closed. She reached over and touched her arm. "Hey, sis. Time to go home."

"You're right. It's been a while since I've been this beat." Maxi pushed herself out of the chair.

"Thanks for coming over and giving me an update, especially when you're so tired." Rose opened the sliding glass door, and they walked into the kitchen.

"I wanted to tell you in person. And you need to let Kirk know what's happened," Maxi said, heading toward the living room.

"Yep, but not tonight," Rose said. "Do you want to be on the call with me?"

"No, but tell him I said hello." Maxi smiled.

Maxi gave Rose a hug and stepped outside. Rose closed the door, then stood in front of the living room window, watching Maxi's Jeep back out of the driveway and turn onto Cedar Street. Her mother had always stood in this very spot at the end of Rose's visits. She'd tap her heart a few times and wave goodbye whenever Rose left for home. Philadelphia.

Rose walked back into the kitchen, her eyes taking in the comfortable space she'd taken to calling home lately. Lake Amelia.

She retrieved her wine glass and topped it off, then returned to the patio and eased back in the Adirondack chair. Gladys half-jumped, half-crawled into her lap. Rose could count plenty of reasons to stay in Lake Amelia. Maxi. Gladys. Bill at the *Dispatch*. Carter at the library. Living in the Adirondacks. This house.

But her life had been in Philadelphia for almost two decades. Her work. Her friends. Her condo. She missed her other life. The injuries she'd suffered when she and Kelsey had taken down Juan would heal quickly. Soon she'd be able to take on more difficult assignments.

Rose had solved the mystery of her father's death. She'd given Kelsey the ten thousand dollars. She'd helped stop Browning and his cronies from hurting any more people.

Maybe the reasons she thought were telling her to stay in Lake Amelia were nothing more than excuses.

Her eyes caught the sliver of moon just above the pine trees. Higher up, a multitude of stars shimmered in the dark black sky. She pulled Gladys closer, feeling the little dog's heartbeat underneath her hand.

She didn't need to give up Gladys. She didn't need to give up this house. But she had to leave both of them, at least for a while, and go back home. To Philadelphia.

Acknowledgments

The more I write, the more books I put out into the world, the more people I have to thank for helping me on this journey. My team grows daily and I couldn't do this without them.

First, to my readers. I love meeting you at events and online. Thanks for your support and feedback. Keep posting those reviews—please!

Thanks to Sharon Parkis and the Colonie Book Club, Pat's Vischer Ferry Book Club, and the original Book Nook book club for fun and feedback.

Big hugs to my beta readers, including Sarah Branson, Leslie Costello, and Cynthia Rybaltowski. Your picky eyes saved me from an embarrassing misstep or two.

My team of skilled writers and editors includes Mark Spencer, Miranda Darrow, Nanette Littlestone, and Hannah VanVels Ausbury. My words are stronger, my stories better thanks to all of you.

Thanks to Carol Pouliot for checking my Spanish dialogue. If there are any mistakes, it's because I goofed transferring them to the manuscript. Also thanks to Heidi McIntyre for her marketing advice.

My professional connections include the Women Fiction Writers Association (WFWA), the WFWA Independent Authors Facebook, and the smaller Indie Author Support Group. Hearts to you for helping me learn the next steps and recover from the wrong ones.

I'm a member of Sisters in Crime, national, the New England chapter, the Mavens of Mayhem Upper Hudson chapter, and the Tristate chapter. Another big shoutout to the Mystery Writers of America. Great writers, great resources.

Back to some of my best friends—Bookstores. Please support your local independent bookstore. I love the big bookstores as well, but the indie bookstores are an indie author's connection to the community. We need them all.

To my loving and encouraging friends and family—especially Cindy, Mark, Ben, Will, Diane, Chuck, and David—my heartfelt thanks for believing in me and supporting my adventures.

As always, thanks to Helen for sharing the journey. And to Mila for the laughs and love.

About the Author

JACQUELINE BOULDEN is a multiple award-winning author whose novels are a mashup of mystery/suspense/women's fiction. A former Emmy-winning reporter and Telly-winning video producer, her stories focus on strong independent women overcoming life's challenges. *Kirkus Reviews* named her second novel, *Family Ties Family Lies* (Lake Amelia Mysteries Book One), a top 100 Indie book of 2024. She lives in upstate New York with her spouse and rescue dog, who's teaching them how to speak Beaglish.

Visit https://jacquelineboulden.com/and sign up for her newsletter. Follow her on Facebook (JacquelineBouldenAuthor) and Instagram (@jacqueline.boulden). If you enjoyed *Lies Lost and Found* or any of my novels, please consider leaving a review. It would mean so much.